bones

gothika #2

eli easton
jamie fessenden
kim fielding
b.g. thomas

Dreamspinner Press

Published by
DREAMSPINNER PRESS

5032 Capital Circle SW, Suite 2, PMB# 279, Tallahassee, FL 32305-7886 USA
http://www.dreamspinnerpress.com/

This is a work of fiction. Names, characters, places, and incidents either are the product of author imagination or are used fictitiously, and any resemblance to actual persons, living or dead, business establishments, events, or locales is entirely coincidental.

ISBN: 978-1-63216-408-7
Digital ISBN 978-1-63216-409-4
Library of Congress Control Number: 2014951383
First Edition October 2014

Printed in the United States of America
∞
This paper meets the requirements of
ANSI/NISO Z39.48-1992 (Permanence of Paper).

TABLE OF CONTENTS

THE DANCE

KIM FIELDING

Chapter One

EVENINGS WERE the worst. Not mornings or afternoons, when some of the deaths had happened, because during the day, Bram could bury himself so deeply in equations and computer screens and beakers that he hardly thought about anything but work. But in the evenings, he couldn't concentrate any longer, and he wandered restlessly around his house, listening to the empty echo of his footsteps.

Tonight was especially bad. Somehow the heat and humidity had only increased after the sun set, and the aging air conditioner was not keeping up. Bram had picked up a book and then a magazine, but the words swam meaninglessly in front of his eyes. He clicked on the TV, but the comedies weren't funny, the dramas were stupid, and the reality shows made him want to punch someone. Even the sports weren't sports—just a bunch of middle-aged has-beens sitting around in ill-fitting suits and terrible haircuts, spouting meaningless statistics. If the temperature had been more reasonable, he would have gone for a long run, forcing himself through mile after punishing mile until his muscles screamed and he was too exhausted to do anything but return home and collapse into bed. Instead, he stalked from living room to kitchen to bedroom to study, his skin tingling as if his nerve cells were multiplying too quickly, his gaze darting from place to place as if he were searching for something.

Thing was, what he was searching for was long gone.

When Bram's circling brought him back to the kitchen, he pulled a bottle of beer from the fridge. Corona. He hadn't realized he had any of the stuff left. He preferred darker ales, sometimes even stouts. He rolled the cold glass across his forehead and leaned back against the counter with his eyes shut.

He used to love the evenings, especially weeknights when there was no real pressure to go out. He would come home and strip out of his polo shirt and khakis, put on sweats if it was cold or boxer briefs during the summer. He and Jim would make dinner together. The kitchen wasn't large enough for two men—they bumped into each other and did awkward dances with hands full of knives and spoons and vegetables as they complained about their workdays. It was wonderful. And after dinner they collapsed onto the couch with music playing or something inane on the TV, their legs entwined. Bram read journal articles or lab notes; Jim went over depositions and motions. They'd interrupt each other with random thoughts and observations, with silly jokes, with chatter about politics or whether they'd paid the electric bill.

"Get a fucking grip," Bram growled. He rummaged in a drawer until he found the bottle opener, and he pried the beer open with an unnecessarily harsh jerk. The Corona tasted like cold piss, but he took a long swig anyway. Maybe there was enough beer in the fridge for him to get drunk. He hadn't done that in a long time.

He finished off the bottle and was about to get another when the doorbell rang.

Tensing, he glanced at the clock on the microwave. It was nearly nine o'clock. Too late for salesmen or Jehovah's Witnesses or the neighbor kids with their endless school fundraisers. None of Bram's friends would drop by unannounced. Not that he had many friends nowadays. He'd managed to push most of them away after Jim's death. They'd really been Jim's friends anyway.

Feeling slightly ridiculous, Bram pulled a large blade from the knife block. On his way out of the kitchen, he picked up the phone lying next to the empty bottle on the counter. He wished he had a pocket, but all he wore was a pair of old running shorts.

He walked into the living room and flipped on the porch light. With the phone and knife clutched in his left hand, he unfastened the locks and opened the door.

"Abraham Tillman?" asked the man standing on his porch.

"*Bram* Tillman."

The man nodded slightly. He looked nervous, which didn't help settle Bram's nerves, but he didn't look scary. Somewhere in his twenties, slender, and a couple inches shorter than Bram's six even, the man wore unremarkable tan trousers and a black tank top. He was, in fact, quite beautiful, with olive-toned skin, tightly curled brown hair, enormous blue eyes, and lips so impossibly lush as to make any starlet mad with envy. When the man chewed nervously on his lower lip, Bram had to look away.

"Can I help you?" Bram asked, staring beyond the visitor's left ear.

"Yes. I mean… actually, I'm here to help you. If I can." The man straightened his shoulders. "I'm Daniel Royer. I'm—"

But Bram hissed like an angry alligator and took a step back, quickly shifting the knife to his right hand. He raised the blade threateningly. "Go away. I'm going to call 911." He wished he'd taken his boss's advice and bought a gun. Not that he'd know how to use the damn thing, but at least he could point it.

Daniel shook his head and held up his hands. "Please! I didn't come here to cause trouble."

Bram hated the familiar feel of adrenaline rushing through his body, making his heart race and his breathing speed up. He managed to keep his voice and hand steady, though, and that was something.

"It was self-defense. I'd never seen him before in my life, and he came at me and I… it was just instinct. Luck. An accident, almost. If I hadn't killed him, he would have killed me. The cops and the DA agreed. It was all caught on the security cameras."

"I know," Daniel said with a sigh. "And I'm not here to avenge my brother's death, I promise."

Brother. Daniel didn't look anything like the man who'd tried to murder Bram three months earlier. But then, Daniel hadn't gotten a good look at his assailant. Hadn't even noticed him, in fact, until the guy came flying down the grocery aisle with a can of peas held tight in one fist. He'd swung the can against Bram's skull with all his might, and when Bram fell, his attacker landed on top of him and kept whaling away with the fucking can. But Bram was bigger, stronger, and apparently had a well-developed sense of self-preservation. He was able to buck the man off. He would have run away, but the man grabbed Bram's leg. And when Bram came crashing down on top of him, the man's head had thudded against the bottom shelf with a sickening crack. He went still instantly. Broken neck, the cops told Bram later. And no traces of drugs in the guy's system. Everyone concluded it must have been a sudden psychotic break.

"I'm sorry for your loss," Bram said to Daniel. He meant it. It wasn't Daniel's fault his brother was messed up. But Bram didn't lower the knife either.

To Bram's surprise, Daniel gave him a sad little smile. "Thank you. Darius was… he did some stupid things sometimes. But he was good, you know? He had a good heart."

"Okay," Bram replied noncommittally. "Look, I—"

"I know why he tried to kill you."

Bram gave Daniel a long, hard look. "Because he was crazy."

Daniel shook his head. "No. That wasn't it. And I know… you're probably going to think *I'm* crazy, but I'm not. Please, Mr. Tillman. If you don't listen to me, you're going to die."

Bizarrely, Bram actually felt a little calmer with the threat. Maybe because death—an eventuality he'd never before given much thought—had been such a frequent visitor lately. He wiped the sweat from his forehead with his upper arm.

"It's late," he said. It wasn't exactly true, but he was tired.

"I'm sorry." Daniel finally dropped his hands and then looked as if he didn't know quite what to do with them. He shoved them in his front pockets and pulled them out again. "It's urgent. My lwa has been trying to tell me for a while, and it wasn't until today I finally understood her."

"Your what?"

Daniel repeated the word slowly. "Lo-ah. My lwa. My mystère."

"I don't know what the hell you're talking about."

"She's… a spirit. An intermediary between humans and Bondye."

"Bondye?"

"The Creator."

Bram waved the knife slightly. "Is this some weird religious thing? 'Cause I'm not going to convert." He was permanently and comfortably secular.

"It's vodou," Daniel replied quietly.

Sweat made Bram's grip on the knife precarious, and his hand was beginning to cramp. He wondered when his life had taken a turn from boring and ordinary to surreal. "You and your zombie apocalypse can go home now," he said. "I'm calling the cops."

"Please, Mr. Tillman. This isn't… this is *real*. A spirit is trying to kill you. If you don't stop him, it'll keep trying until it succeeds." Daniel looked as if he were going to cry.

Bram had a perverse desire to set down his knife and phone in order to comfort Daniel. He wanted to know what the other man would feel like wrapped in his embrace, and he speculated whether those plush lips felt as soft as they looked.

Jesus.

Now Bram was going crazy too.

"You need to leave now," he said, the words coming out more gentle than threatening.

Daniel shook his head and pressed his lips together, and his shoulders slumped a little. As he reached for his back pocket, Bram steadied the blade. But all Daniel did was pull out a worn leather wallet. He opened it and withdrew a slip of paper.

"I was afraid you wouldn't listen. This is my phone number. Please reconsider. I can help you." When Bram made no motion to accept the paper, Daniel sighed and stooped to set it just inside the threshold. He stood again. "My lwa is selfish. She doesn't usually concern herself with other humans, and I don't know why she's trying to protect you. You should listen to her, though. She's never wrong."

As Bram watched, Daniel turned and walked down the sidewalk to the street. He got into a nondescript Honda and drove away. Only when the car was gone did Bram put the knife and phone on a nearby shelf. He wiped his damp hands on his shorts. Before he closed the door, he picked up the paper and stared at it. It showed only Daniel's name and number, written neatly in blue ink. Instead of crumpling the paper, Bram set it on the shelf. *Evidence*, he decided. *In case the guy turns out to be a stalker.*

Bram's sleep was restless that night. He tossed in his tangled, sweat-soaked sheets and woke up repeatedly with his pulse racing, the dregs of nightmares draining from his consciousness. And every damn time he awakened, his dick was achingly hard. At some bleary predawn hour, he gave in—he wrapped his hand around his cock and began to tug. His movements were hard and jerky, his grip tight enough to hurt. And the images that flashed behind his closed eyelids were disturbing: open graves, naked men with featureless faces, a pair of sunglasses with one lens missing, Daniel Royer's soft blue eyes. Bram came with a groan composed of pain as much as pleasure. He wiped his sticky hand on the sheets, rolled onto his side, and finally fell into a deep sleep.

Chapter Two

BRAM USED to drive the nearly three miles to work. But then his car was in the shop for a couple of weeks after the accident, and he got in the habit of running to work instead. He had to leave extra early, and he arrived reeking of sweat. But TintChem offered its employees on-site gym facilities that included showers. Afterward Bram would dress in his company-spec chinos, polo shirt, and white lab coat, and he often detoured by the cafeteria for breakfast.

Today he lingered in the shower. A couple of people were in the gym, staring at TV screens while they used the treadmill and stationary bikes, but Bram had the locker room to himself. He hoped the hot water would wash the cobwebs from his brain, but even as he was toweling off, he felt groggy and out of sorts. He combed his hair without truly looking at himself in the mirror. He knew what he'd see—a sandy-haired guy in his midthirties with dark circles under his eyes. He was a pretty big guy, with heavy bones and naturally thick muscles. In the past few years, he'd put on a few pounds, but when Bram had worried about his waistline, Jim had laughed and given him a squeeze, saying, "I think love handles are sexy."

In the months since Jim's death, however, Bram had lost weight. He wasn't eating properly, and he was pushing his body too hard. He cinched his belt to its tightest hole, and even then his pants slid lower on his hips. Time to buy new clothing. Great. He stopped by the cafeteria but couldn't work up an appetite for even simple food like an orange or a yogurt cup. He ended up buying a large coffee and dumping a lot of sugar into the paper cup.

The brightly lit hallways hurt his eyes—fluorescent lights glaring off white-tiled floors and white-painted walls. He squinted as he walked, his gaze focused just ahead of his feet. He took the stairs to the third floor instead of the elevator.

He shared a small office with Janet Vang, who grunted at him when he entered. He grunted back. That was generally the limit of their casual conversation. It wasn't that they disliked each other—he thought Janet was a brilliant researcher with meticulous habits, and she'd mentioned once that she appreciated his flashes of insight. It was just that neither of them was the chatty type, which was probably why they'd been assigned an office together in the first place.

In addition to Janet's reticence, this morning Bram was also thankful for her dislike of overhead lighting. She had a task light on her desk and so did he. He clicked his on after he sat down and then waited for his computer to boot up. He usually preferred to listen to music while he worked, but today he looked at his headphones and decided not to bother. During his morning jog, all the chords had seemed slightly off, the words of familiar tunes wrong in ways he couldn't identify. He knew he hadn't had much alcohol for months, but he couldn't possibly be hungover from a single beer, could he?

He sipped his coffee and stared at the blue computer screen, and somehow the world seemed distant and almost irrelevant. He imagined this was how an astronaut might feel as he floated in the star-spotted darkness, looking down at that blue-and-white ball so very far away.

JANET MIGHT have been at lunch, or maybe she was in the lab. Bram was deep in a soothing stack of analysis reports, the pretty graphs and strings of numbers and letters swimming around in his brain like tropical fish. He startled a little when he realized someone was looking over his shoulder.

"Oh. Hi, Carla." Carla Castro was the VP of research and development, which made her Bram's boss, but she was also a friend in a motherly sort of way.

She rolled Janet's chair closer to Bram and sat down. "You're way ahead of schedule on these things, Bram. You can slow down."

"I know. I just... I like to get ahead. You know how I feel about deadlines."

"Hmm. Well, they might be called deadlines, but they're not supposed to be fatal. You look like hell, kid."

"Gee, thanks. I love you too."

She drummed her fingers on the armrest. She was a large woman with a bust that strained her blouse buttons, and she smiled a lot. She wasn't smiling now, though. She looked worried.

"Have you been seeing a doctor, Bram?"

"I'm not sick, Carla."

"Not that kind of doctor. We have good insurance. You should take advantage of it."

"We've had this discussion before."

She leaned forward to pat his arm. "I know. I'm gonna keep nagging until I get my way."

Bram rubbed his forehead. "Is that why you came here? To insult me and then threaten me?"

"Yep." She grinned. "And also I have a gift for you."

"What?"

"Hawaii."

He lifted his eyebrows. "I didn't realize you had the power to give away an entire state, Carla."

"Sure. Me and Kamehameha? We're like this." She held up her first two fingers, twisted together. "Anyway, it's more of a loan than a giveaway. There's a conference in Honolulu in three weeks."

"Send Janet."

"It's your turn. She went to the last one, remember?"

"The last one was in Akron, Carla. That doesn't count." He gave a small shrug. "Besides, I'm not up to it right now."

She leaned back in the chair and regarded him for a long time. "Look, kid. You've been through a hell of a lot over the past eight months. Jim's death, the accident, the—"

"I know." It wasn't like he needed a list to remind him.

"A lot of people don't face that much stress in a lifetime. You're strong, Bram, but you're not unbreakable. You need help."

"I'm doing my job!" he snapped. He felt slightly guilty about his outburst but didn't tone down his glare.

Carla looked neither cowed nor offended. "I know you are. It's not your work I'm worried about. Lean on someone, honey. I know you don't get along well with your family, but you have friends. And there are professionals who can give you a hand too."

"Professionals," he growled.

She looked sad as she stood. "At least a vacation. Palm trees. Drinks with paper umbrellas. Cabana boys in sarongs."

Despite himself, he smiled at her. "Sounds like you've been fantasizing, Carla."

"A girl's gotta dream." She patted him again. "Think about it. I won't mention the conference to Janet until Monday."

HE DID think about it. Not right away, but later, while he jogged home through air so thick and hot he could practically drink it. He and Jim had visited Hawaii a few years earlier. Not Honolulu, though—Maui and the Big Island. They hiked lava fields and rain forests, they sunbathed, and Jim attempted to teach Bram how to surf. They watched romantic sunsets from their lanai. They ate piles of tropical fruits. They made love to the sound of pounding waves, then cuddled in bed together and daydreamed about buying a retirement condo on one of the islands.

Although Bram was exhausted, he didn't run straight home. He put in an extra mile or two, his feet pounding the tarmac and the sweat blinding him, his lungs laboring for every molecule of oxygen. By the time he staggered into the house, his legs were so shaky they could barely hold him. He came damned close to blacking out and couldn't make out why—until he drank some water and remembered he hadn't eaten anything all day.

"Not good," he said as he headed to the bathroom. He stripped off his sodden clothes and ducked under the shower before the water warmed. The cold spray made his breath catch, but he stood there anyway. "Stop punishing yourself," he said as the rivulets chilled his body. "It won't bring Jim back." Wouldn't make the whole last year unhappen.

He cooked a decent meal that night—a big cut of pan-seared steak, a salad, a bunch of cherry tomatoes his next-door neighbor had grown. And no beer, just ice water.

The only thing he disliked more than cooking alone was eating alone. He refused to take his dinners in the dining room, where he and Jim used to entertain occasional guests, or even at the smaller table in the kitchen. Instead he sat in the living room with the plate perched on his lap as he pretended the television made good company. After washing up, he channel-flipped until he found an ancient Spencer Tracy movie. An early bedtime, he decided when the movie was over. He'd get some decent sleep to make up for the previous night. And the many nights before that.

He even smiled a little when he slipped naked into bed and heard the first rumblings of a distant thunderstorm. Rain would be good. Might cool things down.

HE DREAMT of a rainstorm. He wandered through a graveyard at night, searching for something, hunching his shoulders in a vain attempt to keep the water from running under his collar and down his back. When he came to a large mausoleum with its door wide open, he ducked inside. The interior smelled like wax and dust. It was a much bigger space than it should have been—so big and dark he couldn't see the walls. In fact, as he turned around, he realized he could no longer see the door. A small pool of bluish light illuminated the space immediately around him. The floor was sandy like a beach, and his bare feet sank in, making walking difficult. The light followed him as he slowly struggled forward.

"Hello?" he called. There was no answer, not even an echo.

He walked for what felt like miles, but nothing ever changed. Maybe he was going in circles. He collapsed, sat with his back bent, and sifted the sand through his hands. If he could only deduce the sand's chemical composition, maybe he could find his way out.

"Calcium carbonate?" he mused. "Basalt? Quartz?" No, he realized with a start—with that weird but definite knowing common to dreams— the sand was made of crushed coconut shells.

"I do like coconut," someone said before stepping into view. He was a very skinny man with very dark skin. He wore a long black duster, a purple feather boa, and a black top hat. Bright lipstick accented his lips, and his eyes were dusted with gold and purple eye shadows. He had an unlit cigar in one hand and an ornate black-and-gold walking stick in the other. His hips swayed as he walked closer. He stopped when he was almost within reach, and then he smiled coquettishly. "Do you like coconut too, Abraham?"

"Bram." The correction was automatic.

The man had a trilling laugh. "All right, then. Bram it is."

"I want to go home."

"You *are* home, *mon cher*. You are curled up very beautifully in your bed. This is only a dream, yes?"

"Then I want to wake up."

"Why? Is your waking life so good you cannot bear to leave it?" The man sank gracefully into a cross-legged sit opposite Bram. He balanced the stick across his bony knees. "I think maybe you have been trying to escape that life for some time now."

"I don't...." Bram wasn't sure how to respond, so he shook his head. "I'm confused."

"Humans often are. You chase yourself in such tight circles, you never see the truth. You don't take enough time to celebrate what you ought to."

"What should I be celebrating?"

The man smiled at him. "Life. Death. It's all one thing, *mon cher*, all part of the dance." His expression turned more serious. "But we must take our steps in time. I think now for you, it is time for life."

He picked up his cane and tapped the end against Bram's chest. The metal tip was either very hot or very cold—Bram couldn't tell which. Either way it burned him, and he yelped but couldn't move away.

One more tap and the man resettled the stick in his lap. "Death seeks you now. It is not time yet for you to die, *mon chou*, so I have been helping you. I might continue." The corners of his lips lifted into a grin that was more like a leer. "But you must ask me nicely. You must *please* me. Then perhaps I will help you more."

"I don't believe in you!"

The man threw back his head and laughed. "As if your belief matters to me," he said, still chuckling. He rose gracefully, executed a deep curtsy, then turned and walked away. But even after the darkness swallowed him, he called back. "I like coconuts and white rum. Or you could sacrifice a black goat!"

Chapter Three

BRAM WOKE up sandy-eyed and sticky with sweat. The sun had not yet risen, but when he squinted at his alarm clock, he decided it wasn't worth trying to get more sleep. Besides, he had to piss. He untangled the sheets, stood and stretched, then shambled to the bathroom, where he emptied his bladder with a satisfied sigh. At the sink, he splashed water on his face while he considered whether to take a quick shower—just enough to wake himself up—or get into his running clothes and jog to the office early. Maybe he could put in a little time with the weights at the gym.

He was idly mulling over this conundrum when his hand strayed to his chest.

"Ow! What the—" His surprised yelp faded away when he saw the marks near his sternum: two angry red circles the size of silver dollars, their edges slightly overlapping. He bent his head for a closer look. Blisters. The marks were fucking *blistered.*

He ran back to his bedroom and rummaged through his bedding in a frenzy, but some part of him knew the truth. He wasn't going to find any weird bugs or mysterious electric devices or anything else that could have burned him while he slept. But only when his mattress was bare did he sink down to the floor in defeat.

It had to be psychosomatic. He'd taken a psych class back in college, and he vaguely remembered a lecture about how certain extremely pious Christians sometimes developed stigmata, their deep religious convictions translating to physical marks on their bodies. Not that Bram was a devotee of anything, but the mechanism could be the same. As Carla had pointed out, he'd been under a huge amount of stress lately. And that visit by Daniel Royer had been unsettling at best. Surely Bram's sleeping mind could be forgiven for taking a quick vacation into Bizzaro-land. Christ, maybe he should take Carla's advice and see a shrink.

The explanation made him feel a little less unsettled, so he stood and set his bedroom back in order. After that, he returned to the bathroom, where he smeared aloe vera gel on the marks and covered them with bandages. Another thought hit him as he pulled on his T-shirt.

Maybe he wasn't even a little bit nuts—maybe he was just developing hives. He'd recently switched brands of laundry detergent, so that could be the culprit. He'd pick up some hypoallergenic stuff after work.

He felt much better as he jogged through the dawn-lit streets. And after he got to the office and spent thirty minutes in the gym, he felt better yet. There was a slight hiccup in his relief when he hit the showers and removed the bandages on his chest—the water stung the burns—but he forcefully pushed the worries out of his head. His work was engaging enough to keep him occupied all day; so much so, in fact, that he skipped lunch again. Maybe he should stock up on some protein shakes or something, or at least remember to bring a sack lunch. Janet had one of those dorm-sized fridges on her side of the office, and Bram was reasonably certain she'd share if he asked.

By the time he left work, he had a plan. It was almost six on a Friday night. He'd go home and shower, then hit the mall for some new clothes. He'd take himself out to dinner afterward. And then he'd go to the grocery store and stock up on stuff he could eat while he worked— and new laundry detergent as well. Finally, he'd head back home and wash his sheets.

Yeah, he was all about the wild weekends.

As pathetic as his plan was, he felt pretty good about it because it meant he wouldn't spend the entire evening at home, brooding himself into a variety of skin conditions. The plan was a good omen—a sign that he was coping with life's setbacks in a reasonably healthy way. He was so pleased with himself that he upped the volume on iTunes. Jim used to make fun of Bram's exercise playlist, but if the Go-Go's and the Cars kept his feet moving at a swift pace, Bram figured the music was doing its job.

At a quiet intersection not far from home, Bram ran in place while he waited for the light to change. He hummed along with the J. Geils Band and, for lack of anything better to do, tried to make sense of the lyrics. What the hell was a lipstick reflex anyway?

Through the din of the music, he heard an angry engine. He turned to the left, where a dip in the road obscured oncoming traffic. And that was when a red sedan came racing up the hill and through the intersection, jumped the curb, and headed straight for Bram.

Through pure reflex—not the lipstick kind—Bram threw himself to the side. He caught a blurry glimpse of the driver, a middle-aged white lady with bleached-blonde hair and a manic grin, and as he fell and rolled, the car zoomed past with only inches to spare. He tumbled through the grass and onto the street. Brakes squealed. He tried to get up and run, but his legs wouldn't obey. The car's motor gunned, and he bunched into a fetal ball, waiting for the impact. With a squeal of tires, the car sped away.

Bram stood slowly, cautiously. He yanked the tangled headphones out of the jack and shoved them into his pocket. The phone remained undamaged in his armband. He instinctively thought to call the police, but what was the point? He hadn't gotten the car's license number, and his description would be vague and uncertain at best. As far as he could tell, nobody else had witnessed what had happened. The car had left physical evidence—skid marks on the tarmac and tire tracks in the grass—but that was all. The cops would likely chalk up the whole incident to reckless driving. But although Bram had seen the driver's expression for only a split second, he had no doubt that she intended to run him over.

He conducted a quick self-assessment. Grass stains on his clothes, gravel and dirt embedded in his skin. He was going to feel bruised and achy by morning. And those fucking burns on his chest—they stung like a sonofabitch. But he wasn't dead.

Yet.

He walked the rest of the way home instead of running, took a long cool shower, then ate a bowl of pasta with chicken meatballs. He walked into the living room, picked up the slip of paper he'd left on the shelf near the front door, and called Daniel Royer.

BRAM CHOSE Chili's as a meeting place because it was the most mundane location he could think of. On a Friday night, it was also crowded and noisy. Toddlers tossed food from their high chairs while their older siblings squabbled over crayons. College kids shouted happily at each other over glass beer steins. Waiters scurried back and forth with food-laden dishes, and in the bar, TV screens flashed baseball and soccer.

Yet somehow Daniel Royer managed to exude an aura of calm as he sat in a corner booth, a little island of quiet within the tumult. He wore tight blue jeans and a plain red T-shirt, and he sipped from a glass of iced tea spiked with several packets of sugar. He was even more beautiful than Bram remembered, and once Bram sat down, he had to fight the wild urge to reach across the table and stroke Daniel's face.

"It's not about zombies or sticking pins in dolls," Daniel said. Although his voice was soft, it somehow carried well.

"Yeah, okay. I got that. But this is Chicago. It's not New Orleans or, or…." Bram flapped his hands.

"Or exotic Haiti. Or deepest, darkest Africa." Daniel looked amused. "I know. I was born here. We're white-bread, NASCAR, football-on-Sundays, church-picnic, red-white-and-blue-wearing folks here."

"I'm… I'm a man of science." Christ, that sounded pompous and ridiculous, but Bram kept talking anyway. "When I was a kid, my friends had posters of sports teams, rock stars, pinup girls, movies…. I had Albert Einstein and Isaac Newton. They asked for video games for Christmas; I asked for chemistry sets and microscopes. I won science fairs. I have a PhD!"

Daniel shrugged. "I was the county-wide spelling bee champ three years running, and I have a master's degree. That doesn't change anything." He took a pull of iced tea through his straw.

Bram sank against the upholstered seat back. "A master's in what?" he asked, as if it were especially important right now.

"Social work."

"Oh."

"You don't think that counts because it's not a hard science." Daniel's mouth twitched into a crooked grin.

"No, I'm sure it's, um…." Bram squirmed uncomfortably. "I'm not here to judge your academic credentials."

"Why are you here, Mr. Tillman? Excuse me. *Dr.* Tillman."

"It's Bram. You said someone's trying to kill me."

"I did. And you didn't believe me. What made you change your mind?"

Bram ran his fingers through his hair, and when that didn't help settle his thoughts, he started folding a paper napkin into complex origami shapes. "Things have been pretty… weird lately."

"Not just my brother?"

Bram shook his head. "No. A few weeks after that, I was in a car accident. This man… I was driving to work, and he swerved right into me.

Head-on. Bang." He shuddered, remembering the sickening reality of the collision, the horrible sounds of crunching metal and shattering glass.

"What happened?" Daniel asked gently.

"He died. My airbag saved me. He was a retired guy on his way to have breakfast with his buddies. Nobody knows why he lost control like that. Except I saw his face right before he hit me, and he *didn't* lose control. He was aiming for me."

Daniel didn't look doubting—just sad. "Another death."

"Yeah. And today when I was jogging, some lady almost ran me over. She was trying to hit me too. She didn't die, though. She just took off really fast after she missed."

"You've had very good fortune."

"Good fortune?" Bram shook his head. "That's three times I almost got killed."

"*Almost.* Three times you just barely escaped. I'd say that's amazingly good luck."

The perky waitress appeared with a plate of nachos and a refill for Daniel's iced tea. "Anything else, guys?" she chirped.

They declined and waited for her to bustle away before they continued their conversation. Daniel took a tortilla chip, and when he stuck out his tongue to catch a bit of melty cheese, Bram was transfixed.

"There's something else," Bram said, more to distract himself than because he really wanted to share the next part.

Daniel swallowed and lifted his eyebrows expectantly. "Another near-death experience?"

"Not exactly. I had... I had a dream last night." His cheeks heated, and he realized he was blushing as furiously as if he were admitting to a wet dream. "There was a strange man, and he said the same thing you did—someone's trying to kill me. He said he might help me if I pleased him, whatever that means. Something about a goat. And, uh, he touched me. With his staff." Yeah, that particular choice of terminology didn't decrease his embarrassment one bit.

At least Daniel looked neither amused nor scandalized. Instead, his eyes were wide and shocked. "*You* had this dream?"

"Yes. And, well, look." Feeling more ridiculous by the minute, Daniel unfastened the top several buttons of his shirt. He deliberately hadn't worn anything underneath, so now when he parted the fabric as much as restaurant propriety allowed, the circular burns were easily visible.

Daniel leaned forward to stare at his chest, and although there was nothing sexual in Daniel's interest, Bram's heartbeat felt a little unsteady and his cock hardened uncomfortably against his jeans. Jesus. It had been far too long since he'd gotten laid—since he'd been so much as touched by another man.

"What did this man look like?" Daniel asked, still focused on Bram's sternum.

"Thin. Dark. Sort of... ageless, I guess."

"And what did he wear?"

This was, without a doubt, the strangest conversation Bram had ever had. Possibly the strangest conversation ever exchanged inside a Chili's. "A black coat and feathers. Makeup."

"Ghede Nibo." Daniel murmured the words quietly, almost reverently.

"What?"

After a long pause, Daniel looked up into Bram's eyes. "He is a lwa. You remember I told you about them?"

"Intermediary spirits," Bram answered promptly.

That earned him a bright smile. "You do learn a lesson quickly, Dr. Tillman. Yes. The ghede in particular concern themselves with death. And with sex."

Bram remembered what the man in the dream had told him. "All part of the dance," he repeated.

"Yes! Exactly!" Daniel ate a celebratory nacho, and Bram had one too. He was hungry. Then he buttoned up his shirt.

"You see," Daniel said after he'd swallowed, "Ghede Nibo is very powerful. He's a very good lwa to have on your side."

Of course, Bram still didn't believe a word of this. Except.... Daniel was obviously sincere. And the burns, the brushes with death, those were all objectively real. "Why would this Nibo guy give a shit about me? I'm a white guy!" He winced at his words, half expecting Daniel to toss his iced tea in Bram's face.

But Daniel only raised his finely sculpted eyebrows. "Three of my grandparents were white too."

"I… I didn't mean…." Bram rubbed his face. "I'm sorry. I only meant that I'm not into vodou and I've never met anyone before who was. So why would a vodou spirit have anything to do with me?"

"I don't know. It's unusual that he'd speak to you like that. But he does tend to take an interest in young men threatened with untimely death." His crooked smile reappeared. "And he has an eye for handsome men too."

Bram blinked at Daniel for a moment before looking down at the table, pretending to busy himself with more cheesy chips. "He said it wasn't my time yet to die."

After a thoughtful nod, Daniel took a long sip of his tea. "So then the question is who's trying to kill you."

"But… I don't get it. Your brother tried to kill me. And the guy who rammed into me, and the lady in the red car today. It's beginning to feel like everyone wants me dead, and I don't understand why. Is it some weird Mob thing? Is someone paying these people to… to off me?" That was a ridiculous notion, of course, but then so was the idea that he had an invisible target painted on him.

Two tables away, a small child screeched, distracting them both. When Bram turned back, Daniel was frowning. "Let me tell you about Darius," Daniel said softly.

Even though his questions remained unanswered, Bram nodded. "All right."

"He was… he was my baby brother. I was seven years older, and he always looked up to me, always wanted to do whatever I did. And even though he was nearly twenty-three, he hadn't yet outgrown that."

Automatically, Bram did the calculation in his head. Daniel must be thirty, or close to it. Bram wouldn't have guessed that. Or maybe he would have, if he'd looked carefully, because there was a certain… solidity to Daniel's eyes that spoke of more age and experience than kids usually possessed.

"Our mama was a manbo," Daniel said. "A priestess. When I was younger, I was too busy to bother much with vodou. And too stupid. But a few years ago, not long before Mama died, I had some dreams… I became ounsi. An initiate."

"What does that mean?"

Daniel was silent a moment, his gaze assessing. Maybe he saw whatever he was looking for in Bram's face, because he nodded once. "It means I bound myself to my lwa. We became partners of a sort. When there is a ceremony, sometimes she rides me."

Momentarily, Bram pictured Daniel fucking a beautiful woman—and he was shocked and ashamed by a sharp pang of jealousy. "Ride?"

"It's... like possession. She takes over my body for a while."

"I'd hate that," said Bram, who detested losing control.

"It's not a bad thing. I remain present when she rides me, but she's momentarily in charge. I trust her. And in return, she protects me and gives me her counsel." He grinned. "And she knows how to have fun, my Ezili Freda." But then his expression turned serious again and he added, "It was Freda who told me what happened with Darius, and who sent me to warn you."

The waitress appeared just as Bram was about to ask another question. "Can I get you guys refills? Something else to eat?" Daniel handed her his nearly empty tea glass, but Bram just shook his head. He was nursing a beer.

"What happened with Darius?" Bram asked as soon as she was gone.

"He was jealous of me, I think. Of Freda. He'd been trying for some time, but none of the lwa had come to him. I kept telling him to wait, but he was never patient." Daniel sighed loudly. "He decided to hurry things along."

"How?" Bram felt as though he was playing twenty questions. He didn't mind, though. He liked being in Daniel's company. Since Jim died, Bram had barely conversed with anyone outside of work, and certainly nobody as attractive as his current companion.

"My brother began to visit graveyards at night. It's not advisable. The ghede walk then, and they will try to escape the burial grounds in the bodies of the living."

"The ghede. Like Nibo?"

"Exactly! But although I wouldn't mind being Nibo's horse, I—"

"Horse?"

Daniel gave a small, elegant shrug. "That's what a person is called when a lwa rides him."

"Oh." Giddyup.

"It's just a word, Bram," said Daniel, probably sensing Bram's unease. "And Ghede Nibo, he's powerful but not unkind. Some other ghedes are more dangerous. Some of them scare the hell out of me. But Darius wanted a lwa to ride him."

The nachos had almost disappeared. Bram ate two more chips and pushed the plate toward Daniel, who finished off the rest. "Should we order some more?" Daniel asked, smiling.

"Sure. Why not." The waitress appeared just then with Daniel's tea, and she was happy to take their order. Bram wondered how much longer Daniel was going to last without a bathroom break. He was drinking a lot of liquid.

Daniel laughed softly as he poured sugar into his glass. "I'm usually better about watching what I eat. But I guess I can live it up a little. It's the weekend."

Bram glanced guiltily around their table at the other customers, all of whom seemed to be having a fun evening out. "I'm sorry if I ruined your plans for tonight," he said to Daniel.

"My plan for tonight was to turn on my air conditioner full blast and read a book that takes place somewhere really cold. Siberia. Antarctica maybe. You didn't ruin anything. I'm enjoying the company, actually." He locked his gaze with Bram's for a moment before looking slightly away.

"Oh," said Bram. He'd heard of drowning in someone's eyes but thought the idea was bullshit. Now he wasn't so sure. "I'm, uh, glad." And then, because he was more comfortable talking about vodou spirits than flirting, he returned to the previous conversation. "So your brother was hanging out in cemeteries."

"He was. But... I'm sorry. I'm going to have to explain a little more to you. You don't mind?"

"No. Go ahead."

"Everyone has two souls. When we die, one of them—the ti bon anj—returns to the Creator. But the gwo bon anj might remain here, to wander. Sometimes the gwo bon anj might watch over the family, especially if it's captured and kept in a spirit pot. But sometimes if the gwo bon anj isn't captured, it can cause trouble. It can ride men too, as a lwa does. It might be angry about being dead. Or just confused." He stirred his tea for a few seconds before looking up again. "Freda told me that a gwo bon anj was riding my brother, and that is why he tried to kill you."

Bram had struggled a little in following the story with all its unfamiliar words. "So... some dead guy was angry at me and possessed Darius?"

"Yes. And after Darius died"—Daniel winced slightly but went on—"after Darius died, the gwo bon anj rode someone else. The man who crashed his car into you. And then the woman today."

They were both silent for several minutes while Bram thought about this. He couldn't possibly believe in all this nonsense—yet he remembered clearly the identical expressions on all three assailants, and he could still feel the tightness of the burns under his shirt.

The waitress brought their second order of nachos before scurrying away.

"If this is true," Bram said slowly, "then I'm screwed. I've been lucky so far, but eventually this ghost is going to get me."

"They can be very stubborn," Daniel replied sadly.

"Well... fuck."

"You're not defenseless, you know. Ghede Nibo offered to help. I'll help too."

A silly warmth bloomed in Bram's chest. "Why do you care? Because your lwa told you to?"

Daniel shook his head. "I don't do everything she tells me to. She's very demanding. If she had her way, I'd wear pink and white dresses all the time and practically bathe in fancy perfume."

"Dresses?"

"I don't really enjoy cross-dressing, so I put my foot down on that one." He reached across the table and covered Bram's hand with his own. "I'll help because I want to."

Bram's throat was suddenly very dry. He didn't remove himself from Daniel's grasp, but with his free hand, he lifted his glass and took a big swallow of beer. He made a face when he tasted it, though. He wished he'd ordered something else. Rum.

"So how have I pissed off a dead guy so badly that he wants to kill me?"

Daniel squeezed Bram's hand before grabbing a nacho. It crunched loudly as he bit it. He chewed thoughtfully and swallowed. "I don't know. But I know how we can find out."

Chapter Four

THE WEATHER wasn't exactly chilly the following day, but it was a little cooler. Bram celebrated with a Saturday midmorning jog. He flinched every time a car drove past, but hell if he was going to stay housebound due to the possibility of a homicidal phantom. Besides, if this spirit was really that eager to get rid of him, surely it could find ways that didn't involve grocery stores or vehicles. It could firebomb his house when he was asleep or poison his water. It could possess someone with a gun and do a drive-by. So he went for a run. At least if the spirit continued to come after him, Bram would be in shape.

Besides, he needed to clear his head, and hard exercise was a good way to achieve that. Bram and Jim used to like those real estate shows where couples had to choose between three houses, each with different pros and cons. There was never a perfect home, and the couples always said the same thing after they saw their third option: "We have a lot to think about." Well, today Bram had a lot to think about.

The previous night he and Daniel hadn't really discussed vodou over their second plate of nachos. Daniel had outlined a plan and urged Bram to consider it. And then he'd steered the subject away entirely, asking Bram about his job, his family, his taste in music. They'd sat there for a long time, and the experience had ended up feeling oddly like a first date. Now Bram even had that whole fluttery pulse thing going when he thought about Daniel. It had been years since he'd felt like that. And he kept telling himself to cool it; this wasn't about romance, after all. But Daniel had found little excuses to touch Bram's hand, and he leaned forward over the table as if he were really interested in Bram's boring life.

Daniel told a little bit about himself too. He was a social worker who specialized in helping LGBT teens and young adults. He worried a lot about the kids and put in long hours, which made a social life difficult. But he loved his job, loved making a difference in people's lives. During his time off, he liked to read, garden, and do small home improvement projects. He was, Bram thought, smart and earnest and, when he wasn't counseling people or discussing vodou, a little bit shy.

Someone's lawn sprinklers jetted against Bram's legs as he ran by, which felt good. A lot of children were out this morning, riding bikes and playing ball while grown-ups washed cars or mowed the grass. Bram turned a corner and passed an elementary school. The building was closed for the summer, but kids played soccer and frolicked on the playground swings. Everything appeared as normal and ordinary as it could possibly be.

It was strange, then, how believable Daniel's tales of lwas and double souls still seemed. Maybe if Daniel weren't so attractive, Bram would have laughed him off. But Daniel *was* attractive—like a rare-earth magnet—and Bram found himself believing every word.

The farther Bram jogged, the more it seemed as if everything in his neighborhood was simply a thin veneer of normalcy overlaying something darker, stranger. That lady walking her golden retriever and those girls doing cartwheels on their front lawn—they were no more real than Disneyland animatronics. And the sunshine was far too bright.

Tears streamed from his eyes. His lungs burned, and his muscles screamed. He wasn't jogging anymore—he was sprinting as if Death were hot on his heels. His heart rate was much too fast. *You're going to die*, said a voice in his head. *But everyone does, eventually. Why hurry things along?*

He arrived back home just short of total collapse. In fact, once he was inside, he *did* collapse, crashing face-first onto the couch so hard that he nearly toppled it backward. He tried to roll over to ease his breathing but couldn't muster the strength. Finally, though, he managed to draw in enough oxygen so he could truly relax. Still sticky with sweat, he fell asleep.

GHEDE NIBO clicked his tongue. "You are very strange, *mon cher*."

Bram blinked at him. Ghede Nibo wore a black duster, a purple-and-gold feather boa, and a coordinating hat with a long black feather. His lipstick was crimson, as were his long fingernails.

"All right," said Bram, who concluded that pointing out a death spirit's own oddness was probably not a good idea.

They were back in the mausoleum, which smelled of fish and coconut. But maybe Ghede Nibo had been decorating, because sparkly streamers hung from the ceiling, and the walls had been painted with colorful murals. Off in one corner, a black rooster scratched at the floor. Bram sat cross-legged in the center of the room, wearing his smelly running clothes.

Ghede Nibo sat opposite him. Bram tensed a little over the walking stick, but Ghede Nibo simply set the cane across his skinny legs. "Why do you run, Abraham?" He gave the name its French pronunciation.

"Exercise."

"Exercise!" Ghede Nibo crowed with laughter. "You work in your garden—this is exercise. Or you lift stones to build a house. Then you will be strong *and* you will eat well and be safe from cold and rain. Your running, it serves no purpose."

He had a point. But Bram shook his head. "My house is built already, and I don't have a garden."

Ghede Nibo's smiled toothily. "Ah, but your ami Daniel, he has a fine garden indeed. A garden in need of plowing." He laughed again and thrust upward with his hips a few times.

"Uh, okay," said Bram, blushing furiously. He wasn't sure he'd ever blushed in a dream. "Look, could you just tell me who's trying to kill me? And how I can stop them."

"Tsk tsk. You cannot simply demand things. We must have a partnership, yes?"

"What do you want?"

The spirit didn't answer immediately. Instead he regarded Bram with an amused sparkle in his obsidian eyes. Then he leaned forward and traced a single red-tipped finger down the center of Bram's chest—right down the middle of the burn marks, which tingled—down Bram's stomach, and to his nylon-covered crotch. Bram tried to move away, but the only mobile part of his body turned out to be his cock, which perked up immediately, tenting his shorts and making Ghede Nibo laugh.

"This is what I wish to see," Nibo said, stroking lightly. "A boy who is big and eager."

Bram made a strangled noise. If the touch continued much longer, he was going to come. He hadn't had a wet dream since he was a teenager, and none of them were ever this weird.

But after crooning something in Creole, Ghede Nibo drew his hand back. Bram moaned his disappointment.

"Talk to your friend Daniel," said Ghede Nibo. "He will know how you may please me."

"You can't just tell me yourself?"

"What would be the pleasure in that?" responded the spirit with a grin. Then he leaned forward and touched Bram's dick again, just a soft caress with a single fingertip.

Bram shuddered and bit his lip hard enough to draw blood. "Please...," he moaned—

—and woke up on his couch, salty with dried sweat and aching with need.

He rolled onto his back, shoved his hand down his shorts, and with three firm strokes, came hard enough to see stars.

BRAM DIDN'T call Daniel that day. He spent the afternoon puttering around the house, doing a dozen small chores. It was weird how a life could be turned completely upside-down, and yet the garbage still needed to be emptied and the laundry done. He'd slept through lunch, but he made himself a big omelet for dinner with some steamed veggies on the side, and then he settled on the couch with a spy novel and the last Corona. He went to bed early and didn't dream.

On Sunday he felt restless. He didn't go running, though. It was the first day in months that he'd skipped it. He did a few errands, braving the mall for new pants and the grocery store to restock his fridge. But after he put his purchases away, he couldn't settle. He tried, but he felt as if something—or someone—might appear from another room at any moment. He'd experienced that frequently in the weeks after his lover's death, as if Jim might pop into the living room, laughing over the huge joke he'd played. Jim wasn't really a prankster, though, and he never did show up.

Bram tried going outside instead, first sitting on his porch and then strolling around the little paved area that passed for a backyard. But the sun was again too bright and the shadows too sharp. He drove to a coffeehouse a couple of miles away, an independently owned place with funky furniture, surly baristas, and delicious desserts. He and Jim used to go there on weekends and sit at one of the tables, sipping and nibbling, reading over their various documents from work. Bram hadn't been there since Jim died.

Maybe the barista recognized him, because she looked slightly startled to see Bram standing at the counter alone. "Yeah?" she demanded.

"I'd like a large dark roast, please." He and Jim always went out of their way to be super polite no matter how the baristas growled and snarled at them—sort of a silly game they liked to play.

The girl filled a paper cup, slammed it on the counter, and poked viciously at the cash register. She didn't even tell him how much to pay, just held out her hand impatiently. Clearly she felt that customers ought to read the total on the cash register screen themselves.

Bram handed her three one-dollar bills, which she snatched away. "Thank you," he chirped. "Keep the change." He grabbed the coffee and walked to an empty table.

The place wasn't especially crowded, maybe because the weather was fine. Bram hadn't brought any work to do, so he played with his phone for a while, then gathered and read abandoned newspaper sections from other tables. He still felt disconnected from the world around him, and his mind kept wandering—to the dream he'd had the previous afternoon, to the expression on the face of the woman in the red sedan, to the way Daniel's inviting lips curved when he smiled.

After Bram returned home, he spent a long time standing in his living room, staring at nothing. Then he picked up his phone and dialed Daniel.

Chapter Five

FOR THE first time ever, Bram called in sick on Monday. And it wasn't even much of a lie, seeing as how his stomach was tied up in knots and his skin felt clammy. It didn't help that the weather had turned sultry again or that all he'd managed to choke down for breakfast was a piece of toast and some coffee. He hadn't even attempted lunch. At least the low-hanging dark clouds prevented the sun from bothering his eyes as he drove across town.

Daniel lived in a quiet neighborhood where older houses perched on large lots. His house looked resolutely ordinary—a neat little brick bungalow with overflowing planter boxes hanging on the porch railings. Instead of grass, the front yard sported an attractive mixture of green, yellow, and purple foliage.

Daniel stepped onto his porch, smiled, and waved as Bram parked. Daniel was shirtless, and due to the porch wall, Bram couldn't see what he was wearing below the waist, making it easy to imagine him naked.

"Get a grip," Bram growled as he cut the engine. He grabbed the paper grocery sack from the passenger seat, exited the car, and proceeded up the walkway.

"Nice house," he said as he climbed the front steps. He was both relieved and disappointed to see that Daniel wore shorts.

Daniel beamed. "Thanks! I grew up here. It used to be kind of a mess, but I've been fixing it up."

"And gardening." Bram gestured at the front yard.

"Yeah. Did you know everything you're looking at is edible or medicinal? And there's lots more in the back. I've got—" Daniel stopped himself with an embarrassed smile. "Sorry. I get a little carried away. I know you don't care."

Except for some reason Bram *did* care, maybe because Daniel was so adorable in his enthusiasm. "I think it's pretty cool, actually. Maybe you could show me around after, um...." He waved the paper bag slightly.

That made Daniel beam. "I'd love to." He had a more businesslike expression as he gestured at the bag. "Did you get everything?"

"Yeah. It was a really weird shopping list, though."

"You're lucky. I already have several items we'll be needing. I sometimes give offerings to Ghede Nibo too. He's good for abundant crops."

"The whole life-death thing, huh?"

"Yes. He's a healer as well."

They stood for a moment on the porch, Bram feeling a bit awkward. He wiped sweat from his forehead.

"Do you want to come inside and have something cold to drink first?" asked Daniel.

"No, thanks. I'd rather get it over with."

"It's not a dental exam, Bram. Vodou ceremonies are joyous, especially when a Ghede is involved. Ghedes like parties."

Bram gave a wan smile. "I've never been much of a party animal." Sometimes Jim had dragged him to some celebration or another, but Bram tended to skulk in the corners, clutching a drink and glancing anxiously at his watch.

"Well, this will be a very *small* party. Just you, me, and the lwas. Come on." Daniel had offered to invite some of the other members of his spiritual group, but Bram had demurred, not feeling very social. He trailed Daniel down the front stairs and onto a narrow path that followed the side of the house. Daniel opened a gate to the backyard and ushered him through.

"Wow!" Bram exclaimed as they rounded the house. "You weren't kidding. You have a farm back here."

"It's less than an acre."

"Maybe. But it looks like every inch is crammed with plants." Not to mention butterflies, buzzing bees, and twittering birds. Spiderwebs decorated the branches of some low bushes, and a squirrel chattered at them from the branch of an apple tree.

"It's what I enjoy doing," Daniel said with a smile.

"Is all this stuff edible too?"

"Most of it, yes."

"What do you do with it all?"

Daniel plucked a sprig of something and handed it to Bram with a small flourish. Bram recognized the scent even before he took it—mint.

"I use a lot of it." Daniel chewed on a leaf he'd picked for himself. "And I donate most of the rest to the youth center where I do some of my work. Some of those kids, that's their only chance to eat something that isn't junk food."

"That's... that's really nice," said Bram sincerely. He remembered what Ghede Nibo had told him about exercise with a purpose. No disadvantaged kids ever benefited from Bram's jogging—that was for sure.

Daniel ducked his head slightly, looking pleased and embarrassed. Then he motioned toward the back of his property, at a long, low wooden building. As they got closer, Bram saw that the area in front of the building was free of vegetation, just hard-packed dirt covered by a thatched awning. Several brightly painted wooden poles supported the awning, and the front of the building sported murals done in vibrant colors.

"We use this as a dance space, a meeting space," Daniel explained when they reached the clearing. "If the entire société were here today, we'd do the ceremony here instead of inside the ounfò."

It felt like a friendly space. Cozy without being cramped, and surprisingly cool even in the day's heat. "Did you build this?"

"My parents did. But now I keep it in good shape."

"Your parents...." Bram vaguely remembered Daniel speaking of his mother in the past tense.

"Gone. Papa died when I was in high school, and Mama passed a few years ago."

"I'm sorry."

"It's not so bad. They still speak to me sometimes. Your parents?"

Bram snorted. "They're still alive, but they don't speak to me at all."

Daniel patted Bram's arm lightly. "Well, then *I'm* sorry." He opened the door, which was bright blue and covered in yellow and red words Bram didn't understand. "Please. Come inside."

Nobody had ever told Bram what to expect inside a vodou temple. When Daniel flicked the overhead lights on, Bram saw a room with a dirt floor and wildly painted walls. A thick pillar rose from the center of the floor to the ceiling, every inch of it covered in complicated paintings. Daniel walked to the pillar and patted it fondly. "The poto mitan. The lwa can use it as a path to the earthly world."

"Oh."

"We'll return here in a moment. But let's give the lwa their gifts first. We'll begin with Ezili Freda. I don't know if she'll join us today, but I have to pay my respects. She gets jealous." He pointed at the grocery sack still clutched in Bram's sweaty hand. "Leave that out here. Freda won't like a ghede's things in her room."

"She has her own room?"

"More or less." Daniel grinned. "The lwa are a bit like humans— they don't all get along. They have families too. Most of the other families tend to look down on the ghedes. Too crude, I think. So we give them their separate spaces, and everyone's happy."

That made sense, Bram supposed. He placed the bag on the floor near the pillar, then followed Daniel through one of several doorways. They entered a small close room that smelled strongly of floral perfumes. The walls were turquoise and lemon, a large table draped with a pink-and-white cloth—an altar, Bram assumed—took up most of the space. Bottles of perfume stood in neat rows on the bedspread, accompanied by a white vase of fresh pink roses and several brightly embroidered squares of cloth. Three bowls brimmed with food. Daniel pointed at them. "Rice with cinnamon. Fried bananas. Coconut pudding. My lwa has a sweet tooth."

Bram remembered all the packets of sugar Daniel had poured into his tea, and he smiled.

Although the room seemed scrupulously clean, it was crowded with other items as well, the purposes of which were unclear to Bram. Pictures of a female saint surrounded by hearts. A gilded mirror. Makeup. Things that looked like bottles covered with pink sequined fabric and topped with dolls, feathers, and artificial flowers. Several fancy dresses, mostly pink and glittery, hanging in plastic bags from hooks on the wall.

As Bram hovered near the open door, Daniel turned to give him a quick smile. "Just a moment, please."

"Do you want me to leave?"

"No, of course not. This is about you, after all." Daniel turned back to the altar. He swept the edge of his hand along the free spaces on the cloth as if brushing away dust or crumbs. Then he uncapped a small glass bottle and sprinkled some droplets of liquid onto the altar. Not water—the liquid smelled like sweet oranges. Daniel used a silvery lighter to light a fat pink candle. Then he murmured for a while, something quiet and rhythmic. Bram couldn't tell whether it was in English, but he suspected not.

Then Daniel began to speak clearly. "I've brought you gifts today, Ezili Freda. Do you see the new bottle of perfume I've left you? And your favorite foods. I made my mama's pudding, the kind you like so much. And I ask that you help me and my friend Bram today. Help us find out how to protect him from danger. If you do this for us today, I will give you this ring." He dug in his shorts pocket for a moment before pulling out a small gold circlet that glittered in the candlelight. "It's a very good ring, lady. Beautiful, like you. Serve us today, and I'll leave the ring here for you." He slipped it back into his pocket. Then he blew out the candle and exited the room with Bram.

"See?" Daniel said when they were back in the main room, the door to Ezili Freda's room closed. "No zombies."

"You were... bribing her. Can you do that?"

"Oh you have to, or she'll become spoiled. She has a taste for expensive things, and she's a little greedy."

"But that seems... I don't know." Daniel struggled to find the word. "Sacrilegious?"

"The lwa aren't gods, Bram. They're spirits and they have needs and desires, just as we do." His eyes were big, and he stood very close to Bram. It seemed to Bram that they were suddenly speaking about something quite different from jewelry and sweets. His throat felt a little thick, as if the air were heavier than normal, and sweat glued his T-shirt to his torso. Daniel was sweaty too, but in his case, the droplets slid down his skin, glistening like jewels.

Daniel's voice was a little raspy when he spoke next. "Let's pay our respects now to Ghede Nibo."

The ghedes' room was larger than Ezili Freda's and contained several altars, as well as a canopy-draped bed. "Do you sleep here?" Bram asked. Squeaked, really, because his voice came out a good octave higher than usual, mostly because he pictured Daniel lying naked atop the bright yellow quilt.

"Not usually. But once in a while, when I want a message from the lwa." His gaze lingered on the bed, making Bram wonder what Daniel was picturing there. Then Daniel shook his head slightly and gestured at an altar. "This is Ghede Nibo's."

Judging from the items on the altar—cards, dice, poker chips, and a tidy stack of cash—Ghede Nibo liked gambling. In addition, the altar contained cigars, a straw hat, and several gourds decorated with beads.

"What's that?" asked Bram, pointing at a bottle.

"Rum with habanero peppers. A drop of that stuff could probably peel your skin away, but Ghede Nibo likes it."

Bram wasn't especially fond of spicy food, but he licked his lips.

Daniel made a slightly strangled noise. "Let's give him his gifts," he said quickly.

After fetching the bag, Bram unpacked the items he'd brought. He handed each to Daniel, who set them carefully on the altar. A pair of sunglasses with one lens broken out. A bag of pistachios and a jar of pickled herring. A package of coconut cookies. A yard of shiny purple nylon fabric, a plastic bag of black feathers, a stuffed black-and-white toy goat. And a bucket of KFC Original Recipe, which Bram had bought the day before and refrigerated overnight, per Daniel's instructions. Bram was relieved that fast food would do and that he wasn't expected to sacrifice something instead.

"That's good," Daniel said after he'd arranged everything. "Now some money, please."

A tiny voice inside Bram's head spoke to him—the last gasp of the Man of Science, maybe. *See? That's what he's been after all along. It's a scam.* But he ignored the voice as he took out his wallet, pulled out three twenties, and handed them to Daniel. This would have been an awfully elaborate setup for a mere sixty bucks. Besides, money was barely a concern to him at the moment, when what he most wanted was to lick the salty moisture from Daniel's bare skin.

Daniel fanned the bills out slightly when he put them on the altar. Then he drizzled some liquid from a bottle onto the stuffed goat. This stuff was sharp and acrid—medicinal, like something a person might swallow to treat a bad cold.

He chanted briefly before speaking in English. "I know you favor my friend Bram. Thank you. And look at what he's brought you. But if you help him, we'll bring you more. Tell us how to keep him safe, okay? Then I'll throw you a party."

Daniel took Bram's hand and led him into the main room. "Is that it?" Bram asked.

"No. That was just the preliminaries. Sort of an invitation to the lwa. Now we do the ceremony itself. Well, I do. You get to sit and watch." He pointed to a few metal folding chairs sitting open and lining one wall. But before Bram could walk away, Daniel grasped his shoulder. "I'm going to call the lwa. They might send me a message. But also, Ezili Freda might ride me. She often does. If she chooses that today, don't be frightened. It's not scary for me."

Daniel's palm was very hot, even through the cotton of Bram's T-shirt. "How do I know if that happens?"

"You'll know," Daniel replied with a chuckle. He released his hold on Bram's shoulder. "Now, just get comfortable, all right?"

Bram followed instructions, crossing the room and sitting on the center chair. The room, dimly lit in general, was even more shadowy near the seating, which suited him fine. However, as Daniel moved around the space, lighting candles and fussing with various small things Bram couldn't identify, it was almost as if Daniel were on stage. This felt very real, though—a sharp contrast to the regular everyday world, which had seemed so artificial these past few days.

A small CD player perched on a shelf. Daniel pressed the buttons and drums began to play, a smooth and rhythmic pounding that seemed to echo in Bram's heartbeat. "If more people were here, we'd have live drumming instead," Daniel said. "But this will work." He opened an ornately carved and gaudily painted wooden armoire and took from it a garment that he slipped over his shoulders and buttoned up the front. It was a long cotton robe with wide sleeves and a deep V-neck. The fabric was a slightly dizzying design of fuchsia, white, purple, and canary. Daniel now looked like a vodou priest instead of just a beautiful social worker in a Midwestern city, and he flashed Bram a quick smile before reaching beneath the robe and stepping out of his khaki shorts. He picked up the shorts, set them on a shelf inside the armoire, and shut the door.

Objectively, Daniel was now clothed in more fabric than ever before in Bram's presence. Yet Bram imagined the lithe bare body that was hidden beneath the loose robes, and he had to swallow three times just to clear his throat.

An enormous boom made Bram startle violently, but Daniel only looked up at the ceiling and smiled. "Thunder. That's good. Ghede Nibo likes storms." Then he picked up a gourd rattle from a shelf and began to chant and sway to the drumbeat. He watched Bram as he did so, and although there was nothing erotic about Daniel's movements, he was easily the sexiest person Bram had ever seen. Bram shifted a bit in his chair as his cock filled, and Daniel gave him a small and knowing smile.

And then Daniel's eyes turned brown.

His hair was suddenly lighter and straighter, and it hung in a thick curtain down his back. His cheeks grew slightly rounder and his chin softened. His smiling lips brightened—not crimson, like Ghede Nibo wore in Bram's dreams, but a shiny pink like the Barbie aisle in a toy store. It was difficult to discern his shape beneath the flowing robe, but Bram could see Daniel's chest swell until a pair of high, round breasts strained at the fabric.

Then Bram blinked, and it was just Daniel again, handsome and definitely male. But he held his back exceptionally straight and his head high, and his movements became more delicate and graceful. Still smiling, he danced closer. His steps were small and graceful. He stopped when he was within arm's reach and smiled down at Bram, swaying his hips in time to the music. He smelled strongly of citrus and roses.

When Daniel said something in French, his voice was higher pitched and less raspy than usual.

"I'm sorry," Bram whispered. *His* voice sounded like broken concrete. "I can't understand."

Daniel gave a bell-like laugh and tilted his head inquisitively. *"Tu es très beau,"* he said very slowly. *"Très charmant."*

"Uh… merci."

With another trilling laugh, Daniel reached forward and just barely brushed his fingertips against Bram's cheek. Bram wouldn't have been surprised if the touch left scorch marks in its wake. But the heat also sank into his skin, spreading through his nerves at almost the speed of light, pooling in his belly like a sea of molten lava. He had never in his life been so desperately hard, so hungry to touch someone else. He whimpered and sat on his hands.

Without turning his back on Bram, Daniel danced slowly away. He stood near the large pillar, moving his hips sinuously and murmuring in French.

Bram's chest began to burn too.

He looked down, half expecting to see glowing circles through his T-shirt like a poor man's Iron Man. He saw nothing out of the ordinary. But even as he considered peeling off the sweat-sodden fabric, another thunderclap crashed, and as the sound faded into the beat of the recorded drums, something like an invisible veil draped over Bram's body. He couldn't move. But something was moving inside him, settling on his bones and inhabiting his skull. It was cool—a comfort in the sweltering heat—and heavy, and it smelled of freshly turned earth.

When Bram rose to his feet, it wasn't of his own accord.

He should have been terrified to lose control of himself like this, but the presence inside him was comfortable and friendly, confident in his movements in a way Bram had never been. It was almost a relief to give up his body to someone else—like letting another driver take the wheel after many hours on the road.

Bram danced smoothly across the floor, each step bringing him closer to Daniel and making him throb more urgently with need.

Daniel's eyes grew wide with surprise.

"You look good," said Ghede Nibo with Bram's voice. He spoke in Creole, but Bram understood.

"What are *you* doing here?" replied Ezili Freda in French.

Nibo laughed and pumped his hips obscenely. "What do you think?"

Freda looked as if she couldn't decide whether to laugh or be offended, which made Nibo hump the air a few more times. Then he danced past her—hips swiveling—and into the ghede room. He cackled when he saw the bed, but he went straight to his altar, uncapped the bottle of pepper-spiked rum, and took a very healthy swig. Bram was distantly aware that the stuff went down his throat like the flame of a blowtorch, but he didn't really feel the pain. With Freda watching from the doorway, still shaking the rattle, Nibo drank several swallows more.

"What do you think, my peach?" he said to Freda. "Are you ready for a real man now?"

Freda snorted elegantly. "Who says *you're* a real man? You're just a gravedigger. You stink of the dead."

"Oh, I'm a man all right, baby. I'll show you." Nibo ripped off his T-shirt and threw the shreds to the side. They landed on someone else's altar, which made him laugh. He kicked off his shoes. And in one smooth movement, he pulled down his shorts and briefs, then stepped out of them. His cock—Bram's cock—was fully rampant, and it bobbed as he rocked his pelvis. "You see?" he crowed. And then, perhaps to prove his point, he poured several ounces of the rum over his groin.

Deep in the recesses of his own brain, Bram swore. That fucking stung. But it also inflamed his lust—Nibo's lust; he couldn't tell the difference—to new and dizzying heights. Nibo lunged forward and grabbed Freda by the waist. She dropped the gourd rattle and screeched, but Bram couldn't tell whether from true outrage or in play, especially since she undulated her body against Nibo's in a manner that nearly drove Bram wild.

With a vicious yank, Nibo tore Freda's gown open. Buttons pinged as they hit the floor. He tugged the fabric from her and tossed it to the ground, leaving her as bare as he was.

Daniel's body was nearly hairless, just a neat little thatch of dark curls at the base of his cock, which was long and slender, and fully hard. His cock and balls were a few shades darker than the rest of him, except for the moisture-slicked tip, which was bright pink. Bram wanted to fall to his knees and lick the shaft, taste whether Daniel was sweet or salty, feel the heat of those high, round balls cradled in his palm.

But that wasn't what Nibo wanted, and Nibo was in charge. He held Freda tight against him and mouthed at her neck and collarbone while squeezing her tight, round ass. Freda and Nibo panted words at each other in French and Creole—endearments, threats, blasphemies, and promises. And God, the way Daniel was pressed against Bram, groin to groin and chest to chest, both of them slick with sweat and rum, smelling of alcohol and fruit and flowers.... Bram almost lost himself completely. He very nearly came.

Freda squirmed out of Nibo's grip, Daniel's blue eyes wide and mouth in a perfect O. She tried to dart away, but Nibo caught her neatly by the arm, tugged her close, and then dragged her across the floor to the bed. He threw her onto the bright bedspread and landed heavily on top of her, rutting hard into the hollow of her hip. She scratched his back and tugged his hair, but she also allowed her legs to fall wide open and she arched upward, perhaps attempting to get better friction against Daniel's cock.

Nibo scooted down slightly so he could suckle on Freda's nipples. Bram loved the pebbly feel of Daniel's flesh against his tongue. He wished he could stroke Daniel's cock, but Nibo wasn't interested in that part of the body beneath him. Oh, but Nibo liked the shallow navel, which he licked as if it were a tiny cup. He liked the sharp tips of the hip bones and the little groove where the torso met the leg. And he liked the puckered rosette between the sweet globes of Daniel's ass.

Freda squirmed and swore and attempted to get Nibo to penetrate her more deeply with his tongue, and then with his spit-moistened finger. "What kind of a man is that?" she said, panting. "That's all you can put inside me?"

"I have much more for you," Nibo retorted, rearing up on his knees and pulling Freda's dusty feet onto his shoulders. He took his cock—Bram's cock—in hand, gave it a few hard strokes, and pressed the slick crown tightly against Daniel's ass, but not quite inside.

Daniel's body went very still. If Bram could have held his breath, he would have. He knew he wouldn't last more than a few seconds inside that tight heat.

But what Bram saw on Daniel's face shattered him: large tears pooled in Daniel's blue eyes, dripped down his face, moistened the yellow fabric beneath his head.

"No!" Bram shouted. With a tremendous burst of will, he recommandeered his own body and tore himself away so violently that he tumbled onto the dirt floor. He scrambled backward with his hands and feet until he bumped against the wall, where he huddled into himself tightly. *I won't rape him!* he insisted.

Nibo's voice came out of Bram's throat. "But it is not rape. Did you not see? She was begging for me to fuck her." He waved at the bed, where Daniel had sat up and was wiping the tears from his eyes.

Maybe she was. But that's Daniel's body, and he didn't ask for any of this.

"He wants you too."

I don't know that. And I certainly don't know that he wants me to fuck him without lube and without a rubber. As far as Bram knew, he was free of STDs. But he hadn't been tested in a while, and Daniel certainly deserved some say in the matter.

Nibo made an exasperated sound. "Ah, you are a foolish man." He sighed. "But I think you are a good man. A man who keeps promises, yes?"

Yes.

"Then I will tell you who is trying to kill you." He waited several moments, probably to draw out the suspense, and then chuckled. "You are impatient, *mon chou*. He was your man, once. Now he is dead. It is he who you must fear." And with a visceral tug that made Bram gasp and shudder, Ghede Nibo was gone.

Chapter Six

UNDER OTHER circumstances, Bram would have admired Daniel's cozy living room. It had built-in bookcases and bright artwork, polished wood floors, a thick Persian carpet, and a tidy fireplace with a carved mantel. The furniture was nice too—a little shabby, maybe, but in a well-used, well-loved kind of way. And very comfortable. Bram slumped in a leather armchair, shirtless but with his shorts and shoes back on. Daniel sat on the couch opposite him, wearing jeans and a black sleeveless tee. Bram couldn't meet his gaze.

"I'm sorry," Daniel said very quietly.

Bram snapped his head up. "*You're* sorry?"

"I had no idea Ghede Nibo would ride you today. It's rare for a lwa to mount someone who's not an initiate."

"I…. Jesus, Daniel. That's not your fault."

"It must have scared you."

"Not really." Bram frowned. "I can't really explain it. It's almost like I'd been expecting him for a while."

Daniel gave him a small smile. "Because he's chosen you. I told you before, you're lucky. He's a very powerful lwa to have on your side."

"He tried to rape you!" Bram shouted.

But Daniel shook his head. "No. He tried to have sex with Ezili Freda. And believe me, she was very willing. She doesn't often want much to do with the ghede, but today she found Ghede Nibo very attractive."

"But she was in your body."

After a long moment of silence, Daniel said, "I find you very attractive."

"You were crying."

Daniel stood, walked the few feet that separated them, and knelt in front of Bram. He settled a warm hand on Bram's bare knee. "Ezili Freda was crying. She always does. I told you she's greedy, right? She cries because she realizes she's not going to get everything she wants." He gave a small grin. "It's like having a very spoiled child."

Bram looked into clear blue eyes and saw no anger or recrimination. "So you... you didn't mind?"

"It's not exactly how I would have planned our first encounter, Bram. But I was enjoying it at least as much as she was. I would have told you that if I could have."

"I would have hurt you."

"No." Daniel patted Bram's knee. "Did you feel pain when you poured that rum on yourself?"

"I felt... something. But it wasn't really pain. Or, I don't know. It was a good kind of pain." Bram frowned. He wasn't normally into that kind of thing.

"It would have been the same for me. Although I'd probably have been sore for a couple days afterward, I suppose." He paused, then winked. "I think it would have been worth it."

Relief made Bram feel boneless, and he slumped back in the chair. He ran a slightly shaky hand over his brow.

"How about you?" Daniel asked. "Did *you* want it?"

"I wanted you." He'd never wanted anything quite so badly, as a matter of fact.

Daniel's face broke into a huge and sunny smile. "Good." He leaned closer, squirming his way between Bram's legs. "Do you still?"

Bram's answer was immediate and honest. "God yes!" But then he shook his head. "But I think I should get my problem fixed first. Otherwise it's just... too weird."

"All right," said Daniel with a soft laugh. "I can understand that. Let's make sure that next time it's just the two of us, okay?"

"Yeah. A foursome is a bit much for me. Especially when one of them is female. I've never had sex with a girl."

"Never?" Daniel raised his eyebrows.

"Nope. I was still in the closet in high school, but I was such a total nerd that nobody even noticed. I tried making out with girls a couple times in college—scientific curiosity, I guess—but they did zilch for me." In a fit of honesty, he added, "I haven't really been with that many guys, actually."

Daniel stroked Bram's face. "You're so handsome. Why aren't men all over you?"

Bram leaned his head slightly into Daniel's touch. "I was a late bloomer, I guess. I fooled around a little, but in case you haven't noticed, I'm a little socially awkward. And most of the time, getting laid seemed like more trouble than it was worth." He closed his eyes for a moment. "And when I was in grad school, I met Jim. We lived in the same apartment complex near campus. He was in law school."

"Is that... is he the man Ghede Nibo spoke about?"

"Yes."

Bram pushed Daniel gently away so he could stand. He walked to one of the windows and gazed outside. The sky had darkened even more while they were in the ounfò, and rain had begun to fall. They'd both gotten wet during the short dash to Daniel's house, and as Bram stood dripping on the back porch, Daniel had brought towels so they could dry off. That meant that Daniel's curls were now a wild and appealing mess, while Bram's hair was probably standing up in weird spikes. And outside, the rain sheeted down. Bram hoped the storm didn't ruin Daniel's garden.

Daniel padded over to stand quite close. "Is Jim buried in Saint Mary's Cemetery?" he asked.

Bram didn't turn around. "Yeah. Wouldn't have been my choice, really, but his family has a plot there. Jim and I never talked about what we wanted if one of us died. I wasn't prepared. His parents insisted on burying him there, and I just kind of caved." He shook his head. "I was numb."

"That's understandable." After a brief pause, Daniel added, "Saint Mary's is where Darius was spending his evenings trying to find a lwa."

"Great."

"Do you want to tell me about Jim? You don't have to."

Although Bram had thought about Jim daily over the past eight months—brooded over him, sometimes—he'd spent very little time speaking of him. Not only because the topic made him uncomfortable, but because he doubted anyone would care.

Bram turned around and gave Daniel's shoulder a quick squeeze before returning to his chair. "He died in a car wreck," he began.

IT HAD been a cold, clear Friday evening with the moonlight shining on freshly fallen snow. Bram cuddled up on the couch in a sweatshirt and flannel lounge pants, a fleecy blanket over his shoulders and a pile of journal articles on his lap. On nights like this, he wished they had a fireplace for the crackling logs and the smell of wood smoke.

Jim was puttering around in the kitchen, maybe washing the dishes or preparing a midevening snack. He meandered into the living room and leaned in the doorway. He wore jeans and a red sweater that brought out the warm brown of his eyes.

"You want anything?" he asked.

Bram gave him what he hoped was a winning smile. "Hot chocolate?"

"We're out." Jim ran his fingers through his dark hair. "Do you want to go out, Bram?"

"Tonight, you mean?"

"Yeah."

"It's cold out."

Jim rolled his eyes. "We can wear parkas and gloves and hats and scarves. We can go somewhere warm."

"It's warm here."

With an impatient puff of air, Jim peeled himself from the wall. He walked back and forth a few times before collapsing next to Bram with a thud. "I'm bored."

Bram put down the article he'd been reading. "Do you want to watch a movie? We can see what's in our Netflix queue."

"I know what's in our queue. Nothing interesting." Moving quickly, he grabbed the papers from Bram's lap and tossed them to the floor.

"Hey!"

"Jesus, Bram. You're making paint, not curing cancer. Can't you forget about the damn job just for one night? We could go to a bar. I can call Mick and Bobby and see if they want to meet us somewhere. We can go dancing."

It was true that there was nothing especially pressing about Bram's work. But he bristled at Jim's tone. It wasn't the first time Jim had been dismissive about the importance of Bram's job.

"I don't want to go anywhere," Bram said sullenly.

With a noisy grunt, Jim got to his feet. "And that's the goddamn problem, isn't it? You don't want to go anywhere. We're not going anywhere."

They'd been having variations of this argument a lot lately, and each time, Bram grew more uneasy. He tried to keep his voice steady when he replied. "I thought things were pretty good for us. We have a nice house and good jobs and—"

"Jobs! Jesus, Bram! There's more to life than your chemicals and my fucking depositions." He kicked at the fallen papers, scattering them slightly. "You don't get along with my family. And okay, yeah, I can see that. They haven't treated you that well. But you haven't really made much effort to win them over, have you? You never want to hang out with our friends. It's like you want to turn us into hermits, all locked up in our cave."

"I don't think of our home as a cave." He thought of it as... security. A place where nobody rejected him. And he felt like he and Jim made a comfortable little family of their own. They did go out sometimes with Mick and Bobby or some other friends, but they were really Jim's friends—lawyers, most of them—and Bram simply felt more content without them. Until lately, he'd thought Jim felt the same.

Jim slumped a little. "Look. I know you had a shitty childhood—"

"We don't have to talk about that."

"But maybe we should. I know your parents were huge assholes and they never treated you like you deserved. But the whole world's not like them, baby. There are plenty of good people. And there are so many things to see.... I'm restless, Bram. I'm cooped up."

Bram was trying very hard not to panic. "Okay. We can... I'll put some clothes on. We can go to the coffeehouse, maybe."

"I don't want to go to the coffeehouse," Jim said sadly. He sat down again, this time slowly. "I'm going to take a leave of absence from the firm."

"What?" Bram blinked at him, trying to process words that made no sense.

"I spoke with Costello the other day. She said I can take six months without pay and they'll hold my job for me. I figure I've got enough money saved for that."

"But... but...."

"I've been thinking about this for a long time, actually. I'm thirty-four, Bram. I've finally paid off my goddamn student loans, but here I am. I've been doing basically the same stuff for years, and I'm probably going to keep doing it until I retire. I want... I thought it would be fun to travel. Bum around Europe, maybe. Or hit some islands. Christ, someplace tropical sounds pretty good right now, doesn't it? We could sit on the beach and ogle the boys in Speedos."

"I can't," Bram said. "My job."

"Maybe they'd give you a leave too. Or... fuck, Bram. Just quit. You can find something else later."

Bram shook his head. "I can't." He wasn't even sure what he was denying—giving up his job, leaving his home, venturing out into an uncertain world.

The corners of Jim's mouth had turned down. "And I can't stay here anymore, babe." He stood and brushed imaginary crumbs from his thighs. "I'm going out. I'll see if Bobby and Mick will meet me somewhere."

Bram stood as well. "I'll come with."

"No," Jim replied gently. "Stay here. We'll... we can talk about this some more tomorrow. We have the whole weekend to work something out, right?" But his weak smile said he didn't expect to arrive at a solution by Sunday night.

Clutching the blanket around himself, Bram watched silently as Jim donned his outdoor gear. Jim gave him a chaste little peck on the cheek. And then he left. Bram was still standing when the garage door rattled closed.

DANIEL WAS perched at the edge of the couch, his expression solemn. "He died that night?"

"Yes. He had a couple drinks with his friends. And on the way home, he hit a patch of ice and slammed into a pole. He didn't even make it to the hospital."

"You never got to say good-bye."

Bram angrily blinked away tears. "No." He buried his face in his palms. "If I'd been with him that night, I wouldn't have let him drive after drinking. I never minded being the designated driver."

"Maybe you still would have slid on that ice."

"Maybe. But I was a better driver. More cautious. He was always going too fast." He let his hands drop. "I drove him away that night, and now he's angry."

"I don't think it's like that, Bram. I don't think he's mad at you."

Bram moved his hands so he could give Daniel an incredulous look. "He tried to kill me. Three times."

"Can I explain more about my beliefs? Then maybe you'll understand."

Honestly, Bram had already learned far more about vodou than he'd ever intended. And he was more mentally and emotionally exhausted than he'd ever been, not to mention hungry as hell. But Daniel was looking at him so sweetly and earnestly, so obviously eager to help, and he'd already done so much for Bram....

"Why don't you have a boyfriend?" Bram asked.

"What?" Daniel blinked at the non sequitur.

"You're the most beautiful man I've ever seen, you're smart, you're generous, you're incredibly sweet. Why on earth are you single?"

With a blush coloring his tan cheeks, Daniel looked even more delicious. "I'm busy," he said quietly. "And I'm... I'm a homebody."

"But still."

"When I was younger, I made some bad choices. That was before I listened to Ezili Freda. But then, she doesn't approve of many men." He grinned. "She approves of you, though." He shrugged gracefully. "And most people have trouble with the whole vodou thing. They think it's weird or creepy. Why have you been so accepting of it?"

Bram had to think about that for a while. "I guess because that's the context of how I first met you. I mean, you weren't some random hookup who started chatting about lwa over drinks or something. Besides, with all my brushes with death and near-death lately, I'm not as easily spooked as I used to be."

It must have been the right answer, because Daniel smiled brilliantly before plopping himself in Bram's lap and wrapping an arm around his neck. "Not too hot or squishy for you?" he asked.

"No. You have really good AC." Daniel's weight felt good in his lap, and Bram liked the way skin and cotton leaned against his bare chest.

"Good. My mama said people learn their lessons better when the lessons are sweet. She used to make me cinnamon rice pudding and sugared plantains when I did my homework."

"I like you better than rice pudding," said Bram, giving him a little squeeze.

Daniel made a contented-sounding sigh and leaned his head against Bram's. "So there are two souls, right? I told you this part."

"One of them goes to God." Bram couldn't remember the names.

"Right. The ti bon anj. That soul has the things that make us unique. Our personality, right?"

"Okay."

"That's the part of you that dreams and that gets guidance from the lwa. And the other—the gwo bon anj—that soul is our energy. Our... divine spark. It's Life with a capital L."

Daniel was quiet a moment, perhaps letting Bram process what he'd heard so far. "I think I get it," Bram finally said.

"You know, some people say a zombie is made when a bokor, a sorcerer, steals a person's ti bon anj and locks it away. All that's left to inhabit the body is the gwo bon anj. The body is alive but without its own will."

That was news to Bram, who'd been taught that zombies were the brain-eating undead. But the explanation made sense in its own way, so he nodded.

"At death," Daniel continued, "usually the gwo bon anj goes to the underworld. Not hell. Just... the place of the dead. But sometimes it gets lost, especially when a death is very sudden and untimely."

"Like Jim's."

"Yes. I think the soul becomes confused. It's drawn to things—and people—that feel familiar. And it might carry some of the person's emotions, especially strong ones felt near death. But it doesn't really have the ability to plan a vendetta."

"So Jim...."

"It's not Jim. It's a piece of him, that's all. And it misses you very badly, but maybe it also remembers that you two were having some problems. It's not really evil or malicious. In a vague sort of way, it probably wants you to join it."

Bram groaned. "So basically I have a ghost zombie stalker."

"Basically."

He could fall asleep like this, on soft cushions with Daniel cuddled up against him, still smelling of Ezili Freda's perfume. Sheltered dry and cozy indoors as rain pelted the windows. Nobody judging him or demanding anything of him.

He sighed. "He'll keep trying, though, won't he? And he's been responsible already for two other deaths, Daniel. Including your brother."

"I know."

"Can we stop him?"

Daniel leaned forward a little so he could look at Bram's face. "We? Even after what happened today, you want to be involved?"

"I *am* involved. You're the one who could gracefully bow out if you wanted to."

"I don't want to."

Bram smiled at him. "Good. Thank you."

They spoke briefly about their plans, but most of the discussion floated over Bram's head. The day had simply been too much already—he couldn't absorb anything more. Daniel must have realized this at some point, because he gave Bram's cheek a quick kiss.

"You want something to eat? Or a nap?"

Gently pushing Daniel off his lap, Bram shook his head. "I'm gonna head home."

"You sure?"

In truth, Bram was sorely tempted to stay. But he needed his head clear, and he was fairly certain that wasn't going to happen with Daniel nearby. His weary brain kept flashing to images of Daniel's naked body spread beneath him—the sleek muscles beneath smooth skin, the lovely cock and peaked nipples, the sharp angles of his cheeks and hips. Bram had already ripped the guy's clothes off once that day. He needed to get out before he did it again.

"I'm sorry," Bram said. "I'm no good to anyone right now."

"Are you okay to drive?"

Ghede Nibo had guzzled a lot of rum, but it hadn't made Bram drunk. "I'm fine. But I hope I don't get pulled over." A shirtless guy with burns on his chest and fingernail scratches on his back, reeking of booze, steering home through a storm on a Monday afternoon. Yeah, that would entertain the police.

Daniel walked with him onto the porch, and they stood and watched the rain for a few moments. Then a thought struck Bram. "Did you give Ezili Freda her ring?"

"Not yet. I think I might give her two. She's not going to be happy we interrupted her thing with Ghede Nibo." He chuckled. "And I have to plan a party for him. But first we fix your problem. See you Saturday?"

On impulse, Bram grabbed Daniel in a fierce hug. "Yeah," he breathed into Daniel's ear. "Saturday."

"Be careful, okay?"

When Bram pulled his car out of the driveway, Daniel still stood on the porch, waving at him.

Chapter Seven

SHORTLY AFTER Jim started working at the law firm, when Bram was still in grad school, they'd picked out a house together. It had been a compromise. Jim wanted a condo within walking distance of shops and restaurants; Bram preferred something with a lot of privacy. They ended up buying a clapboard cottage with a tiny yard and high fence, only a short drive or run from their offices. They'd abandoned their shabby student furniture and picked out new things. They'd agreed on paint colors and prints to hang on the walls. Bram liked the house—it was the first place he'd lived that truly felt like home. Even after Jim's death, he'd been happy to continue living there. As difficult as the lonely evenings were, he'd been grateful for his familiar refuge.

But this week he couldn't enjoy his house at all. The walls were too boring. The food was too bland. Nothing there caught his interest, not even his journal articles or his DVD collection. And it was lonely.

On Wednesday evening he jogged home from work, showered, and went out for Thai food. He ordered everything extra hot, even though it made his nose run and his eyes burn. And when he'd finished eating, instead of returning to his house, he went to the coffeehouse with the rude baristas.

The guy behind the counter had floppy bangs, a scraggly beard, and black spikes in his ears, as if he couldn't decide whether to be emo, hipster, or punk. He looked as if he intended to die of ennui before Bram got his order in.

"I have a question," Bram said.

"What?"

"I'm looking at the menu board, and you've got, oh, maybe two dozen kinds of coffee drinks listed. And that's not counting the teas, the smoothie things, the hot chocolate...."

"So?"

"Do there really need to be that many kinds of caffeinated beverages? Isn't that overkill?"

The barista rolled his eyes. "Whatta ya want?"

"Water. I want a big cup of plain old water."

"There's water bottles there." The barista poked a finger in the direction of the refrigerator case.

"But I want mine in a cup. And I want you to call it something fancy. Aguaccino or something. You'll think of something, right? You're an artist."

The barista glared at him for several moments before spinning around, jerking a paper cup from a stack, and filling it at a sink. He plunked a lid on it. Then he marched back and slammed it on the counter. "That's two eighty-five."

"I won't pay unless you give me the fancy name. Because that's the part that's worth the money, right?"

After brushing his hair from his eyes and looking hopelessly at the ceiling, the barista puffed out a breath of air. "Here is your eau de la tappe, sir. Two eighty-five."

Bram set a five-dollar bill on the counter. "Eau de la tappe. Not bad. You can keep the change in compensation for the attempt at French." He picked up the cup and turned around to survey the tables.

Only a few of them were occupied. In a cushy chair near the window, a middle-aged man slouched with a book. Near the wall, four teenage girls huddled with their cell phones, giggling loudly. Not far from them, a woman and man in their early twenties sat across from each other, but their eyes were on their phones. And close to the door, one woman knitted while her companion tapped at a laptop.

Bram sat down at the table with the young couple. "Hi," he said mildly when they goggled at him.

They exchanged quick glances. "Um, hello," said the girl.

"I'm drinking overpriced water. How about you guys?"

"Coffee," the guy answered. He looked a little frightened, which was pretty funny. Bram wasn't a petite man, but nobody had ever mistaken him for an axe-wielding murderer.

"Well, that makes sense. Coffee in a coffeehouse. So, are you guys married or just dating?"

"Look," the guy said, bristling. "I don't know what you want, but—"

"I'm just making friendly conversation, like people do. Anyway, I saw you sitting here, and I was wondering what stage of your relationship you're in. 'Cause if you're married, okay, although it's still kind of early in a marriage for you to be ignoring each other. But if you're just dating? I'm pretty sure you should be talking to each other instead of texting your friends and checking your Tumblr accounts. There should be flirting, maybe a little bit of veiled innuendo…. You should be building up the sexual tension until you're both ready to go home and fuck like rabbits." He sat back in his chair and gave them a cheery little smile.

Neither of them seemed capable of formulating a coherent response. Bram took a sip of water. It tasted like paper.

"Why is coffeehouse music always so tragically pretentious?" he asked, waving a hand vaguely in the direction where the speakers might be. "It always tries to be cool without being offensive, but that's bullshit because truly cool music isn't bland. Besides, every time someone orders a cappuccino, all we hear is that obnoxious *zhoop*. Maybe they should just play the sound of toilets flushing, considering all the liquid that gets consumed."

He stood and walked away, abandoning his expensive water.

Sitting in his car in the parking lot a few minutes later, he began to shake. He'd never pulled a stunt like that, and he had no idea why he'd done it now.

No. That wasn't true. He had a definite idea, and it was named Ghede Nibo. The lwa wasn't riding him now—Bram could feel the difference—but it was if he were hanging around nearby, egging Bram on. As if Bram were a teenager whose new best friend was a bad influence.

But Ghede Nibo's effect on his behavior wasn't bothering him right now. What had his heart racing and his hands feeling clammy was that he'd *enjoyed* making a small spectacle of himself and yanking a few chains. And he'd suddenly realized he couldn't remember the last time he'd done something just because it was silly and fun.

BY FRIDAY Bram's coworkers were giving him very strange looks. Janet was spending more time than usual in the lab and keeping her earbuds stuck in her ears when she had to come back to their shared office. She fled entirely when Carla showed up late Friday afternoon.

Bram looked up from his computer screen and grinned at her. "How they hangin', Carla?"

She sighed heavily and plopped down in Janet's chair. "What's going on, Bram?"

"Nothing. I'm just looking over these reports."

"That's not what I mean." She poked at her smartphone for a moment. "Yesterday morning you proposed a toxicity marathon to see who could withstand paint fumes the longest. You also went downstairs to the gym and told everyone they should be plowing fields instead of using the treadmill." She glanced over at him. "I'm told you accompanied the suggestion with some graphic movements."

He shrugged.

"You've been telling dirty jokes in the lab," she said. "You stood next to Brian Billings and pretended he was overloading your Gayometer."

"Brian Billings is a homophobic idiot. I bet he's compensating."

"You sent out a mass e-mail containing thirty science-related puns. This morning you asked the cafeteria manager why the packaged pastries contain more chemicals than most of our paint products."

"Have you seen the ingredient lists on those things?" he asked, smiling.

"You wrote a memo to the CEO complaining that our hallways are too bland and demanding they be painted with rainbows."

"We make paints, Carla. We should not have white walls."

She tucked the phone into her jacket pocket and gave him a long look. "You spent thirty minutes this afternoon roaming the building, asking everyone you met whether they were working hard or hardly working. And when they were men, you emphasized the hard. Are you taking something, Bram?"

He sputtered a laugh. "No. I'll pee in a cup for you if you like."

"Something prescription, maybe? Sometimes those medicines have unexpected side effects."

"Not even aspirin. I am fully capable of operating heavy machinery."

"Then what the hell is up with you?" she yelled. Carla never yelled.

Bram set down the pencil he'd been toying with and scratched the back of his neck. "I was just livening things up. Carla, we literally watch paint dry for a living. We need more levity."

"Peeking on your coworker over the top of a bathroom stall isn't levity, Bram—it's sexual harassment."

"It's not like he was taking a shit. He goes in there every day to play Candy Crush and update his OKCupid profile."

Carla slowly stood and crossed her arms. "Are you trying to get fired?"

"No. I like my job." That was an honest answer, although the prospect of unemployment scared him much less than it would have the previous week.

"Okay. As of now, you're on vacation. You have a lot of it saved up anyway. I don't want to see you back here for at least two weeks. See a therapist, Bram. Then go find somewhere fun and exotic, with lots of cute and easy boys hanging around."

Maybe she expected him to throw a tantrum or say something inappropriate, because she looked slightly apprehensive. But Bram only nodded. As she watched, he shut down his computer. He hung his lab coat on the coatrack and grabbed his gym bag from under the desk.

"Thanks, Carla," he said. "I'll see you later."

He'd driven to work that morning because jogging had seemed like a waste of effort. Now, he peeled off his shirt as soon as he was inside his car. Then he started the engine and cranked the AC to the max. Even with his sunglasses on, he squinted. Without really making the decision to do so, he pulled out his phone and called Daniel.

Daniel answered after two rings. "Are you all right?" he asked right away. He'd been checking up on Bram twice a day, which was sweet and comforting.

"Nobody's trying to kill me at the moment. That I know of. But do you have a few minutes?"

"Sure. But hang on—let me go somewhere more private." After a brief pause, he said, "Okay. This is good."

"Are you at the shelter?"

Daniel worked in several different locations, but he spent a lot of his time at a shelter for LGBT teens. He'd talked about the place during their evening phone calls over the past few days, Bram huddling comfortably on the couch.

"Yeah," said Daniel. "And I'm actually in a closet right now, which is pretty funny. But nobody's going to be listening in."

"I won't keep you in there for long." Bram watched a sparrow land on a nearby tree. "Um, I wanted to ask you something."

"It's a little early for a marriage proposal, and this isn't remotely romantic."

Bram's laughter was loud in the car, even with the noise of the fan. "I think we need at least one official date first. The thing is, this week I've been kind of… off."

"What do you mean?"

"I've been doing stuff I would never have pictured myself doing. I mean… nobody's *making* me do anything. I'm in control. But I'm finding myself wanting to do some pretty weird shit, Daniel."

"Yeah." Daniel was quiet a moment, perhaps gathering his thoughts. "When I was a kid, I was pretty wild. I did a lot of stupid things. But then Ezili Freda chose me, and after a while, I started listening to her. I calmed down. I started putting effort into school. Stopped sleeping around."

Bram closed his eyes and leaned back against the headrest. "Sounds like your lwa is a lot more responsible than mine."

"Well, Ghede Nibo's a lot cruder than she is, that's for sure. But my point is that I *needed* to do those things—I needed to grow up and chill out. But you've already done plenty of growing and chilling. *You* needed to loosen up a little. Ghede Nibo's helping you."

"Daniel, there's loosening up and there's acting like a psycho. I came really close to getting fired today. Carla *should* have canned me after the shit I've been pulling. And I don't even care all that much."

"Sweetheart," Daniel said. Bram's heart lurched and his breath caught. And Daniel repeated the endearment as if he wanted to be sure Bram didn't miss it. "Sweetheart, you've been a champagne bottle. Now you're opened and there's bound to be some initial foaming. You'll settle. Give yourself a little time. You've had an awful lot of excitement lately."

Excitement. That was one way to put it. But Daniel's words soothed Bram. "You think?"

"I think. You'll find your balance. You'll still be a little bubbly, but… but I think I've taken this metaphor about as far as it will go. You know what I mean."

"Yeah. Okay. Thank you."

"I'll be done here in an hour. You want to get together?"

Bram did want that. But he declined. "I think I'm better off foaming solo. I'll see you Saturday morning, okay?"

"And you'll be careful until then, right?"

Bram smiled so widely his cheeks hurt. "I will," he said.

Chapter Eight

SATURDAY MORNING was bright and sunny, but by nine o'clock, the temperature was already far too hot. Bram had dressed lightly in running shorts and T-shirt, a slightly ratty old one with a faded emblem from his alma mater. He hoped the lwa wouldn't be offended that he hadn't dressed up, but considering what happened to his clothing last time, he decided to play it safe.

Daniel was shirtless again, beaming at him from the porch. "Nobody killed you!" he called out as Bram approached.

"Not that I noticed."

When Bram reached the top of the steps, Daniel grabbed him by the waist and pulled him close for a scorching kiss. It took Bram by surprise—he dropped his paper bag—but it was by far the nicest surprise he'd ever received. Daniel's lips felt as soft and lush as they looked, and he tasted of mint and sugar. His hair was silky, his muscles flexed beneath sweat-sheened skin. He laced his fingers behind Bram's head as they kissed, and he made deep little grunting sounds that went straight to Bram's cock. They'd met so recently, and they didn't really know each other that well, but Daniel's touch soothed something deep inside Bram; healed a wound, filled a lifelong hole.

"You're a good kisser," Bram observed after they parted.

When Daniel grinned like that, he looked even younger. "But practice makes perfect."

"I'd like to aim for perfection."

Daniel gave a lock of Bram's hair a gentle tweak. "Now?"

Oh, Bram was sorely tempted. But he wanted to get the business with Jim settled first. "Later, okay?"

"Done."

They walked around the house again. If the rainstorm had done any damage to Daniel's garden, it wasn't evident now. If anything, the blooms seemed brighter, the leaves more vibrant, the vines more heavily laden. Daniel pointed at a plant as they passed by. "I'm going to have to leave covert zucchini on my neighbors' porches again, or I'll never get rid of it all."

"Sounds evil."

"Well, I am a vodouisant. I'm supposed to be scary, right?"

As Bram laughed, he thought about how Daniel terrified him less than anyone in the world.

The temple looked the same as last time but smelled strongly of flowers and alcohol. "I hope you don't mind," Daniel said as he switched on the lights. "Some members of the société came over last night, and we had a little ceremony. We asked the lwa to guide us today."

"I don't mind," said Bram, touched by the effort. "It didn't bother the other people to ask for help for some stranger?"

Daniel had been arranging some small items on a shelf. He looked back at Bram over his shoulder. "You're not a stranger. You're my friend. They'd be happy if you decided to join the société, you know." He shrugged. "No pressure. I just want you to know you're welcome."

"Thanks." Bram wasn't sure if more formal vodouing was in his future, but he appreciated the offer. He'd never belonged to much of anything.

As they had before, they entered Ezili Freda's room first. Her altar was crowded with recent offerings—a brand-new bottle of perfume, several dishes of sweet food, a pretty necklace.

Before Daniel approached the altar, Bram caught his arm. In a quiet voice, Bram said, "I, um, brought her a couple of things. I don't know if that's appropriate, but—"

Daniel beamed. "She'll be very flattered! It was really nice of you to think of her."

"I was feeling sort of guilty about, uh, interrupting her fun last time."

"She told me she understands. Actually, she was pleased you were concerned about me. She's my protector, remember. She says she thinks we make a good ma—" He shut his mouth with an audible snap and blushed.

"A good what?"

His cheeks still pink, Daniel looked down at the floor. "A good match," he whispered. He raised his head quickly, appearing worried. "That doesn't mean you owe me anything or you have to do anything, okay? It's just her opinion."

If he hadn't feared sacrilege, Bram would have shouted with joy. He wasn't sure if a lwa was a good judge of whether two people would make a good couple, but he was hopeful. Ezili Freda was supposed to be an expert on love, right?

Bram squeezed Daniel's shoulder. "Good."

That delighted grin again, stretching from ear to ear. Daniel tugged him close, gave him a peck on the cheek, and then stepped away. "Why don't you give her the gifts?" he said.

Feeling slightly awkward, Bram drew a bouquet of pink roses from the paper bag. It was an expensive bouquet, although he thought the flowers from Daniel's garden smelled better. He examined the altar uncertainly, not sure what to do until Daniel stepped in to help. "You can just set them there for now. I'll fill a vase later."

Bram obeyed. Then he took out a bottle of perfume. "I hope this is okay," he said. He'd never bought women's scent before, and he'd had to ask the girl in the store for help. She assumed it was for his girlfriend. It was expensive, pink, and came in a fancy bottle with a lush satin bow.

"Perfect," said Daniel.

Finally, Bram pulled out the last gift for Freda. It was a bracelet made of small heart-shaped links. It had set him back over two hundred bucks, and the salesgirl was convinced he was the most thoughtful boyfriend ever. He placed it next to the necklace.

"You chose exactly the right things," said Daniel. "No wonder she likes you."

Bram stood back while Daniel completed the ritual. Afterward, they walked to the ghede room. Bram glanced at the bed, feeling slightly guilty. The bedding had been straightened since his last visit.

Bram had brought presents for Ghede Nibo too, of course: a little bag of hot peppers, a container of the spiciest curry his favorite Thai place could dish up, a spool of purple ribbon, a deck of cards, a black top hat. The hat had taken considerable searching, but Bram found it at a shop that sold adult dress-up clothes and upscale sex toys. Passing the shelves of toys had made him blush, which was silly.

"I brought cash too," he said and placed a pile of crisp twenties on the table.

"This is costing you a lot of money. Is that all right?"

"It's fine." Bram's bank account was healthy. He and Jim had never been big spenders, and he'd been the beneficiary of Jim's life insurance. It seemed fitting to spend a little of Jim's bequest on helping get rid of the homicidal soul.

Daniel chanted as he poured from a fresh bottle of rum, and Bram silently implored Ghede Nibo to help them put Jim's soul to rest.

They walked back into the main room. "Daniel? Will Jim be all right? His gwo bon anj, I mean. Getting stuck in a jar isn't awful?"

"It's a lot better than wandering. The jar is like… like a home. Someplace to feel safe. And eventually the gwo bon anj will settle beneath the waters, where it belongs. Someday it may become reincarnated, or it might even become a lwa."

Bram nodded. He could understand feeling better in a safe place. He'd be terrified if he were homeless. "Okay."

Smiling gently, Daniel took a jar from a shelf. It was about the size of a mayonnaise jar but more rounded and wrapped in blue cloth. Red sequins spelled out Jim's initials. "One of the société ladies helped me make it," Daniel said. "I'm not very good at arts and crafts."

"Those were his favorite colors."

"I know. Ezili Freda told me." He patted Bram's arm. "Go ahead and have a seat, if you want."

Back on the same folding chair as before, Bram watched Daniel place the jar on the floor near the big central pillar. He felt a twinge of guilt when Daniel removed the fuchsia robe from the armoire. "I didn't ruin it?" he asked.

"Nope. Just popped the buttons. I sewed them back on. That much crafty I can handle by myself."

This time Daniel took off his shorts before he put the robe on. He stood naked and unselfconscious, smiling at Bram.

"Jesus," Bram said with a moan. He wanted to run across the room and settle his hands on Daniel's slim hips, drop to his knees on the packed dirt ground and nuzzle at his groin, feel Daniel's cock harden in his mouth. Even as he watched, Daniel's cock twitched and grew half-hard.

"I think we're thinking the same thing," said Daniel. "And it has nothing to do with vodou."

"I'm mostly thinking you better put on that robe before I do something stupid."

With a soft laugh, Daniel complied. He turned on the CD player. Drums pounded, this time more quickly, and people sang on this recording. Daniel picked up his beaded gourd from next to the CD player and shook it like a rattle. He closed his eyes and moved his feet quickly in time with the drums. His chant joined the recorded ones.

Ezili Freda appeared almost instantly. As before, Bram saw just a flash of the lwa over Daniel's body, and then only Daniel again, but now with a more sinuous movement of the hips. She gave Bram a sexy smile. "*Bonjour, mon cher. Je suis heureuse de te revoir.*"

Although Bram wasn't sure what she'd said, he nodded respectfully. "Bonjour, ma'am. And, uh, merci for recommending me to Daniel."

She had a throaty laugh. "*Mon plaisir*, Abraham. *Merci pour les cadeaux.*" And as if a thought had just occurred to her, she danced her way into her altar room. When she came out a minute or two later, the new necklace was around her neck and the bracelet glittered on her wrist. She'd tucked one of the roses behind her ear.

"*Très belle*," said Bram, exhausting his stock of French phrases.

Without breaking her rhythm, she gave him a regal curtsy. Then she moved closer to the pillar and the spirit jar and danced in circles around them, sometimes waving her arms, sometimes seeming to address the jar with her singing.

Bram was neither surprised nor frightened when Ghede Nibo possessed him. It was an oddly familiar sensation and somewhat comforting, like having a trusted friend take over a difficult task. With the lwa in charge, Bram rose from the chair and pulled off his shirt. He skipped into the ghede room, where he plunked the pair of single-lensed glasses on his face and the top hat on his head. He chortled happily before guzzling several ounces of the chili-laden rum and then—pulling forward the waistband of his shorts—pouring some of the liquid onto his rapidly hardening cock. The heat of the rum thrummed in his veins and sweat poured from his body, the salt of it stinging his eyes.

Bram had never been much of a dancer. Unless he was allowed to clutch his partner and sway to a slow song, he felt awkward and gangly. But not only was Ghede Nibo an excellent dancer, he could somehow sway and prance and leap without dislodging his glasses or hat. Bram sort of hoped that later on his body would remember how to move like this.

Ezili Freda smiled at him when he reentered the main room. Ghede Nibo took off the hat before he bowed deeply for her. "You are beautiful as always, my lady," he said in Creole as he replaced the hat.

She answered in French. "And you are a terrible flatterer and flirt, as ever, gravedigger."

"As ever. I take it my boy meets your high standards?"

"He's a good boy."

"And very pretty," said Ghede Nibo, swiveling his hips from side to side. "Dance with me, my lady. Let us make such a wonderful spectacle the gwo bon anj cannot help but be drawn to us."

Bram hadn't realized that was the plan. Maybe it wasn't—maybe it was just Nibo's scheme to get his hands on Freda again. If that was the case, his scheme was successful, because she swayed to him and settled Daniel's garden-callused hands on Bram's shoulders. Ghede Nibo took her hips and tugged her a bit closer.

Their dancing resembled a tango, but faster and much, much bawdier. They rubbed against each other, dipping and spinning. Bram's cock strained at his shorts, and Daniel's hard length ground against him. It was as close as they could get to sex without taking their clothes off. They were exceptionally graceful and never missed a beat. Although their skin was slick with sweat and their lungs worked hard, their steps were flawless. And the damn hat remained perfectly in place.

Ghede Nibo had his arms wrapped tightly around Freda as he mouthed at her long neck. She scratched his back with her fingernails, just enough to sting beautifully. Their groins were pressed tightly together, and Bram's head filled with the scents of citrus, rum, growing things, and sweat. He bucked his hips forward, meeting Daniel's answering thrust, and realized he was very close to climaxing. Judging by the wild look in Daniel's eyes, so was he.

But a breeze eddied around them all of a sudden, stirring the dust that their dancing had kicked up. A strange feeling accompanied the breeze—a cry not quite heard, an embrace not quite felt.

Still not faltering in their dance, Ghede Nibo and Ezili Freda moved apart until only their hands touched. They stepped closer to the jar. Freda released one of Nibo's hands so that instead of facing each other, they now danced side by side, both of them watching the jar.

"Come," Ezili Freda sang. "Come home now, my little one. The waters await you."

On the other side of the jar, a vague shimmer appeared in the air, like a heat mirage over a stretch of hot road.

Ghede Nibo sang, his voice resonant. "Come. It is time for you to leave this boy. It is time for you to leave this world and go beneath the waters. It is time."

The shimmer seemed to hesitate. For a very brief moment, it coalesced into a transparent figure: Jim, naked and pale, staring at Bram and crying.

Despite the lwa riding him, Bram tried to lurch forward. He wanted to hold Jim one final time, comfort him, tell him good-bye. But Ezili Freda kept a fierce grip on Bram's hand and Ghede Nibo wrenched his body back a step.

Jim's image disappeared, replaced by an agitated waver of the air. "No," Ghede Nibo said firmly. "He is not yours any longer, spirit. And it is not Abraham's time to die. Go! Go under the waters. This is where you belong now."

The shimmer jerked forward. Bram was certain it was going to envelop him, to ride him just as Ghede Nibo was. Could a man be ridden by two spirits at once? Bram had the conviction that the experience would destroy him, body and soul.

But Ezili Freda raised her free hand, palm outward, and screamed. "No! You may not have him. He belongs to my Daniel now. You are not wanted here any longer. You will never be happy here. Go!"

Bram felt the gwo bon anj's shriek more than he heard it. The shimmer grew smaller before sinking into the jar. The jar rattled slightly and then fell over. And Bram collapsed to the ground.

Chapter Nine

DANIEL'S BED was covered in a clean-smelling cotton sheet, as cool against Bram's bare skin as the damp washcloth on his forehead. Although the air-conditioning battled mightily, it was not the cause of Bram's gooseflesh as Daniel looked down at him with concern.

"Are you all right?" Daniel asked.

Bram took a deep breath and let it out. "I've never fainted before."

"It happens sometimes. It can be a shock when the lwa leaves your body. You were only out for a few seconds."

"I'm still feeling a little... woozy." He'd had to lean heavily on Daniel as they walked from the temple into the house, and now Daniel was fussing over him as though Bram was an invalid. "Is Jim...?"

"He's settled. He won't bother you anymore."

Although Bram was relieved to hear that, a fresh pang of grief struck him. Jim's spirit might have been murderous, but it was also the last bit of his lover left on earth.

Maybe Daniel read Bram's thoughts, because he crossed the bedroom and took a framed photo from atop his dresser. He brought it back to the bed and held it so Bram could see. The picture showed a smiling family on a beach: a handsome man in his forties with his arm around a pretty woman about the same age. A teenage boy with wild brown curls stood beside her, and a younger kid with a smudge of dirt or sand on his face stood in front.

Bram sat up a little—Daniel adjusted the pillow to prop him up—and took the photo for a closer look. "A beautiful family. You look a lot like your mom."

"I know. But I have my papa's eyes. When he got older, Darius looked just like Papa, but with Mama's eyes."

"God, Daniel. I'm so sorry about your brother."

"I mourned him. I loved him, and so much of his potential was wasted in this life. I mourned my parents when I lost them too. But you know, I'm sad mostly for myself, because I miss them. I'm not sad for them. Their souls are where they belong, and they're at peace. Maybe they're even together." Although Daniel's voice was soft, his expression was untroubled.

"And you think Jim is at peace too?"

"Yes. It's terrible you had to lose him so soon, but—"

"I was losing him anyway," Bram admitted. It was time to face the truth he'd known all along. He and Jim had become a couple because they were comfortable together, because their relationship provided a safe haven from an uncaring world. But although they loved each other, they'd never felt the same passion that Bram now felt for Daniel. By the time Jim died, their protective shell had grown brittle and claustrophobic. They would have broken it soon. It was cracked already.

Daniel took the photo back, smiled at it for a moment, and replaced it on his dresser. The mattress dipped when he sat beside Bram. "We certainly don't welcome death most of the time, but in vodou we take a different view of it than a lot of people do. It's not just an end but also a beginning. So in a way, it should be celebrated."

Bram remembered what Ghede Nibo had told him, and he repeated it out loud. "Life, death. It's all the same dance."

"Exactly," said Daniel, stroking Bram's cheek with the pads of his fingers. "I guess the important thing is to keep dancing."

Bram grabbed his hand and kissed the back of it. "I like dancing with you."

Although Daniel smiled widely, his eyes looked suspiciously glossy and he blinked rapidly. "I'm going to tell you something sappy, overblown, and premature."

"Sounds wonderful to me."

"I'm sorry about the deaths—Jim, Darius, the man who tried to run you over. But they brought us together, and that's... amazing. I have *never* felt about anyone the way I feel about you. Uh, that's the premature part. We haven't even had a real date."

Still holding Daniel's hand, Bram gave it a squeeze. "But we've had two possessions each. I think we can skip the first date part."

Daniel gave him a very long look. "I didn't scare you away with what I just said?"

"You're a vodou priest. You're supposed to be scary."

Daniel's shoulders relaxed and relief flashed across his face. "I'm not a priest yet," he said. "Just an initiate."

"Same difference." Bram tugged Daniel closer and looked him straight in the eyes. "I don't know if you guys believe in fate. I'm not sure I do. But I believe you and I can have something... something really good. Something really real."

Laughing, Daniel clambered to the center of the bed and straddled him. "Are you saying this is the beginning of a beautiful friendship, Bram?"

"You're a *Casablanca* fan?"

"God yes! I practically know the script by heart. Mama and I used to watch old movies together, and that was one of my favorites. Well, anything with Humphrey Bogart."

"*Maltese Falcon*," Bram said, pretending to swoon.

"*African Queen*. You too?"

Bram nodded. "I know this is weird, but he was my first crush. He wasn't really all that good-looking, but he was so... I don't know. Manly without being an asshole."

Daniel looked completely delighted. "I know! When I saw him on the screen, I wanted to be Bergman, Bacall, Hepburn. I wanted someone to talk all clever and gruff to me and then crush me in his arms."

"Like this?" Bram grabbed Daniel's shoulders, pulled him down until their bodies were flush, and held him tightly.

"God, yes," moaned Daniel, undulating slightly. "Like this."

But Bram had an unhappy thought. "I reek." He did—sweat and rum. And dirt stuck to his skin.

"Me too. Don't care. We can shower later."

And then Daniel kissed him.

They'd kissed earlier, but this was far better. Bram's spirit-related problem was solved. And now, conveniently enough, they were on a bed, with Daniel's weight pressing so gorgeously against him and with nothing between them but a couple pairs of shorts. And even then, Bram was able to squirm his hands under Daniel's waistband to cup that round, smooth ass with his palms.

"I've been dreaming of you," Daniel whispered in his ear.

If Bram hadn't been hard already, that would have done the trick. It was almost as if he were a lwa who had managed to ride Daniel just a little bit—just enough to visit him in his sleep. And speaking of riding....

"Do you have rubbers?" he asked. Because it hadn't occurred to him to bring any.

Daniel laughed into the crook of Bram's neck. "I bought some this week. Just in case...." Then he lifted his head so he could lock eyes with Bram. "After the stunts the Iwas pulled with our bodies, you probably think I'm kind of easy, but I'm not. I haven't done this in a while."

"We don't have to do much of anything, actually. I've been turned on practically since we met. I think my fuse is going to be really short."

Was that a giggle from Daniel? Bram was pretty sure it was, and it made him laugh too. "What?" asked Bram.

"Mine too. I was worried I was going to embarrass myself. How about if we get the first act over with, break for intermission, and then have the chance for a leisurely second act? What do you think?"

Bram thought he was already falling in love—but he didn't say so. Instead he squeezed Daniel's butt and arched up a little with his hips. "Can we at least undress?"

"Done!" Daniel hopped off, shimmied out of his shorts, and pounced back onto the mattress. Almost before Bram could blink, Daniel divested him of his clothing too. Then Daniel was back on top of him, their cocks in direct contact.

When Bram and Jim used to have sex—especially during their last couple of years together—they did it at night with the lights off. That had been Jim's preference, and Bram had wondered if it had something to do with the little love handles he'd grown or the bits of gray that were beginning to appear in Jim's dark brown hair. Sometimes Bram even wondered if Jim was imagining himself with a different partner— younger, sexier, more interesting.

Now sunlight streamed through the bedroom windows, and Daniel certainly didn't seem discontented with the man beneath him. In fact, he kept interrupting their kisses to rear up a little and examine Bram's face. And each time he did, Daniel smiled widely.

As for Bram, the feel of Daniel was heady enough, as was his citrus-and-sweat scent. But the sight of him made Bram whimper with need: Daniel's sweet, supple body flexing above him. His tan skin contrasting with Bram's paler tone. His blue eyes almost obscured by shining pupils. His opulent lips parted in noisy gasps. His long, sleek neck; his peaked brown nipples; his muscled, sweat-slick torso. And oh God, his rosy-headed shaft moving so deliciously against Bram's.

Bram came first—a hitch in his chest, a neutron bomb in his core, a long moan from his throat. He heard the echo of Ghede Nibo's laughter. Or maybe it was his own—it was a little hard to tell.

Seconds later Daniel dug his fingers hard into Bram's shoulders, pressed his hips forward, and cried out raggedly before collapsing onto Bram's chest.

Only after they had caught their breath did Daniel roll to Bram's side. They both laughed at the gross squelchy sound they made when they parted.

"Now we really need that shower," said Daniel, snuggling up and throwing one leg over Bram's.

"Is yours big enough for two?"

"Mm-hmm." Daniel yawned.

"But maybe a nap first?" Bram chuckled. "It's been sort of an exciting morning."

"Nap, shower, late lunch, act two. How's that schedule sound?"

"Like heaven."

Daniel played idly with the hair on Bram's chest, moving it around and tweaking it gently, but it was clear from the way his brow furrowed slightly that he was thinking about something.

"You know," he finally said, very slowly, "my shower's big enough for two. So's my bed. In fact... so is my house. I know we're new. I know you love your home, but—"

"I don't love my home. I mean, it's okay. It's nothing special. I just love what it represents to me." Comfort. Refuge. But lately more like a self-made prison.

"Could you imagine another house representing those things? My house, for instance?"

Because the sight of Daniel was too distracting—too tempting— Bram closed his eyes. He pictured himself sitting on Daniel's comfortable, slightly shabby furniture. Puttering around in the kitchen with the turquoise-and-lemon walls. Coming home from work, changing into casual clothes, and helping Daniel out in the garden. Cuddling with Daniel in front of the fireplace in winter. Visiting the temple in the backyard and meeting the members of the société. Climbing into this bed at night and scrunching up close to Daniel, just as they were right now.

He opened his eyes and smiled. "I can imagine it very well, actually."

This time, Daniel's smile spread slowly, but it lit up his entire face and made his eyes sparkle with joy. "Good," he said hoarsely.

If Bram truly did have two souls, at the moment they were both at peace.

Daniel moved his finger to the burn marks on Bram's chest and traced around their edge. "I think this is going to scar."

"That's all right." Bram glanced down at himself and for the first time realized the marks looked like a sideways figure eight. "A lemniscate." A symbol a chemist knew well.

"What?" Daniel sounded sleepy and content.

"Ghede Nibo branded me with an infinity symbol. What do you think he meant by it?"

"I don't know. Maybe nothing. He likes to joke sometimes." Daniel yawned loudly before settling his head against Bram's bicep. His hair was soft and a little tickly.

Maybe it was just a joke. But when Bram glanced at the dresser, the photo was obscured by a shiny black top hat—the same hat that had tumbled from Bram's head when he fainted. As far as he knew, Daniel had left it in the temple when he helped get Bram into the house.

If you looked at it right, an infinity symbol looked like a pathway. Like the steps to a dance that never ended. Two halves—equal and opposite—looping endlessly into one another.

"Thank you," Bram whispered. He made a mental note to buy more flowers and rum after act two. Unless a third act intervened.

Smiling, he drifted into a sweet afternoon nap.

KIM FIELDING is very pleased every time someone calls her eclectic. She has migrated back and forth across the western two-thirds of the United States and currently lives in California, where she long ago ran out of bookshelf space. She's a university professor who dreams of being able to travel and write full time. She also dreams of having two perfectly behaved children, a husband who isn't obsessed with football, and a house that cleans itself. Some dreams are more easily obtained than others.

Kim can be found on her blogs:

http://kfieldingwrites.blogspot.com/

http://www.goodreads.com/author/show/4105707.Kim_Fielding/blog

and on Facebook:

https://www.facebook.com/KFieldingWrites.

Her e-mail is dephalqu@yahoo.com, and she can be found on Twitter at @KFieldingWrites.

By KIM FIELDING

Alaska
Animal Magnetism (Dreamspinner Anthology)
Bones (with B.G. Thomas, Jamie Fessenden, and Eli Easton)
The Border
Brute
Don't Try This at Home (Dreamspinner Anthology)
A Great Miracle Happened There
Housekeeping
Men of Steel (Dreamspinner Anthology)
Motel.Pool.
Night Shift
Pilgrimage
The Pillar
Snow on the Roof (Dreamspinner Anthology)
Speechless • The Gig
Steamed Up (Dreamspinner Anthology)
Stitch (with Sue Brown, Jamie Fessenden, and Eli Easton)
The Tin Box
Venetian Masks
Violet's Present

BONES
Good Bones
Buried Bones
The Gig
Bone Dry

Published by DREAMSPINNER PRESS
http://www.dreamspinnerpress.com

THE BIRD

ELI EASTON

I'VE ALWAYS been fascinated by Voodoo and by the West Indies. This story was inspired by classic old films like *I Walked With A Zombie* and *White Zombie*. It was also inspired, in no small part, by the steamy erotic vibe of the film *Wide Sargasso Sea* with Nathaniel Parker and Karina Lombard.

Special thanks to my beta readers Nico Sels, Kim Fielding, Kate Rothwell, and my ever patient husband.

The snatch of song Major Pivot sings is from "The Lost Chord" by Arthur Sullivan, 1877. He later quotes Shakespeare's *King Lear*, Act IV.

~1~

March 3, 1870

My Dearest Richard,

I arrived safely in Jamaica, and I write to you as my very first act at Crosswinds, just as I promised. The passage was eventful. We hit a storm that was so fierce I was convinced I was going to die. I was about to write that you would have laughed to have seen me on my knees, white as a sheet, and praying for my life as the ship rolled. But that isn't true. You are so soft-hearted, you would never laugh at another's distress, much less mine.

Remember when we studied the things soldiers think about before battle in our military strategy class? Well, I thought of you as I stood at death's door, of how I'd miss our friendship. Happily, it was much ado about nothing in the end. As you may have surmised, I did not die.

Onward and upward and all that. I will write again as soon as I have taken the measure of this place. Give my good wishes to your family, and tell your brother that he owes me a pint, as I was not sick once, not even during the worst of the storm.

Your ever devoted,
Colin

March 10, 1870

My Dearest Richard,

I just received my first packet of letters from you. You must have written the day after I left London! It's like a breeze from England to read your familiar script in this strange place. Please keep pen to paper, and I promise to do the same on my end.

I already have quite a bit to tell. Yesterday I was forced to fire Mr. Tuttle, our plantation manager. Everything Father had been hearing about him was true. He tried to put on a good face when I showed up, but it was clear he was a drunkard and a brute. The laborers hated him. I sent him packing and had a firearm at my side whilst I did it. He put up a fuss, and our argument was a fine spectacle for everyone on the plantation. I wonder if any of them wagered on the outcome.

The long and short of it is, Tuttle is gone. Which means I must run this blasted place. Father gave me two years to turn the plantation around, and I mean to do it if that's what will get me home and back to you and to Elizabeth. I've been speaking to some of our neighbors. The plantation closest to mine is run by a man named Lester Pivot, the sort of devout church mouse who runs services in his house for the natives. He lives with his brother, Major Pivot, who is not altogether in his right mind, poor chap. Lester believes sugarcane is on the wane and bananas and coffee are where the future lies. Of course, you know how Father feels about sugarcane, but it wouldn't hurt to diversify. I plan to convert several acres and see if I can impress Father with the return.

Now here's the thing I've been itching to tell you about. After Mr. Tuttle left, I went to his quarters, which consisted of three rooms in the east wing of the house. I wanted to see if he'd done any damage to the place, he was so furious when he left. The drawers of the dresser and the closet stood open and empty, and he had, indeed, wrenched the door nearly off its hinges in anger. His mattress was bare and slightly askew. Suspicious, I turned it up. The mattress rests on a wooden bed frame. On the slats, just under where his head would have rested, was a bundle that included several chicken feet, the head of a rooster, twigs and dried herbs of some malodorous variety, and the whole bound in twine splattered with dried blood.

Remember old Dr. Hodgets? He'd get so excited when he lectured on what he called "primitive beliefs" that his neck would stretch up above his collar like a tortoise. I thought of him when I saw the bundle and how his eyes would undoubtedly light up at the sight of it. How he would love to be able to explore the native practices here. They call it Obeah, and it is a type of folk magic that has its ancestry in the African slave trade. It's illegal in Jamaica, with a penalty of whipping if you are caught, but it's practiced all the same.

Who placed the bundle under Tuttle's bed? One of the household staff? One of the laborers? What was its purpose? Was he supposed to sicken? Die? Be driven away? And did I, by my own actions, fulfill the curse for the curse maker?

I can see you now, Richard, smiling your indulgent smile and shaking your head at my fancifulness. Well what, then, is a former student of philosophy to think about when in a strange land? Man does not live by sugarcane alone.

To be honest, I'm uneasy here. It is hot and windy, and I feel restless in my own skin. There's a mystery to this place, a sense of being watched, of there being things hidden just below the surface of these smiling faces. Yet truly the servants have been nothing but polite and seem relieved that Tuttle is gone. I'm on probation, I think. Should I fail to live up to their silent demands, I shall no doubt be rewarded with a bundle of my own under my mattress. Perhaps they will curse me with gout or a fit of giggles. But no matter, there shall be no need for a curse, because I am determined to turn this place around and earn my father's permission to marry Elizabeth and get on with my life back in England.

Assuming the young Miss Elizabeth waits for me. How is she? Are you keeping an eye on her as you promised? I know I can depend on you, even though you have never been fond of her. I hope the two of you will become friends in my absence—please try, for my sake?

Your ever devoted,

Colin

~2~

Jamaica, 1870

IT WAS damn hot riding in the sun. The heat shimmered above the land as the laborers stooped, placing the short pieces of cane with a bud eye into the prepared planting rows. In the field next to them, the cane crop was already knee-high. My father had instigated rotational planting years ago, when the plantation had been like a new toy to him, and he'd spent several years here himself. As long as you avoided having the cane ripen during the rainy seasons—too much moisture could ruin the crop in its final days—you could stagger the planting and guard against market highs and lows. In theory.

Sugar, I could still hear him lecturing over the dining room table, *will be money in the bank long after Entwhile has ceased to be. Sugar is a drug. The whole world craves it. And unlike opium, we don't even have to feel guilty about it. Why, grandmothers give babes in arms something sweet to calm their fretting. But it's a drug nonetheless. Never forget that.*

Despite my father's passion for sugarcane, my mother refused to leave England, and so he'd run the plantation by correspondence for years. Several lazy and unscrupulous overseers had turned Crosswinds from a productive enterprise into a liability. I knew that if I could turn it back from ruin, I would at last be the favored son. Let my older brothers, Rupert and Harry, toady along at my father's side at Entwhile. Father's heart was in Jamaica.

Tuttle had let the rotational cropping go, too drunk to rouse himself or the laborers more than once a year for planting. The field we were working now had been reclaimed by the wild grasses and ferns, and it had been an almighty struggle to plow it. It made me angry. Three months since I'd arrived, and I was still angry at how Tuttle had abused my father's trust, claiming in his letters to be doing work that had never been done. And, from the whispers I'd heard, taking advantage of the laborers too. We paid them a pittance in wages since slavery had been abolished, but they still needed the money. There were few ways to earn your daily bread in Jamaica. A ruthless man could use that leverage to force the poor wretches to do whatever he wanted.

Looking at their bent bodies working away, sweating in the sun, the idea turned my stomach. The women came in all hues, from a medium caramel to nearly black. They wore full skirts in faded colorful cotton, tucked up to their knees to avoid the mud, billowy, long-sleeved shirts, and handkerchiefs tied around their heads. The cotton was their shield from the sun. I could not fathom wanting to rut with such bodies. The older men covered themselves too, but the younger ones... some of them tied the long sleeves of their tunics around their waist so that their sweat-slicked muscles were exposed.

I tried not to look at them at all.

I called a break at noon, and Sally and Morning went among the laborers, passing out buttered bread and fried plantains. It did not seem to bother the natives to sit in the sun, but my own head, accustomed to the English gloom, was spinning. I made for the shade of the trees that edged the field.

Crosswinds lay at the foot of a small mountain so that one could walk up into the forest and look down on the property and on out to the distant sea. The plantation looked perfect from up there—idyllic and green—until you got up close enough to see the neglect, to see the green was out of control and threatened to swallow us all up again.

I had just tied my horse and taken the water from my saddle when I saw a woman—Tiyah was her name—approaching the trees. She acted like she didn't see me, her face fiercely intent on her internal thoughts. She disappeared into the forest.

I would normally have let her go, assuming she was going to relieve herself or spend the short break out of the heat. But the look on her face stirred my curiosity. And also, it was Tiyah. She was a tall woman, not young but not yet old, and handsome for her people. She had a commanding presence that, to be honest, intimidated me, though I would never admit it. I'd heard whispers among the servants in the house—about going to Tiyah for aches and pains, blessings or advice. She was an Obeah woman, a practitioner of that folk magic that so fascinated me. My mother would have been horrified at such heathen ways and refused to have her on the plantation. But I had the advantage of an education at Eton and Cambridge, where my mind had been opened to the wonders of the natural world, of travel and exploration.

Oh, the long nights Richard and I had spent, up talking until dawn about distant peoples and places we'd read about in the tales of Marco Polo and lurid magazines.

This would make an interesting letter to Richard. That made up my mind. Leaving my horse safely tied, I followed Tiyah on foot.

She took a well-trod trail through the forest up the hill. I stayed as far back as I could, but she was oblivious to me. At times I caught snatches of her muttering. It was nearly a chant in a singsong voice, but I couldn't make out the words.

The tree cover was thick and buzzing with insects, and I nearly stumbled right on top of her before I saw that she had stopped.

To the side of the trail was a small ridge where a narrow footpath edged out to a looming rocky face. There was a natural depression in the face of the rock that was the size of a large steamer trunk. It had been made into a sort of shrine. Tiyah knelt in front of it and lit a half-dozen candles. In and among the candles were a host of items—a bottle of rum, a beaded necklace, small bones, a loaf of bread, coins, scraps of brightly colored cloth, and a statuette of what looked like the Virgin Mary, only with a black face and hands.

I watched from the cover of the trees, delighted to be seeing the native practice with my own eyes.

After lighting the candles, Tiyah spoke in urgent patois. I'd picked up a few words from hearing my servants speak. The patois the natives spoke was a mix of English words and African, though the pronunciation made the English words challenging to recognize. But there was no mistaking the pleading tone of her request, or the main thread of it.

"Erzulie, I beg you! Erzulie, save my daughter!"

Tiyah took a white handkerchief stained with blood from a pocket and placed it on the shrine. Then she removed a plantain leaf and carefully unwrapped it to reveal a small chunk of ice.

I knew there were ice ships from the north that visited the docks, but I could not imagine how she'd managed to keep such a thing from melting through her morning work. Perhaps it had been much larger to start. She offered it with both hands, placing it in front of the candles.

Ice?

I was still pondering it in my mind when she rose and turned toward me, done with her prayers. I started to dive back into the trees, but I realized it was too late and I would only look like a namby-pamby fool. So I straightened my spine and stepped out.

"Tiyah," I greeted her firmly, not wanting to appear apologetic. "Get along back to the field now."

She didn't move. Her eyes stared into mine with both confusion and a kind of challenge. "You follow me, Missah."

I thought of making up a lie, but such instincts had been beaten out of me in my youth. My father had never tolerated a liar. "I did. I was curious. You're not in any trouble. Go join the others."

She took one deliberate step closer to me and tilted her head, her eyes narrowing as she studied me.

I refused to be afraid of her, Obeah woman or not. I might be curious, but I was no gullible fool. Like many folk beliefs—curses, the "evil eye"—Obeah was based on sympathetic magic. As a man of learning, I knew it was all folderol in the end, even if it was rather fascinating.

Then I realized the look in her eyes was not threatening. At least not that way. She looked like she wanted to… lick me. I felt my body blush. I was no gullible fool for that either. I had no interest in picking up a paramour, as some of the English here did.

If she wasn't going to obey my order, I'd simply turn and go myself, haughtily, as if I expected her to follow as a matter of course. As I started to leave, she spoke.

"You curious, Missah? About dis?" She waved at the shrine.

I raised my chin. "From a scientific standpoint, yes."

She laughed. "Den ask what you will, young *scientist*."

She was mocking me, but it didn't feel ill-meant. And why should I not ask, if she was willing to tell me? I thought of what Dr. Hodgets would do.

"Why the ice?"

Her face grew grave, a shadow passing over her. "My… daughter. She very ill. Fever. Seven days now. If it do not break soon, she die. De gods burn her up."

"So the ice is… a sign of what you want them to do—cool her down. Is that right?"

"Yes." She looked at me fiercely. "I speak to de loa, but actions, *tings*, are better than words. Words!" She spit it out like it was poison. "Words make promises and break dem, like a lamp trown at de wall."

I had nothing to say to that. It was true enough, I supposed. I wanted to ask more about the gods, about the shrine, but I could see she was troubled about her daughter and it was not the time.

"Has she seen a doctor?"

Tiyah shot me an angry glare. "White medicine—only for those with plenty white money." With that she pushed past me and headed down the trail.

~3~

THAT NIGHT, the drums were relentless. I knew they signaled some sort of exercise of that pagan magic that Tiyah practiced. *Obeah*. I had no idea what such worship looked like, but the drums were positively indecent. They conjured up images of naked bodies dancing and thrashing about in some sort of religious ecstasy.

Richard always said I had too much imagination. I missed him—missed the chance to whisper with someone about the drums. He would calm my fears and my overthinking. He would make me laugh. But Richard was not there.

They were probably holding a ceremony for the girl, Tiyah's daughter. But what good would such magic do? A fever had struck Entwhile in the year before I was sent off to school. I was the first to fall and the first to recover. I remember wandering the silent halls, looking for servants who were all sick abed. I watched as our family doctor, competent Dr. Lowerly, tended my younger sister, ordering a cold bath for her and dosing her with salicylic acid, a derivative of willow bark that did wonders for pain and fever.

I thought of the chip of ice Tiyah had guarded so carefully to place at the shrine. She probably spent a week's wages on it. The ice ship from the New World delivered to Kingston Bay several times a year, and I knew there'd been a recent shipment. But it was a costly luxury.

The drums beat on. I tried hard to ignore them and sleep, but the night was so hot, even with the doors to the veranda open. I could not stop thinking how much worse the heat would be if I had a fever. Heat builds upon itself like a vine climbing a tree. The girl would likely die. Children died, it was the way of things. Still, I could not forget Tiyah's face as she spoke of the fever. And since Tiyah worked for me, her family was my responsibility, or could be seen as such. On the other hand, I couldn't be seen to play favorites, nor did I want to start a riot of people asking for medical help day and night. This was a plantation, not a hospital.

God, the drums!

I gave sleep up for a loss and got dressed. I roused my house man, Philip. "Send Simi into town to buy five pounds of ice." I handed him coins. "And ride yourself for Dr. Fornay. Tell him it's urgent."

TIYAH'S DAUGHTER, Lily, stayed in the house for almost a week. Her fever broke on the second day, thanks to ice baths and Dr. Fornay. But she'd been ill a long time, was emaciated, and too weak to stand. Tiyah worked in the fields all day, so it was agreed Lily would stay with us, where Philip and Sally could tend her hourly until she was strong enough to be on her own.

I heard the whispers. The natives believed Tiyah's power had convinced me to take Lily in, that the loa had answered Tiyah's prayers. It was a notion that made me smile, and I couldn't help writing to Richard about it. I didn't bother addressing it with the servants, of course. It's best to pretend one doesn't hear idle gossip. One must be above it if one is to maintain any sort of order.

When Tiyah came to get Lily, she asked to speak with me. I was in my office, writing my correspondence, and I told Philip to show her in. I figured she wanted to thank me, and I didn't want that to happen on the veranda, where the servants would hang on our every word and find ways to add more fuel to their speculations, no matter how innocuous our exchange.

"What can I do for you, Tiyah?" I asked her briskly.

"Missah." To my shock, she came around to my chair and fell to her knees in front of me.

"Come now!" The sight made me extremely uncomfortable. "There's no need for that. Take a seat."

But Tiyah, as she was wont to do, ignored me. She stared up at me, her face tight with emotion. "You saved de life of my daughter, Missah. Tis a great debt I owe."

"Nonsense." I felt my face heating, and so I did what I always did when I was at a loss: tried to imitate my father. "I only did what I could easily do. Your continued well-being is thanks enough. Now—"

"No," Tiyah said fiercely. "You do not understand. Lily, she also de daughter of Erzulie."

I stared at her, confounded. That was the god she'd been praying to at the shrine, wasn't it? I'd heard the name mentioned by other servants as well. It was a female deity, I was pretty sure, one they associated with statues of the Virgin Mary.

"Lily, she made when I was ridden by Erzulie. Erzulie chose de father, and she make de baby."

Good Lord! The images that conjured up. I really didn't need to hear this. "Er... I don't think—"

"De loa pay their debts, and so do I," Tiyah insisted with a prideful shake of her head. "I ask Erzulie what is de proper payment. If you see her in your dreams tonight, do not be afraid, Missah."

I realized my mouth was hanging open. I was at a total loss, but I knew that to refuse a gift was an insult. Assuming this was meant to be a gift of some kind. Hellfire. In my dreams!

"Yes. Well. Er... I hope Lily remains healthy. It was, uh, no trouble at all. You may go."

I could swear Tiyah was smirking when she left.

I WAS swimming in the small bay near Crosswinds. It was night, and the moon was full. It hung, as dark as an orange, above my head and reflected in the black water of the bay as if in a mirror. The water was warm, and I was... naked? I could feel the water caressing my bare skin in little eddies that made me shiver with delight.

I swam effortlessly, strangely at peace with being in the bay alone at night, at having no clothes on my body. The water lapped at my chest like warm fingers. I floated onto my back.

Something brushed my leg. The terror came in an instant, with a cold, sick rush. I jerked up in the water and looked all around me frantically. But the water of the bay showed no disturbance.

Below. It's down there, underneath me.

The peaceful moment was gone. I swam for the shore as hard as I could. I could see the distant beach, but no matter how frantically I stroked, it came no closer. The water, now cold and merciless, was dragging me out to sea.

Something scaly slithered along my leg in a caress.

I screamed and thrashed my limbs, trying to scare off the creature, and then I swam for shore again, huffing with fear. Adrenaline coursed through me, giving me a burst of power. And still, no matter how frantically I swam, the shore receded.

I was going to die.

The thing touched my foot and then curled around my leg. *Tentacle? Snake?* It felt rough as sand, pulling at the hairs on my leg as it slid upward. By now I was too exhausted to fight it. I could only tread the water and wait in terror for whatever it would do to me. I was in its environment, and I'd never felt so helpless.

The thing coiled up my leg. It seemed to grow in diameter, getting rounder and fatter, as if preparing itself for attack. It reached my groin and slid between my legs, causing chills that were equal parts erotic response, horror, and dread. It took a turn at my lower back and curved around my waist.

And still, the thing trailed off my foot. Dear Lord, how huge it was—how monstrous! My arms tread fitfully as I peered down into the water, trying to see it, my fear all-consuming and my heart crashing in my chest.

And then I did see it—a snake's head, large as a grapefruit, eyes red, skin so bright green it shone like emeralds in the water. It reared back, opening its mouth to expose a pure white interior and razor-sharp teeth and—

I screamed! The snake struck me on my left breast. Its long incisors buried themselves deep in my flesh, and I could swear I felt them pierce my heart. It drew in, sucking the blood from the chambers of that organ, sucking out my soul!

"MISSAH COLIN!"

Philip woke me in my bed, where I had been thrashing and screaming. The sheets were soaked with water, clammy against me as I sat up, trying to reconnect to the bedroom, to the real world.

"You have beaucoup nightmare, Missah Colin," Philip said worriedly. "Is you all right?"

Was I? My chest burned. I opened my nightshirt, ripping it in my haste, and stared at the bare skin of my chest. It was unmarked. "I—" I blinked up at Philip, striving to calm my breath. "I need a drink."

Philip shook his head in that "these people are crazy" way of his, but he said, "I go fetch it." And he left.

I sat all the way up and swung my feet from the bed. The planks of the floor felt solid and good under my feet. I pushed aside the mosquito netting and walked to the veranda. It was still dark, the middle of the night, but I had no interest in going back to bed or, indeed, of ever sleeping again.

What a horrible dream!

Philip brought me a glass of scotch, and I thanked him and sent him to bed. Then I put on my robe and went to the study. I would write to Richard, tell him about my nightmare, about Tiyah's warning that I would see Erzulie in my dreams, and about my confounded imagination. I was more gullible than I'd thought, and I was not pleased about it. But even the idea of writing to Richard steadied my nerves. It would put things in their proper perspective and remind me of who I was.

I was Colin Hastings, third son of the Earl of Huntington, graduate of Eton and Cambridge, engaged to Miss Elizabeth Simons.

I rubbed my hand over my chest and tried to hold on to that.

~4~

TIYAH CAME to me the next day after I dismissed the laborers from their work. It was late afternoon, and the sun was like a fat egg yolk sitting on top of the tall, sickeningly green palm trees. We'd cleared another field that Tuttle had allowed to go fallow, and I was staring over the land, thinking about how best to measure out for the young banana tree saplings I'd purchased. I felt a chill, then realized Tiyah was standing by my side.

I only just managed not to startle. Her attitude was subservient, with her eyes lowered, but nevertheless I felt a twinge of the fear I'd had in the nightmare. I pushed it away with determination. I absolutely refused to fear Tiyah.

"What can I do for you?" I asked coolly.

"Tis what *I* can do for you." She raised her eyes. Her face had an expression somewhere between smugness and satisfaction, as if she knew something I did not.

"Yes?"

"Missah Hastings, Erzulie tell me de gift she offer you for saving Lily. Tis a very special ting, a great honor."

"Yes?" I asked, as if it meant nothing to me, but I could not help swallowing convulsively.

"She offer you a life of passion, Missah. De desire of your heart, dis she give to you."

"What?" A stupid little laugh escaped me. I could feel my face burning.

Tiyah spoke with disgust. "I see de English marrieds. Man and wife like two cold fish. He spark quick only to make baby. And she not at all. Dis no life, Missah."

My face had no idea what to do with itself. I had no doubt it was frozen in some ghastly rictus. I could not believe this woman stood there and spoke to me of such private matters. "Er, I-I don't think—"

"No! Do not insult her, Missah. You tink well on it. Your heart's desire. Love. Great passion! Dis what Erzulie offer you. I know many who would kill for de same, but Erzulie, she offer it to *you*."

I shut my mouth and thought about it.

The nightmare had been so real, the feeling of the snake between my legs, the way it had *bit into my chest, as if sucking out my heart's blood.*

I stared at Tiyah. "My heart's desire?"

"Yes."

"H-how does Erzulie know what my heart desires?"

"She taste it. Do you not remember?" Tiyah tapped my chest.

There was something sly in her face, like she knew damn well about the nightmare. Had Philip mentioned it? I wouldn't put it past the servants to gossip over my night terrors. But then it occurred to me that I'd never mentioned the snake biting my heart to Philip or to anyone else. And when Tiyah had put the idea in my mind, that Erzulie might come to my dreams, she'd never said anything about my heart either. So how had she planted that particular suggestion in my mind? How could she possibly know?

"Tink on it, Missah. Tomorrow you answer. We must make de ritual dis Saturday when Erzulie's power is full with de moon. Den or not at all."

With that solemn warning, Tiyah strode away.

GOOD GOD. I thought about it.

This is the power of suggestion. Some part of my internal compass had spun off True North and down into the darkness. I didn't believe Erzulie had come into my dreams and tasted the secrets of my heart. But I didn't *not* believe it either.

I wished Richard were here so I could talk to him. I knew him so well that I often could hear his voice in my head even when he wasn't there. But on this, my Richard was uncharacteristically silent.

Would he say, "What a lark! You must do this, old man, if only in the name of science! Think of the experience, seeing one of their rituals firsthand!" Or would he say, "Oh, Colin—stay far, far away! You're too easily led, my friend. This is dangerous." I could equally imagine Richard saying either, which was no help at all. As for my neighbors, the

Pivots, I knew saintly Lester would advise me most strongly to steer clear of such "devil worship." And Major Pivot, poor fellow, lived in a world of his own and would be of no use at all.

What if Tiyah could really do what she said? What fool, when offered one chance to rub the genie's lamp, refused? I was not that man. No, I was a different grade of fool altogether.

Tiyah was not wrong in her assessment of the English. I'd never seen my parents touch, not in my twenty years of life. There was no affectionate kiss on the cheek, as I'd seen the post master give his plump wife. There was no brush of a hand across the shoulders while passing, no warm look with promises for later.

I thought about Elizabeth, my darling girl. She was everything a man could want in a wife—cheerful, kind, beautiful, graceful, accomplished on the piano, and with a lovely singing voice. I was lucky to have found such an agreeable bride who also came with a dowry. Her family's home, Robin's End, was not palatial, but it was quite a tidy little estate, comfortable enough, and it would pass to me as Elizabeth's husband. As an Earl's third son, I'd inherit no property or title of my own, only a modest allowance. Elizabeth was my salvation in more ways than one.

I loved the girl. I did. I was thrilled when she accepted my proposal and admitted she loved me too. But passion? "Passionate" had never been a word I would use to describe our union.

I'd kissed Elizabeth three times, and I could recall each distinctly. There'd been novelty in the act, and fealty, and a desire to bind her to me. But it had not particularly stirred my blood. Then again, she was young, only seventeen, a sweet, innocent girl. It wouldn't have been right to force myself on her, to play gross with her goodness.

But what if it was never there? What if Elizabeth and I ended up exactly like my mother and father? What if Elizabeth merely tolerated my attentions in bed? Lifted up the hem of a voluminous nightdress and turned her head away? Could I bear such an act?

I'd only been with one woman, at a house of prostitution the Cambridge fellows frequented. Richard and I had gone together for our first time, and afterward we'd agreed the experience had been over too quickly and was horribly underwhelming. We'd both decided we would rather wait for wives of our own. It was yet one more way in which Richard and I were in complete sympathy. But what if, after waiting for a wife, my bed with Elizabeth was cold?

And what if Tiyah could change that?

I drank scotch and paced in the sitting room. It was still so bloody hot, and the open windows and doors scared up but a ghost of a breeze. In the distance the drums had started again, damn agitating things. They made me feel restless in my own skin.

I'd been in Jamaica long enough to see things. I'd seen men and women pair up and walk off at the end of a work day, their shoulders touching, their eyes full of sin. I'd seen husbands grab their wives for a deep kiss, hands groping on the globes of the woman's behind. One night, when I couldn't sleep, I went to the kitchen for a glass of warm milk. I'd heard loud moans and the slam of a bed on the wall from the direction of Sally's room. Philip, I knew, courted her, though they were not married. I'd said nothing, too embarrassed to bring it up with him.

My blood stirred thinking these thoughts, my groin tightening. *Passion*. It was like a miasma here in Jamaica. They were bloody shameless about it.

What if Tiyah's gift could give me that? Make Elizabeth full of passion for me, and me for her? Could we be proper Englishfolk in the day and wild savages at night? Would I even want such a thing?

Yes, by God. I wanted it very bloody much. I wanted love, and lust, and passion, tangled bodies and sweaty sheets, at least once in my lifetime. Sometimes my very clothes seemed to choke me, as if the binding threads of civilization strangled the man in me, the flesh-and-blood *man*. I'd denied my urges for so long, pushing carnal thoughts down or stroking myself guiltily when I could no longer bear it.

I wanted to let myself feel it all, to touch and be touched. I wanted to breathe. I had to be insane for thinking Tiyah could give me that. Then again, this was a strange land, and strange things were possible, were they not?

My mind made up, I wrote a quick letter to Richard, telling him what I was going to do. He would sweat blood waiting for my next missive, telling him what had transpired.

I could hardly wait myself.

~5~

I PREPARED myself for the ritual as best I could. I'd asked Philip what he knew about such things, and he denied adamantly that he'd ever been to an Obeah ceremony—and then proceeded to tell me in detail what he'd "heard" happened there.

I could expect blood sacrifices, apparently. Chickens and maybe a goat. I could expect dancing and drums. If we were "blessed," one or more of the Obeah men or women would be ridden by a loa, an Obeah spirit. This is apparently akin to having one's body possessed by another's will. No matter how frightened I might be, I must take care not to offend such deities, Philip insisted.

I remembered what Tiyah had said about Erzulie "riding" her when Lily was conceived. It was all so... sordid and yet unbearably interesting. I decided I was going to attend the ritual being "ridden" by Dr. Hodgets. How Richard would smile at that notion! But I was going to try to see thing through my old professor's eyes, wearing my "little scientist" hat, and observe to the best of my ability so I could later write it all down for posterity, perhaps eventually publish it with one of the learned societies.

In any case, it was a good excuse to attend the ritual without feeling like a gullible fool. I did not fear for my safety. Although I was white, and therefore held with an impenetrable disdain and aloofness by the natives, I had not been a bad overseer, I thought, and I *had* saved Lily. These people had no reason to do me harm.

Then again, once in a wild frenzy, who could say what might happen? I considered hiding a gun on my person, but the smallest I had was still too large to tuck into one's pocket, and I didn't want to insult Tiyah by coming armed.

I took hold of my courage. I'd go as a man of science, not a soldier.

TIYAH CAME for me herself, dressed all in white—a full long skirt, a loose blouse, and a white cloth twisted and tied around her head. She said nothing and put her hands to her lips to urge me to do the same.

She led me from the house and into the woods on a path I'd never noticed before.

I tried to remember the way so that I could retrace my steps later, in the daylight, but we walked for a long time, with sudden turns that had no discernible markers that I could see. I had the feeling I was being led in circles purposefully to confuse me. And it was dark. The night was lit only by a full moon, and we carried no light with us. The sound of drums grew louder and softer in turn until my head was spinning. There was also a cloying smell, like the smoke of some herb, that wafted through the night. It made my throat burn when I got a strong scent of it. It started to make me feel dizzy.

By the time we reached a clearing, I was no longer scared or even anxious. I felt as though I was in a dream. I was there, but I was detached from it too, a sensation I welcomed wholeheartedly.

There was quite a crowd gathered—at least fifty in the clearing itself and more in the shadows beyond the firelight. The clearing was brightly lit after the dark of the woods, and warm from the heat of a large bonfire. In the center was a pole, about ten feet tall, with carvings and paint covering it in a primitive design. The drums were loud enough here to reverberate in my bones, and it was strange to see the drummers when for so many months I'd only heard the sound from a distance. There were three of them, young native men pounding on African-style drums. They were so lost in the rhythm they were like extensions of the drums themselves.

The crowd parted for us, and I stumbled after Tiyah, blinking rapidly at the brightness of the fire and the stare of dozens of eyes. I felt I should speak, but I had nothing to say. I wished for escape, but I could not very well back out now.

We reached the center pole, and Tiyah turned to face me. She reached out her hands, staring at me all the while, and on either side of me, a man stepped forward. One of them had a goat, bound and struggling weakly in his arms, the other a small pig. Both men slashed the throats of their prey. The dying animals cried in terror and tried to get free—too late. Their blood splashed on Tiyah, on her bronze arms and white clothes and even on her face. She stared at me with a strange toothy grin. I tried to take a step back, disgusted by the sight, but there were people right behind me and they grabbed my arms and held me firm.

Tiyah began chanting to Erzulie, her patois thick and beyond my ability to comprehend. I felt a moment's panic at having my arms held down, like the pig and goat had been held down, but I forced myself not to fight it. It's not like I could leave anyway, not without pushing my way through the crowd like a gutless fool. And once again the sound of the drums and the cloying scent worked to relax me.

I'd seen the sacrifice, I told myself. And really, it was nothing I could not have seen at any butcher shop in England. If that was the worst of it, I would be fine.

That was when Tiyah's eyes rolled back in her head. Her chin came down and her head cocked coyly, regarding me the way a crow might regard a crumb. The very features of her face grew sharper, her nostrils flaring harshly, her lip curling in a caricature of a smile. With only the whites of her eyes showing and her face splattered with fresh blood, it was a dreadful effect.

"Please—" I had no idea what to say.

Tiyah—or possibly Erzulie or some other spirit—stepped toward me. She ran her hands over my body, from the crown of my head to my shoulders and down my arms, then up the underside and down past my ribs, waist, and hips, muttering to herself all the while. She continued down each leg to my ankles and then moved up the inside. The touch was firm and impersonal, like that of a tailor. I blinked but didn't move, well-trained little Englishman that I was. It was only when she went farther than any tailor ever dared and squeezed my privates in her hand, as if testing the weight of them, that I came to my senses and stepped back with a gasp.

Tiyah laughed. She spoke in French, which I'd become modestly competent at in school.

"You do not like when I touch this part of you? But all men like it. Such a pretty face, but you deny your own manhood."

Even as fuzzy as my head was, I was aware that I did not want to have such things discussed in front of a crowd of people who worked for me. I could only hope most of them did not speak French. The concern forced me to try to get my head together.

I stiffened my spine and spoke firmly. "You asked me to come here to offer me something for saving Lily's life. You owe me nothing for that. I was happy to help her. But if you would give me something, I will accept it with thanks."

I thus hoped to hurry things along and forestall any long discussion of passion, or lack thereof. I was beginning to wish I had never agreed to this, as interesting as the ceremony was. I had to get through it with my dignity—and authority—intact.

Tiyah ignored my words. She tilted her head, as if listening to something, and then danced away. The crowd began dancing along with her. I saw a man, a very large man, convulse, his eyes rolling up in his head. He began making strange, jerky movements not unlike those of a rooster. Someone blew smoke directly in my face, sickly sweet and acrid. I coughed. Someone else danced by me, brushing against my back—breasts pressing against me so that I could feel her nipples. I whirled, outraged, but she was already gone, and I could not tell who had done it.

Fear was beginning to trickle in, despite the drums, despite the smoke and the surreal feeling of the whole evening. I'd lost my hold on dear old Hodgets somewhere along the way, and perhaps myself too. I was intoxicated, and I was not among friends. Indeed, I had no idea where I was. I'd also lost sight of Tiyah, and I felt vulnerable and exposed.

Had I really expected anything from this but humiliation? Making up my mind, I turned to go. I'd find my way home one way or the other.

I pushed my way through the writhing bodies toward the forest until suddenly I found myself directly in front of the center pole once again. Tiyah stood before me, legs spread wide, her skirt rucked up to her knees. Her eyes were still rolled back in her head, and her mouth was open in an "O" like a silent scream. She turned her palm up and shoved it, hard, on my stomach. We both froze.

"*It is here,*" she whispered in French. *Il est ici.* "*That which you swallowed. That which you buried.*"

"W-what?" I stuttered.

"Bring it!" she ordered the man at her side. He left and stepped back a moment later with a cage. It was an old gilded bird cage, made in England or France and repaired crudely with wire where it had begun to fall apart. Inside the cage was a bird. It was large—at least the size of a very large crow. But it was not a crow. Its body was white underneath and topped with blue-black feathers. The top of its head was the same deep blue, and its eyes were perfectly round and a brilliant red. It was an exotic thing, like Jamaica herself.

Were they going to sacrifice this bird too?

"*Ici*," Tiyah-who-was-not-Tiyah repeated. The tips of her fingers dug into my stomach over the stiff cloth of my trousers. "*Ici*." Here, here.

Her fingers hurt, but I found I could not pull back. My feet felt rooted to the earth, heavy as lead.

"*Ici!*" She screamed.

The man who had brought the bird stepped forward. In a moment he had unfastened the buttons of my linen vest and pulled up my white shirt. He pushed down the waist of my trousers, exposing my navel and lower belly to the night. I gasped and tried to move, but it was as if I was paralyzed entirely.

It's an illusion, the power of suggestion. You can move. You must move!

But I could not. Not even my tongue would work. It lay flaccid and numb in my mouth.

Tiyah muttered in French, too low and slurred for me to make it out. Her fingers returned, digging into the naked flesh and muscle just above my groin. It was excruciating, and I felt a wave of nausea as her fingers pressed deep. I looked down, transfixed. Bright red blood sprouted around her fingers as if she were penetrating my flesh. I tried to scream and could not.

"*Il est profond. Très profonde,*" she muttered, her teeth clacking as her fingers dug into my belly.

"God help me," I choked out, as another strong wave of nausea wracked me. I gagged. I was being held up now by two strong men on either side, my arms slung around their shoulders. I did not remember getting there, but it was good they propped me up because my knees had given way.

"*Bâtard!*" Tiyah cursed angrily, though whether at me or my belly, I couldn't tell. She hissed and looked into my eyes with those blank whites of her own. "*You must bring it up. It is too deep. I cannot reach it,*" she ordered in harsh French.

I gagged again as her fingers relentlessly pushed, causing pain unlike any I'd ever know.

"*Spit it up, Colin Hastings! I order you! Now!*"

She dug even deeper, and my vision pulsed black with agony. I felt the hot splash of blood running down my stomach and soaking through the fabric of my trousers. I retched and retched again. It felt like my bowels were coming up into my mouth—bitter and sour and tasting of death. And then there was something there, in my throat, something thick and slimy, like uncooked liver. It choked my airway.

Tiyah held out her hand, and I spat the horror into it, repulsed to my soul and gasping for breath.

In her hand was a black orb, black as if filled with dark blood. It was the size of a goose egg, and it pulsed. It looked like nothing I'd ever seen, like a badly deformed heart or a half-formed embryo.

"Ah!" she said, cradling it in both hands with a satisfied air. It was then I realized that her fingers were no longer digging into me. I looked down, but though my belly was smeared with blood, there was no wound.

A parlor trick. It's all a parlor trick. You've been mesmerized, like in those theater shows. This isn't real.

Still, I could not stop staring at the thing in her hands and feeling like it was part of me, both repulsed and attracted to it.

The man who had brought the bird cage opened a little door, and Tiyah reached in with her bloodied hand outstretched.

The bird, *dear God!*, it ate up the thing in her hand in one greedy gulp.

I retched again at the sight, disgusted.

"There. There. *Oiseau doux. Oiseau bon.*" She crooned to the bird as she latched the door shut.

I slumped against the arms that held me up. Sweat sprung up all over my body, like when a fever breaks. The breeze was cool against my face, and I felt a rush of giddy relief. My breathing calmed, and my heart soared. *It is probably the shock*, I thought. But I felt so bloody good.

Tiyah grasped my face in both her hands and looked into my eyes. It was Tiyah now. Her own eyes were brown and a little bloodshot, but they were Tiyah's eyes. "Tis done, Missah. You take good care dis bird. Feed 'im. Treat 'im well. Long as he live, your passion be free. And he live long time, ey?"

I blinked up at her, not knowing what to say.

Tiyah smiled knowingly. "Tis well, Missah. Sleep."

As if I had been waiting for those words, I fell immediately into unconsciousness.

~6~

I HAVE no idea how I got back to Crosswinds, but when I awoke next, I was in my bedroom. I'd been having an amazing dream in which I was soaring high in the sky like a bird, gliding on air currents while looking down on the landscape, searching for prey. Only what I felt was not a hunger of the stomach, but a hunger of the loins. The bird—me—was searching for something to *mate.*

The dream was so real, and so primal, that when I woke up, I sat in bed, trying to hold on to the feeling of being that bird, the indescribable joy of gliding on cool air, the intense focus of my search, the pull of desire.

But, as dreams do, it slipped away. As the bedroom became more solid around me, I found that my body was fully aroused and throbbing in a demand for attention.

I shoved off my bedclothes and tore the nightshirt over my head. I was so bloody hot I was sick with it. I ignored my body's awkwardly swollen state, pushed aside the mosquito netting, and opened the door to the veranda to try to get some air into the room.

Then I realized the heat was coming from within me, not without. I could feel a breeze on my face and a coolness against my skin. It felt like rain, like a storm was coming. I could see the palm trees swaying strongly in the wind. But this did nothing to relieve the burn making my skin moist with sweat and pooling in my groin in a maddening ache.

Passion.

Was this feeling a result of the ceremony? Was Erzulie doing this to me, or was it yet another instance of the power of suggestion?

Oh, God. I didn't care. For once, I felt no need to fight it.

The night was dark, clouds obscuring both moon and stars. Yet still, somehow, I could see, as if there was a dim glow in the air. The distant fields of sugarcane rippled like approaching snakes. There was no one in sight across the open yard in front of the house.

And then there was.

He came walking from the trees, a silhouette, calm and steady. He kept on coming until he was standing in the yard in front of me, maybe twenty feet away. By then I could see the whites of his eyes and the glow of his... *bare skin.* He wore nothing at all. The top curve of his manhood, partially erect, was visible to me, as was the smooth, hairless skin of his chest and two peaked nipples.

Lust roiled in my stomach, making my head reel as if I were still aboard the ship. I heard myself moan before I could control it.

He was beautiful, this male, and I wanted him. I wanted that maleness, in my hands, my mouth, rutting all over me.

I tried to hang on to a scrap of reason. *Who was he?* He looked young, but his face was obscured. He was a native—I could see the dusky color of his skin—and yet, from one blink to the next, it was not dark but glowing white, his chest strangely familiar to me.

Richard.

I knew it wasn't Richard. Richard was in England. But I pushed this knowledge from my head deliberately. I *wanted* it to be Richard. I missed him so much. And I wanted to touch him. I wanted this all to be a dream that I could indulge in without guilt and without fear of consequences. I *chose* for it to be so, willingly. My fear and self-consciousness were not absent, but they were small voices, and distant, overwhelmed in a flood of need.

He opened up his hands in supplication, his cock growing larger as I stared at him. I could not be bothered with the stairs at the other end of the veranda. I scrambled over the wooden railing of the balcony, ran across the lawn, and then he was in my arms.

He stood still as I pressed into him, my arms clutching around his back, my face buried in his shoulder. He was tall, and solid, and smelled of smoke and rain and sweat. He was real in a way that was frightening, reminding me this was no dream. He was lithe, lean, his skin soft. My mind flashed on a native youth I'd seen looking at me before when he worked in the field, a beautiful boy I had purposefully avoided.

Colin, a voice whispered in my mind, Richard's voice. The stiff arms relaxed and came up to embrace me.

I moaned and pushed hard against him. I didn't quite dare to rut, but the pressure of him against me was a necessary thing. His cock grew harder against my belly, and I found the edge of his hipbone and couldn't stop a thrust of my pelvis. Embarrassed at this animalistic urge, I pulled my head back and kissed him. I thought to redirect the need, express something more civilized, but his mouth was all tongue and wetness and sin, and there was nothing civilized about it. He pushed me back toward the veranda.

When my back hit the railing, he broke the kiss to clamber gracefully up and over, pulling me along by my hand. And then we were in my room and on the bed.

There was a sense of secrecy there in the dark, behind the mosquito netting. He placed me on my back and removed my drawers, exposing me to the air. I looked and felt harder than I'd ever been in my life, flesh turned to turgid steel with the force of my blood. I didn't fight him. If anything, I felt proud of my state, the boldness of it. I arched eagerly and reached for him. I could see, as he sat on his heels, a glimpse of his face. He was smooth and mocha-colored, with full lips and long, dark eyelashes. He *was* that unusually pretty youth I had seen before. But his eyes burned with wanting me, and he leaned over and took my cock into *his mouth*, and I couldn't find it in myself to care.

I closed my eyes, my hands clamped on the sheets, and I pretended it was Richard.

His mouth was like nothing I'd ever imagined. It was infinitely better than my own furtive tugging, and I could hardly remember my single time with a woman. This was deliberate, his tongue rubbing rough and flat and perfect against my glans, his mouth suckling like he was a child with a candy. His head moved up and down, and one hand fondled my sack.

I gritted my teeth, squeezed my eyes shut, and gripped the bed harder, not wanting to spend quickly, like a virgin schoolboy. But it was beyond me to resist the suck and drag of that mouth or the bliss that was shuddering through me. I had no idea it could feel like this, that there could be so much rapture in it, that my skin could be so sensitive, the delight so sharp. I savored it as long as I could, which was not nearly long enough. Lightning pulsed through me, hot and transcendent, and I screamed as I spilled into his mouth. He did not pull away but kept at me, extending the sensation until I could no longer bear it and was forced to push him off.

He came over me then, laying his hot skin chest to chest with mine and kissing me deeply. I tasted the bitter musk of my own spend in his mouth, and it didn't repulse me. It was obscene and erotic and almost enough to stir me again. He ground his hard member against my stomach as his tongue played against mine, his hips moving faster and harder. I was barely recovered, but I helped him as much as I could, arching my back and holding myself stiff to give him a firm surface to grind against. I clutched his lower back tight with my hands.

He came with a whimpered cry into my mouth. I felt him pulse wetly against me—hot, liquid spurts.

The feeling and sound of his pleasure roused me, and I wanted to do it all over again. I clutched him and kissed him hard, but before I could reinvigorate my lust, exhaustion crept in and my limbs felt heavy and slow. I let them fall away from him as he kissed my cheek.

I closed my eyes and feel asleep.

WHEN I woke the next morning, the sun was bright and my head was clear. The night came flooding back to me. I had a glimmer of hope that it had all been a dream, but I was naked under the bedclothes and I had spend dried on my stomach. I could still smell him on the sheets and on my skin, a darker musk than my own. I found a short black hair on the pillow, curly and coarse.

It had not been a dream.

I rose and washed thoroughly at the basin. Then I rang for Philip and, not meeting his eyes, ordered my usual tea and breakfast on the veranda. I sat in the morning sun, drinking my tea, my person as tidy and English as it ever had been, and waited for the panic to come.

But it didn't come. I only felt numb and tense.

What was done was done. I'd been caught up in the frenzy of the Obeah ceremony, that drugging smoke, and Tiyah's power of suggestion. I'd been sent the youth for the purpose of seduction, clearly, and seduce me he did. I had no reason to feel shame or that I'd taken advantage. I had not gone to his house and dragged him here. It was he who had placed his mouth eagerly on my cock. It was he who then lay on top of me and took his own pleasure.

At the thought, heat flashed through me again, and I wanted, dear Lord, I wished I could feel it all over again.

I took a sip of tea, my hand shaking.

The issue was where to go from here. I could ignore the sly looks and innuendo I would likely get from the natives. I could pretend I didn't remember. If anyone had the temerity to write to the authorities or my father and reveal my sins, I would deny it. I'd be believed before any of them.

But strangely, these thoughts were like the ghosts of thoughts I used to have. A few days ago, I would have been horrified that I'd kissed a man, let him touch me, would have been humiliated that anyone *might know*. But now, while the thoughts still came, I felt only a mild echo of fear and a great deal of confusion.

I sipped my tea, staring into the green trees.

She sent me a man.

That succeeded in twisting a knot in my stomach.

Tiyah sent me a man, and I wanted him. I loved it.

My teacup clattered to the saucer.

I loved his maleness, wanted it. And when we touched, kissed, I thought of Richard.

I will give you your heart's most secret desire.

I shoved my hat onto my head and went out to work so I didn't have to think anymore.

~7~

Eton, 1859

"VULGARIAN!"

"Boor!"

"Peasant!"

I stood at the kitchen door with the pot of tea I'd prepared for Thorkell warm in my hands. Three of the senior boys were in the hall outside the kitchen, pushing around another junior. I'd noticed the boy before. I was small for twelve, and he was as slight as me. He had an agreeable face and ruddy cheeks that looked like someone had just pinched them. There was a certain congenial shyness about him that had made me want to befriend him at first glance, but so far I'd not even learned his name.

He was doggedly trying not to spill the tray with the cup and pot of tea he'd prepared, even while being pushed around. He said nothing, keeping his eyes on the floor.

One of the boys snatched the pot from the tray, opened the lid and sniffed, then made a face. "Don't even know how to make a proper English tea. You're a disgrace!"

"Do it again!" another ordered. "And make it right this time or else."

I'd only been at Eton for a few weeks, but I'd heard stories from my older brothers, and I knew enough of the way things worked to assume two things. First, the boy was not of the upper classes. He might be a scholarship case or maybe even a foreigner. Hence the bullying. And second, the state of the boy's tea had nothing to do with it. They'd likely reject any pot he made.

All first year boys like me were "fags," or servants, to an upper class boy. Fags made their fag-masters breakfast, midday tea, brushed their shoes, and did whatever other small chores they might need. In exchange, the fag-master acted as mentor and should, in theory, protect a boy from just such bullying. But in fact, bullying was rife at Eton. I'd had my share of it, despite my name.

My name. I straightened my spine and tried to summon the imperial affect I'd seen my older brothers use. "What are you up to there?" I demanded, approaching the group with the pot of tea still in my hands.

One of the senior boys eyed me up and down. "Who are you?"

"Hastings," I said proudly, lifting my chin. "And my brother will not be amused to be delivered cold tea."

I spoke with as much disdain as I could muster, which was considerable. I sounded positively haughty to my own ears. I was taking a chance, though. My eldest brother, Rupert Hastings, was well-known. He was the House Captain of Games, and as heir to the Earldom, he had that sheen of untouchable success that all Etonians, as well as the rest of the world, bowed and scraped to. But he was not the bullied boy's fag-master, nor mine, and his tea had nothing whatever to do with what was happening in the hall. I hoped these boys didn't know that.

The chance paid off. The three boys exchanged wary glances, and with a final flick to the boy's ear, they sauntered off, leaving us alone.

"You didn't have to do that. Thank you," the boy said. He sounded British but rough in his speech. He was from the North, I guessed, working class. His hair had fallen forward over his eyes, and with his hands full, he could do nothing about it.

I quelled an urge to brush it back for him. "All in a day's work," I said, rather stupidly.

"I suppose the tea isn't very good," he admitted sadly. "My fag-master is Wheaton, and he always makes a sort of face when he drinks it. But he's too polite to say so."

"Let me see." I put my own tray on the floor and lifted the lid off his pot. It was the color of piss. "Hmm. Did he ask for it weak?"

"No." The boy blushed. "My father imports coffee, among other things. We never drink tea at my house. Now if Wheaton liked coffee, I'd be on my game. I make the best you've ever tasted."

I smiled at his boasting. "I've never had coffee. I'll like to take you up on that sometime, see what it's like. But for now, why don't I show you how to make a proper tea?"

"Would you?" he looked surprised. "Why?"

"Must do right by poor Wheaton," I said, though I had no idea who Wheaton was. "I'm Colin, by the way."

I was rewarded with a huge grin. He had a small gap between his two front teeth that was rather endearing. "I'm Richard. Richard Wesley."

"Come on then, Richard Wesley. Let's make some tea."

London, August 1, 1870

My Dear Colin,

You know how to give a fellow a heart attack, don't you? Five days have gone by since I received your letter about attending that Obeah ceremony—are you truly mad, old chap? And since then, nothing. You've spoiled me with a letter a day since you left, sometimes two, and then, after such an explosive revelation, you leave me hanging?

Right then, you've done it now. I'm utterly terrified. I booked my passage. I leave today, and I hope to be there by the beginning of September. I'm sailing on the *Libertine II*, so if you are not, in fact, dead, please meet me at the docks.

I hate that I'll have no chance of hearing from you on the journey. If not for the fact that I was praying for a letter, I might have left two days ago. But I can't wait any longer. I'm sending a telegram to Kingston as well, in case this letter arrives later than I do.

I pray you are soon showing me the sights of Jamaica and we can laugh about this. I may even refrain from punching you, if only you are well and abjectly repentant. Please, Colin. Please be safe.

Your friend always,
Richard

AT THE beginning of August, I received a telegram.

Arriving in Kingston early September on Libertine II. Stop. Letter to follow. Stop.
Richard

I was not surprised that my lack of correspondence would drive my friend to such an extreme, though I was surprised it had only taken five days. In fact, I had not put pen to paper to write to him since the ritual. I was unable to even think about him without my whole being seizing up with indecision. I did not know what I wanted to say to him or how to say it.

I was waging an internal battle.

The bird was winning.

It was the full heat of August. In the evenings I sat in the parlor, doors and windows open to catch a breeze, and indulging myself with scotch, a fanning servant, and chips of ice bound in a cloth for my forehead. I burned inside and out until I was sure I would be consumed. Often Major Pivot would come to play cards and, sometimes, his brother Lester too.

West Falls, the Pivots' plantation, was managed by Lester Pivot. He was a small man with a compunction to evangelize to the natives and, if the gossip was to be believed, a weakness for his native housekeeper. John Pivot, whom everyone called Major, was the younger brother, in his late forties. He was a small, round man with an impressive mustache. He had apparently lost his wits during his service in the Second Boer War and been sent to Jamaica to be hidden away like a dark family secret. He believed himself to be an actor and would burst into song at the slightest provocation.

At least he provided a distraction and he was a decent tenor—for a madman.

"*I have sought, but I seek it vainly, That one lost chord divine,*" he sang as he sorted his cards. "*Which came from the soul of the organ, And entered into mine.*"

"It's your turn," I said, having to remind him to draw every single time.

And then there was the bird. I'd had it moved from my bedroom to the parlor, and there it sat in the evenings, watching me. It was hungry, always. The servants fed him crickets and beetles and little fish they bought from the fishmonger. I watched the bird gulp them down by the dozen, its black beak sharp and its gullet bottomless.

And the red eyes—always those red eyes!

Every time I looked at the bird, I thought of the ceremony. Had Tiyah-Erzulie really pulled something from inside me and given it to the bird, or had it all been a trick? Was the bird me? Was I it?

I hated the creature. I feared it. I ordered the servants to give it anything it wanted. I would have gotten rid of the thing, but I was afraid of what might happen to me if I did. No way could I kill the winged monstrosity.

So in the evenings, I drank, and played rummy with genial Major Pivot, and I alternated between ignoring the bird and staring at it.

As for its part, the bird had no such division in its nature. It was always staring at me.

After *that night*, there had been no laughing remarks or sly looks behind my back amongst the servants as I had feared there would be. It was as if nothing had changed. The young native man I thought had been my lover was gone for about a week, and then he reappeared with the other laborers. He did not approach me, nor I him, though at times my eyes drifted to him of their own accord. Even Tiyah went back to her work and did not try to speak with me again, though I could sometimes feel her watching me, wondering.

No one came to me in the night again. I was both relieved and… disappointed.

As the days passed, my fear and confusion lessened under the dullness of routine. I could pretend nothing had happened, but *it had*. And I was left alone to sort it out. It was between myself and the bird.

The nights were the worst. Whatever had been done to me, it had changed me physically. I would lie in my bed, my very skin restless and craving, my body slick with the swamping heat of lust. I could not stop the memory of that night, the feeling of that man, or fantasies of Richard in his stead. I imagined Richard's mouth on me, Richard laying heavily on top of me, his cock hard against my hot flesh. No matter how often I brought myself relief, it was never enough, only a momentary reprieve. It was like an addiction.

Had I really wanted this? To feel passion? Now I was being driven mad by it.

During the day, I drove myself hard in the sun so I didn't have to think. But in the parlor in the evenings, I could not escape it, especially once I'd received the telegram.

Richard was coming. He was on his way even then.

We'd been the best of friends since the day I'd taught him how to make tea at Eton. We'd spent six years together there and another four at Cambridge, where we had rooms side by side.

He'd been such a good-hearted boy, young Richard. He was the son of a self-made businessman from Manchester, and often had to take sly comments about being lowborn and nouveau riche. It did not matter one whit to me. His hair was a light brown, the color of a robin's back, and his cheeks as ruddy as a robin's breast. He was slender and tall and as hopeless at sports as I was, but he loved to walk. The boy could walk for hours and hours, and we'd often follow the River Cam out of Cambridge until we could see hedgerows. Hedgerows, said Richard, were when you knew you were in the country. And how he loved the country.

I missed his shy smile and his laugh, which was open and bright. I missed his whispered confessions—people he liked and didn't like, what he really thought of his parents, our professors, our lessons. I remembered a week when I'd been deathly ill with a stomachache and he'd brought me water and biscuits and sat by my side all evening, reading to me to take my mind off the pain.

Together, we didn't need any other friends, though one would orbit around us from time to time before moving on. We were content just the two of us.

Once when we were fifteen, Richard slipped into my room in the middle of the night. He crawled into my bed, claiming a nightmare. We lay on our sides, facing one another. There was a flush on his cheek and a look in his eyes that was nothing like fear. And after we'd stared at each other for a long time, he leaned forward and pressed his lips to mine, warm and hesitant. Then he lay back and watched me for a response.

My heart had pounded in my chest until I thought I might die. I remembered hating the hope on his face. I'd felt a blind panic. But I merely rolled my eyes and told him to "stop kidding around" and go back to bed. He went pale and left without a word.

But I knew in my heart what he wanted... he wanted us to kiss and touch each other, there in the dark. Maybe I knew, deep inside, that he'd always wanted it, wanted me that way, intimately.

Did he? Or was I wrong? Was he as incapable of conjuring up such a fiery and subversive idea as I was, in the cold and pristine landscape my mind had once been?

Had *once* been—and was no more.

We'd never spoken of it again. He never kissed me again.

I wouldn't have let him; I think he knew that. I had a wall around my heart. I loved Richard more than I'd ever loved any other person. He was part of my soul. But… there was no way I could *be that*. My family… my father… our friends… the very fabric of our society forbade it. They had laws about such things, for God's sake. I was not an outcast! All I wanted was to be successful, worthy, respectable. I would do well in Jamaica so that I could return to England and take up my rightful place, my place among the best of society, be a credit to the Hastings name.

One night, after Major Pivot had gone home and I'd drank too much, I threw my glass in a rage. Crystal and scotch shattered against the wall just to one side of the birdcage.

"Stop staring at me!" I screamed at the bird.

It flapped its wings in alarm. Its wingtips struck roughly against the sides of the cage, hurting it. I felt bad immediately. After it settled, the bird turned its back on me for the first time and sat huddled on its perch, head down.

Blast it. It only made me feel worse.

~8~

"TIYAH! COME here."

She and the others were harvesting the cane in our first crop, heavy, back-breaking work. She stood and shielded her eyes, looking over at me. I motioned for her to come closer.

When she stood beside my horse, I looked down at her, utterly composed. "After the day's work, you will come speak to me at the house, in the study."

"Yes, Missah," Tiyah said, betraying no opinion on the matter. She went back to work.

I MADE her wait in the study while I bathed and changed in my room, disgusted by the day's sweat. I needed all my English armor to deal with her—soap, pomade, and a clean cravat.

I entered the study and ordered Philip bring us cold tea, offering Tiyah a glass as well. Then I dismissed him. I looked at her, trying to find a way to begin.

"I see de bird, he is well," she said.

I frowned. "Yes."

"Tis a good ting." She began to drink from her glass and then drained it in one long draught. She put it on my desk and wiped her mouth with the back of her hand. "No?"

I stared at her. Her eyes were curious. For a moment, I pictured my hands around her neck. Not a healthy level of aggression, I admit. I cleared my throat and looked away from her. "I want you to remove this... whatever it is you've done to me."

She said nothing.

I looked at her. "I can't go on this way," I insisted. "You must take it back."

She sat forward in her chair, her brow troubled. "Give back a gift from de loa?" She scoffed like she didn't believe me, like I was playing a prank.

"Yes, damn it! I can't—" I made myself take a breath. Richard was arriving in a few weeks, and I knew I'd never be able to control myself around him. I couldn't take this terrible *need* anymore. I had to finish things here and get back to Elizabeth, and I couldn't, not with this hunger eating me up. "It's disturbing my sleep, my mind. I'm engaged to be married, for God's sake! I don't want this!"

"I know what tis you want." Tiyah pinned me with her too-knowing gaze. "You want a man in your bed. But you don want to want It. So you push it deep inside you, swallow it down like poison. But dis who you are, Missah. A frog who try to be a bird—he will end badly, no?"

I was shocked at her words, that she would say it out loud. *You want a man in your bed.* I was filled with terrible anger made worse by humiliation. I leaned forward on my desk, trying to impress upon her the force of my will.

"I. Saved. Your. Daughter. You take this off me, or I will not be responsible for what I do to you—to the entire village!"

What I meant by the threat, I didn't know—death and destruction, I suppose. I'd never go through with it, but I was at the end of my rope. I saw disdain flicker across her face before she schooled herself into a cold expression and leaned back in her chair.

She might as well have screamed at me, *You're like all the rest after all.* I didn't care. I hated her, hated myself.

"Maybe I take it away," she said coldly. "But if you insult Erzulie like so, you never feel passion again, Missah. Not even what you feel before."

"I don't care," I said, straightening my spine.

"So it be. Tomorrow night, I come for you."

IT WAS like having the same nightmare twice. The drums began, and soon Tiyah stood in my front yard in the dark, dressed all in white and beckoning to me. She led me into the trees with no light to find our way. Her form glowed like a ghost ahead of me.

Only two things were different this time. First, Tiyah had insisted I bring the bird, so I carried the large cage awkwardly at my side. And secondly, I felt less fear of what was to come and more anxiety to simply get it over with.

Erzulie would take my passion from me? I would have none at all?

Good!

I remembered what it had been like before, how the ideas that had skirted around the edges of my brain had been easy to shut out, like a vague itch I could ignore. I remembered how my body had been far less demanding then, so much less... ripe, lush, hungry. I'd been innocent, like a child who doesn't yet know what it means to be a whore.

Could I get back to that naiveté? And if not to innocence, to numbness at least?

I *had* to. I had a life waiting for me in English society with Elizabeth, and I refused to be the sort of degenerate who dragged male servants off to dark corners. I refused to be a disgrace.

Yet I wanted *so much*. And it was addictive to want like that, heady. Once the desire was gone, would I miss it? Or would it be like a man with one leg who learns how to just get on with his life?

The drums—louder and louder—shivered down my spine. The sharp, cloying scent of the smoke filled my nostrils and sank into my brain. Their effect on me was amplified this time, by the heat that already lived under my skin. I struggled to control it and stay true to my purpose.

THE CEREMONY was much like the one before. We arrived at the circle with the center pole. There were fewer people this time, but still enough to fill the clearing. The man who had handled the bird the first time took the cage from me and vanished with it.

Tiyah shook her head, a frown on her face. "I know not if Erzulie come. She not pleased."

With that, Tiyah moved into the crowd and I was left to my own devices.

What had Tiyah meant by that? Would she refuse to lift this curse from me?

Dancers whirled past me, caught up in the beat of the drums. And now I did feel their looks and their disdain, eyes flashing at me as they went by. Maybe they all knew why I was there, to refuse Erzulie's gift. Well, I didn't care. It was not their life being ruined. I would do what I'd come to do. I pushed toward the center pole, wanting to get it over with.

As I moved through the dancers, my heart beat harder and harder. I felt a tingle of dread, and it quickly became a knot of fear, like a fist squeezing my heart.

No passion, ever. Not even what you had before.

Through the beat of the drums, I felt Richard there, like a ghost following right behind me. I even turned to look, the sensation was so strong. But, of course, he wasn't there.

Except he was. Because what I was doing right now felt like a betrayal of him in a way.

Richard, fifteen years old, leaning forward to kiss me with his soft, dry mouth in my schoolboy's bed.

He'll still be my friend. He will always be my friend. We'll just never have… that.

Never.

But we never would have had it anyway. Even if he did want me like that, it's not something I ever would have allowed myself to acknowledge. So what difference did it make?

I stood in front of the pole, and Tiyah was there, waiting. Her eyes were rolled back in her head, showing only the whites, and she stood rigid, staring at me. In her hands was a knife.

For a moment I thought she meant me harm, that in refusing her gift, I'd angered her to the point of murder. But she only thrust the knife forward, handle first, urging me to take it.

"Tuer il. Tuer l'oiseau. Et tuer votre désir à jamais!"

Kill it. Kill the bird. And kill your desire forever!

The man holding the cage opened it and brought out the bird. Oh, the bird! It had become as familiar to me as my own face in the glass—exotic and horrible and familiar all in one. It did not try to fly away but sat hunched with its black feet curled around the man's fingers. Its red eyes were fixed on mine. It opened its beak in a plea but made no sound. It sat there, chest moving with its rapid breath, waiting.

The knife was in my hand. My palm was slick with sweat against the wooden handle. The man held the bird away from his body, offering it up to my blade. One strike in the breast and it would be done.

Richard. The name echoed around and around through my skull, as if part of me were panicking, wings beating against the walls of my mind. *Richard.*

I saw his eyes sparkling in the sun, his slim, pale chest when we went swimming in the river, his broad mouth laughing. I saw him lying on his side in my bed at school, so young, only fifteen, his eyes staring into mine full of love and hope and fear.

I saw Elizabeth's face, young and polite and good, her hand perfectly poised as she sipped a cup of tea in the parlor.

The knife fell from my hand to the ground. I reached forward and grasped the bird on either side of its wings, lifted it up, and tossed it into the air.

With a loud caw, it flew away.

~9~

I SENT a boy to frequent the docks in Kingston, ready to send me word the moment the *Libertine II* was spotted in the bay. It was September 4th when I received the message, a Saturday morning. I left Philip in charge of getting a coach ready, and I rode into town as fast as I could on my horse.

The ship was real, and it was there, causing my excitement and nerves to soar. *Libertine II* was painted on her brown sides in a jaunty red and blue. Men, and a few ladies, waited on deck to disembark. I jumped off my horse and tied him to a post. Then I strode toward the ship, my hand shading my eyes as I searched the deck.

I saw Richard, backlit by the sun. His tall, trim body was dressed formally in a mustard-colored jacket, his brown hair set off with a beige top hat. He spotted me and waved. I faintly heard his cry of "Colin!"

He looked handsome and so very English, and I swore I could see the relief in the set of his shoulders when he saw me. Poor fellow. If I'd had to go a month or more without knowing if Richard was alive or dead, I'd have done myself physical harm.

It took ages for them to secure the plank. I stood in a small crowd on the docks and watched him—watched him watching me. A buzzing tension invigorated every part of me. I wasn't sure what was going to happen, only that I wanted to see Richard again more than I wanted anything else in the world.

At last he was coming down the plank. I surged forward to meet him.

He wore that heart-stopping grin of his. "By God, Colin, you had me worried. Not sure if I should hug you, hit you, or beg your forgiveness for intruding."

"Hug, most definitely."

I embraced him like a brother. I held on longer than was our custom, and when we parted, there was an uncertain tension in his mouth that hadn't been there before.

"Is it all right that I came, then?" he asked, a bit flustered. "You're not cross about it?"

I studied his dear face, which was so familiar to me, and at the same time, entirely new. Because for the first time, I was gazing at him without a self-imposed wall between us, allowing myself to *feel*.

"It's the best possible thing, that you came," I said, meaning it.

I was rewarded with a brilliant smile. "Well, then. I suppose you have a great deal to tell me."

"I do. But not here."

We chatted about mundane things until Philip arrived with the coach—the weather in London, Richard's voyage, the sugarcane crop. When we were ensconced in the coach, just the two of us, and working our way into the countryside to Crosswinds, he had a hard time keeping my gaze and there was a high color on his cheeks.

"So, will you tell me what happened? With this Obeah ritual?"

"Not here," I said again. I was unable to keep the pleased smile from my mouth.

He looked bemused. He studied me for a long moment. "You've changed."

I thought of that night, of Tiyah-Erzulie digging her fingers into the secret graveyard of my belly and pulling out a piece of me. "I have," I said solemnly.

Richard frowned but said nothing more.

WE HAD luncheon when we arrived, and then I took Richard on a tour of Crosswinds. It was a good distraction, and we both needed it. I tried to behave as I always had, but I caught myself looking at him time and again. And every time he tried to bring up the subject of the Obeah ceremony or what had happened to me in Jamaica, I told him, *Not here, not yet.*

I was knotted up with twisted strands of apprehension and longing, like the two serpents of a caduceus. I felt unsure if I had the courage to do what I wanted to do, unsure if I'd be welcome or if there was no foundation beneath me. But a few times, I caught Richard looking at me in a way that told me I was not wrong.

By dinner, Richard was fading, smothering yawns with his linen napkin.

"You're exhausted from your journey," I said, pouring him a second glass of wine.

"I've no reason to be," he complained. "Not like I could do much aboard the ship."

"I know you, Richard. You were worried about me the whole voyage. You hardly slept."

He grumbled words like "nonsense" and "sea air" but didn't entirely deny it. He was blinking wearily by the time we finished our meal, and I took him to his room.

"Good night, Colin," he said at his door. "You know, you've yet to tell me your story, and if I weren't about to fall asleep, I'd have it out of you."

I leaned against the doorjamb and let my eyes linger on his face. "You'll know it soon enough."

With a final puzzled look, he went into his room.

I LET him sleep for eight hours, though I was unable to get any rest myself. I paced along the veranda, soothed by a breeze from the sea. It was three in the morning when I entered Richard's room. I wore a nightshirt and nothing else. I closed the door behind me, put my candle on the table by the bed, and slipped under the covers.

He stirred, half-sitting up on one elbow and peering at me confusedly in the dim candlelight. "Colin?"

"I had a nightmare," I said, echoing his words from long ago.

"Oh?" He turned onto his side to face me and lay back down on his pillow. "Are you all right?"

"No," I said softly. My heart pounded so loudly, he could surely hear it.

He visibly swallowed and stared at me. The tension formed and curled between us, heavy and dark, like a sleeping beast. When I couldn't stand it any longer, I leaned forward and pressed a dry kiss to his lips, then withdrew.

His breathing bordered on panicked, and his eyes went wide with disbelief. "Colin?"

"Do you remember that night you crawled into my bed in Eton and kissed me?" I asked quietly.

He blushed furiously and looked at my chest rather than my eyes. "I... I...." I'd never seen Richard speechless before. But then, we'd never dared speak of this.

I put my hand on his arm to reassure him. "I should have kissed you back."

He raised his eyes slowly, and I saw everything on his face—fear, desire, hope, longing, uncertainty. He considered my words for a long moment. I could see his brain working, trying to decide what was going on. Richard needed to come to things in his own time. I waited.

"Why are you saying this now?" he finally whispered.

I smiled at the way his mind worked. He hadn't denied it, asking, *What do you mean?* Or *Why are you doing this?* Only, *Why now?* "It's rather a long story. Do you really want to discuss it right this moment?" I teased him with a cocked eyebrow and a long glance at his lips.

A shudder ran through him. "Perhaps later."

"Good thinking."

We stared at each other a moment longer, and then, squaring his chin in determination, Richard leaned forward and kissed me back. His lips against mine were dry and chaste, still tentative. But I pushed into him, moving myself closer until I was pressed against his sleep-warmed body. He grasped my upper arms, pulling me even closer. At that welcome, I felt a hot rush of lust and a heavy ache of affection in my chest.

I'm in Richard's bed. This is happening.

The feelings were so sharp and so sweet that the moment felt worth anything—any price, any punishment, even my immortal soul. I felt no guilt or shame, only the joy of absolute surrender to something I'd wanted for so long, I might have been born already addicted to him. It felt unbearably, perfectly right.

I touched my tongue to his lips and sucked lightly. He trembled beneath me and opened his mouth on a sigh.

I kissed him the way I'd dreamed of doing—wet and deep. He kissed me back desperately.

"I never thought...," he said, when I freed his mouth to attend to his neck.

"Did you imagine it?"

"Yes. God, yes."

Had Richard ever been with another man? He trembled beneath me as if this was new to him, but then, I was trembling too.

I grasped his wrists and pulled his arms up over his head, lying fully on top of him. I fed on his mouth. I could feel his chest firm and flat against mine, with only our nightshirts between us. His cock was so hard it hurt where it dug into my stomach. I'd never felt anything as arousing as Richard's body underneath mine, and I was light-headed at the evidence that he wanted me too, that he was in this as fully as I was.

He broke the kiss and rolled me onto my back. His straight, long hair spilled forward like silk. I couldn't help but run my fingers into it and hold it back so I could see his eyes. The hazel was only a rim around a pupil, bottomless and black.

"You can't give this to me, then take it away," he said, as if it were being forced from his lips.

"I won't. You're the other half of me."

He nodded in agreement, his eyes growing damp with emotion. Then he kissed me hard. We kissed and rolled and rutted, and it was so good, it felt like we could go on forever. But I felt his hands tugging down his own drawers and then lifting my nightshirt, and suddenly I couldn't bear to not be naked with him. I pulled my nightshirt over my own head and then his. He was a sight in the candlelight, his chest lean but strong, his skin a pale field with a lovely glowing blush.

"Will you take me?" he asked shakily. His thighs came up around me, and his hips lifted so that my cock slipped over his bullocks and between his cheeks.

Dear God. "Is that… are you sure?" I wondered if he understood what he was asking, if he had any more experience than I had.

"I've dreamt of it a million times. Please, Colin."

I'd experimented a little with myself in the past few weeks, and I knew we needed something to ease the dryness. I had placed a jar in his bedside table earlier for such an eventuality, though I hadn't really believed it possible. I took a breath and reached for it.

"Have you done this before?" I asked.

"No. I never would, not with anyone but you."

"I'm glad."

We figured it out together, Richard and I, the way we always had done everything. There were smiles and laughter as we did our best to prepare us both, but none of it dulled the sharp lust I felt in every part of my body. Our familiarity and his openness only made me want him more.

At last he laid flat on his stomach, arms and legs outstretched as luxuriously as a cat. I penetrated him carefully and with many sighs and sounds on both our parts. Entering him was like pushing into a fist, he was so tight. We both teased each other with the glacial pace of my entry—him pushing up as I held still, me pushing forward when he moved away. It was like savoring a favorite dessert, that first seating, and we encouraged each other and whispered over it like the boys we once were.

But at last I was buried inside him as deeply as I could go, my ballocks, now tightly drawn, pressing against the sweet curve of his arse. I lay on top of him, knitting his fingers with mine and rubbing the top of my feet over the bottom of his, so that every part of us touched. I nuzzled his neck and, when he turned his head, the sides of his beautiful mouth.

The overwhelming pleasure was like a caught breath, and I could only resist for so long before I had to take the next gasp.

He wiggled against me as I pulled out several inches and pushed back in.

"Oh God, Richard," I groaned as the pleasure nearly unmanned me.

"Colin! Hurry. Don't wait!"

I withdrew and slammed into him. Then there was nothing that could stop our headlong fall, for I was on the cusp already, and from the tension in his body below me and the way he rutted into the mattress, I knew he was too. And so I plunged and withdrew, faster and faster, as Richard moaned without ceasing. Soon I felt him clench tight around me, nearly expelling me from his body as he dug his face into the pillow, gripped my fingers tight, and convulsed. I pushed in deep in a bid to hang on and let myself go, spilling inside him with an intensity that made me cry out.

We lay still for a long moment, until I felt his chest struggling to rise against my limp weight. I rolled off and onto my back. It was a moment I could never take back, and one I would never wish to erase.

LYING THERE in bed, I told Richard about Tiyah and the Obeah ceremonies. We cuddled together, and I wove my tale with whispers and small gestures. It was as if we were boys again, telling strange stories in the night. Only this strange tale was true, and it had happened to me.

He held my hand and listened intently, propped up on one elbow. And when I got to the part about the native boy who had come to me, I didn't shy away from the truth. Nor did I hold back when I told him of my determination to be rid of the gift and the second ceremony.

"What a fantastic yarn, Colin," he said to me when I'd finished. "You didn't make it up?"

"Not one word."

He studied my face. "Why did you change your mind and let the bird go?"

I pulled his hand to my chest and placed it over my heart. "I didn't choose to let the bird live. I chose you."

"And Elizabeth?"

I saw doubt in his eyes, a preemptive withdrawing, as if he expected me to say I'd still marry her and we'd see each other when we could or maybe not at all.

"I've written to her and freed her from her obligation to me as gently as I could. She'll be terribly upset and probably hate me, but she'll be happier with someone else in the end. If I'd married her, we both would have lived half a life."

He fell into me then, slipping his arms around me and burying his face in my neck. "I'm frightened," he said. And in his voice, I heard all the things he didn't say—*I want you, I've always wanted you, and I choose you too, but what will become of us?*

As for me, I was done being frightened. I remembered the sensation I'd had in my dreams of flying high above the landscape, surrounded by nothing but openness, free.

Epilogue

Jamaica, 1880

"To Philip Garvey and the legislative council!" I raised my glass of wine in a toast.

"Hear, hear!"

Beside me, Richard gave Philip a congratulatory pat on the back. Philip's broad face beamed.

We'd invited our neighbors to the small celebration, as well as Philip's family. It was an uncomfortable mix. The natives, dressed in their Sunday best, gathered on one side of the room and the English around the table. Major Pivot was there with a fox stole wrapped around his neck and a flat cap with leaves attached to it on his head. He was on a King Lear obsession lately, and he had fewer good days than bad. I'd told Lester Pivot he was welcome to invite Jena, his housekeeper and paramour, and he'd blustered as if he had no idea why I would suggest such a thing. So be it. I have no right to judge what a man hides in his bedroom.

The capital of Jamaica had moved to Kingston in 1872, and a new legislative council made up of nine islanders had just been formed to advise the British. It was a step toward self-government that was meant to appease the Jamaicans, who were becoming more and more restless with foreign rule. Most of our fellow Englishmen were not happy with the measure. But Richard and I had supported Philip in his bid for the council, and I had hopes that it would be a good move for a peaceful future. Richard and I had made our home in Jamaica, and we had made a success of the plantation. I didn't want that ever to change.

Philip and his wife, Sally, would be sorely missed at Crosswinds. They'd protected Richard and I and kept our secrets well. But Tiyah's daughter, Lily, was going to take Sally's place, and we had Jax, who'd taken shelter with us a number of years ago and learned his trade under Philip's tutelage. Jax had good reason to guard the privacy of a pair of bachelors, for he was of the same inclinations himself.

Major Pivot banged on his glass to get everyone's attention. Lester shot me an apologetic look, but I shrugged. We had little enough entertainment—Major Pivot was welcome to the floor.

"*When we are born, we cry that we are come, To this great stage of fools,*" Major Pivot quoted in his most theatrical voice. "And fools we are, but even fools can stumble upon the right path."

I smiled at Richard.

Major Pivot raised his glass. "To Philip, who deserves this honor. May he be a steadying hand on the wheel. And to the estimable Misters Hastings and Wesley, who have been most excellent neighbors and friends. They've shared their success with all of us, and we are most grateful."

"Hear, hear!"

Lester gave me an inscrutable look, though he drank to the toast. Lester suspected, or probably more than suspected, that Richard and I were not merely friends. But he kept his own council. We were not the only pair of English bachelors living in Jamaica. There was something to be said for inhabiting the fringes of the British Empire.

"Our little bird is leaving the nest," Richard said to me sotto voce and with a teasing smile.

"Philip would have your head if he heard you say that."

"Very well, our fifty-year-old little bird is leaving the nest. It won't be the same without him."

"No. But we'll be fine."

"Better than," he said, giving me a look that made me wish we were alone. He was even more handsome now than he'd been when he first came to Jamaica. His skin was golden brown from the sun, and his hair had lightened to a dark tawny gold. I loved him, and that was worth everything.

"Better than," I agreed, letting my eyes say the rest.

I WAS closing up the doors to the veranda later that night when I saw a shape perched on the railing in the dark. I froze and felt a frisson of terror wash through me. I knew that shape even though I hadn't seen it in ten years. With trembling fingers, I pushed the slatted doors farther open so the candlelight from inside fell on the familiar form.

The bird's black feet were wrapped around the top rail, and it was hunched in on itself, its white and blue feathers ragged, a smear of blood on one wing. Its red eyes stared at me fixedly. Its black beak opened in a silent caw.

"Everyting well?" Jaz asked, coming up behind me.

"Send for Tiyah. Hurry," I ordered, my voice quaking.

I didn't move until she arrived. I stood and stared at the bird, and the bird at me. I'd wondered, over the years, what would happen if the bird ever came to ill. Would I sicken and die with it? Was my fate and the bird's irrevocably linked? It had not been an easy road, these past ten years, but we had made a place for ourselves, Richard and I. I did not want to lose it, or him.

Tiyah appeared at my left hand. "Yes, Missah?"

"It's the bird."

"Yes, Missah."

"Is it...?" I couldn't finish that thought.

She pushed my arm from where it had been frozen on the handle of the door and moved quietly past me. She approached the bird, but it didn't look at her. It continued to stare at me.

"*Oiseau doux. Oiseau bon.* Give it to me." She held out her hand to the bird, palm up.

The bird shuddered so violently, I startled, sure it was dying right then. But it stayed on its perch and bent its head toward her palm. With two heaves of its chest, its open beak dripped a trail of bright blood and then something slithered from its gullet into her hand. It was the thing, the blood-rich blob that the bird had swallowed all those years ago.

I put a hand over my mouth to hold back a cry of horror.

"*Oiseau bon. Vous êtes libre. Allez-y,*" Tiyah crooned to the bird.

It raised its ragged wings weakly and flew off, its flight uncertain. It was dying, that much anyone could see. And it had come to return what was mine. A clammy nausea suffused my body.

Tiyah turned to me, the thing in her hand. It was smaller than it had been, the size of a small egg now. It was redder too, more flushed with blood.

Involuntarily, I took a step back. "What.... What happens now?" I asked, my voice weak and my hands slick with sweat. I felt light-headed, as if it was I who was dying instead of the bird. Or maybe I was dying with it.

Tiyah said nothing, just stepped close to me, her dark eyes serious. She held her open palm and the object up to my lips.

I closed my eyes and shook my head in a harsh jolt.

"You must," she said fiercely. "Take it by your own will, Missah, and nuttin' will change."

Take it by your own will.

Richard was down the hall waiting for me. I closed my eyes and opened my mouth.

"Swallow it whole," Tiyah instructed.

I felt her palm come over my mouth, the blood-rich organ bitter on my tongue—its scent and taste repellent. I gagged, took a breath, swallowed.

When I opened my eyes, Tiyah was gone. With the veranda door still open and no sight of either Tiyah or the bird, I could almost believe I'd dreamed it—if not for the taste of copper in my mouth. I poured myself a finger of scotch and washed it away.

"Colin?" Richard leaned in the doorway, watching me. "Is everything all right?"

"Yes, love. Everything is fine," I said. I walked over to him and took his hand. "Let's go to bed."

ELI EASTON has been at various times and under different names a minister's daughter, a computer programmer, a game designer, the author of paranormal mysteries, a fanfiction writer, an organic farmer, and a profound sleeper. She is now happily embarking on yet another incarnation, this time as an m/m romance author.

As an avid reader of such, she is tickled pink when an author manages to combine literary merit, vast stores of humor, melting hotness, and eye-dabbing sweetness into one story. She promises to strive to achieve most of that most of the time. She currently lives on a farm in Pennsylvania with her husband, three bulldogs, three cows, and six chickens. All of them (except for the husband) are female, hence explaining the naked men that have taken up residence in her latest fiction writing.

Her website is http://www.elieaston.com.

Twitter is @EliEaston.

You can e-mail her at eli@elieaston.com.

By ELI EASTON

Bones (with B.G. Thomas, Jamie Fessenden, and Kim Fielding)
Closet Capers (Dreamspinner Anthology)
Heaven Can't Wait
A Prairie Dog's Love Song
Puzzle Me This
Steamed Up (Dreamspinner Anthology)
Stitch (with Sue Brown, Jamie Fessenden, and Kim Fielding)

SEX IN SEATTLE
The Trouble with Tony
The Enlightenment of Daniel
The Mating of Michael

Published by DREAMSPINNER PRESS
http://www.dreamspinnerpress.com

THE BOOK OF
ST. CYPRIAN

JAMIE FESSENDEN

Chapter One

THE BOOK was evil. It was said that to own it—or merely to *touch* it—was a great sin. An ancient tome attributed to St. Cyprian of Antioch, yet containing magical spells so dark that those who did own a copy took precautions to constrain its influence. Alejandro knew the moment he laid eyes on the intricately carved wooden box, wrapped with a metal chain in the shape of a cross and secured with a rusted padlock, that he'd stumbled across it: *El Gran Libro de San Cipriano.*

"Do you have a key to this lock?" he asked Miss Passebon.

The willowy young woman turned from surveying the rows of dusty shelves of books, candles, jars, and other items in the abandoned botanica to eye the box in his hands with disinterest. "I really don't know. I suppose it might be on the key chain." She searched in her purse for the keys she'd tossed into it after opening the front door. She fished them out and handed them to her guest, clearly indicating he could take the time to search for it, if he cared to.

Alejandro examined the keys closely while Miss Passebon walked down the aisle, an expression of dismay on her lovely face.

"Most of this will probably have to be thrown away," she muttered. She pointed at a row of saint figurines, some of them over a foot tall. "I suppose these will cause me all kinds of bad luck if I chuck them in the trash?"

"Definitely," Alejandro replied. He could tell she didn't believe, but he knew his grandmother would throw a fit if she heard anyone talking about throwing those figurines away. "We can pack them up and ship them back to Abuela if you can't sell them," he continued. He didn't have a fortune to ship the entire contents of the botanica back to New Hampshire, but he would salvage what he could. Old *Grand-père* Passebon had been a close friend of the family when Abuela had lived in New Orleans. Alejandro hadn't even been born then. But the old man had instructed his granddaughter to contact a number of his close acquaintances and allow them to take whatever they liked from his possessions. That included both his house and the botanica.

Alejandro hadn't been the first to arrive—the old man had known several people still living in New Orleans—so the truly valuable furniture and artwork had already been taken. Some specific items had been removed from the botanica. Alejandro wasn't sure what they'd been, but there were intriguing spots on the shelves where circular or square patterns in the dust indicated something had recently been carried off. Still, he felt a bit guilty grabbing something that could be very valuable. The others appear to have missed it because it had been tucked far back on a top shelf behind the counter. "Do you know what this is?"

Miss Passebon shook her head.

"Well, I'm not sure until I get it open...." One of the smaller keys fit the lock. He turned it and met resistance, but a slight pressure caused it to rotate with a scraping sound like fingernails on a chalkboard. Then the lock snapped open. He set the box on the countertop and pulled the chain away. Holding his breath, he lifted the wooden lid.

There it was, discolored and brittle with age, the cover made from paper glued onto cardboard, peeling away now, and bound to the pages with loose stitches of heavy cotton thread. Somebody had made this copy by hand a long time ago, crudely reproducing an illustration of a sorcerer surrounded by skeletons and devils on the cover. He'd seen a reproduction of that etching online, from the 1893 Portuguese edition in the Library of Lisbon. The fact that it was a copy was a little disappointing. It probably wouldn't be all that valuable to a bookseller. But what was really important was whether or not the spells inside had been copied down faithfully.

Alejandro lifted the cover carefully to look at the first page, a strange sensation going through his body when he did so, as if he'd eaten something that disagreed with him. The pages seemed to be... greasy somehow, though he knew that was impossible. Grease would make the paper translucent, and it wasn't. He knew what his grandmother would say about something making him cringe when he touched it, but at nineteen, he was still skeptical about some of her beliefs, even though he respected them. He shrugged the unpleasant feeling off.

The book was in Spanish, thank God, which possibly meant the person who copied it had also translated from Portuguese. Alejandro might be able to struggle his way through a Portuguese edition, but this was so much easier. His family spoke Spanish at home.

Miss Passebon peered over his shoulder and laughed. "It looks like something a kid put together," she observed.

"No," Alejandro said, shaking his head. "Somebody copied it by hand, and translated it, maybe. But I recognize some of it from fragments I've seen online. I think it may be complete."

"A complete what?"

"*The Great Book of St. Cyprian*. It's a very old book of magic—black magic. A lot of the spells are used today in hoodoo magic, but it's really unusual to come across a complete copy. Many people wouldn't *want* to see a complete copy."

She gave him a look of disbelief. "Why not?"

"They say you should never touch it, if you value your soul. And if you dare to read the whole thing from cover to cover, the devil will come for you."

She laughed, obviously not taking any of that seriously. "Oh well, then you'd better get it out of here!"

"Are you sure?" he asked. "You might be able to get a good price for it."

She put one hand on her slender hip and waved the other in the air to take in the shop that had been locked up since Grand-père Passebon passed away a month ago. "I just want to unload all of this stuff and get back to New York. Grand-père was a sweet old man and I want to carry out his wishes, but I don't have time to get appraisals or anything like that. Take what you like, and the others can take whatever they want. First come, first served."

Alejandro carefully closed the book and placed the cover back on the box. He'd been hearing about this book his entire life, but he'd never seen it. There were no more than fragments of it online. The feeling of excitement that welled up in him now was almost overwhelming. Still, he had enough presence of mind left to realize he had one big obstacle to overcome if he was going to bring this book home with him.

His grandmother would never allow it into the house.

MATTHEW HAD known the Varela family since he moved to New Hampshire six years ago. Alejandro had stood in the doorway of his apartment building, leaning against the weathered green frame as he watched the moving van being unloaded. He was barefoot and shirtless, his skin smooth and tanned, his torso thin but well-defined. And he was handsome. *Very* handsome. Short, dark brown hair and eyes so brown they seemed black, set under an angry-looking brow.

Matthew had just hit thirteen, but he already knew he preferred boys to girls. And it was only the fact that his new neighbor scared the crap out of him that prevented him from saying hello. Instead, he helped his mother and her current boyfriend, Frank, carry stuff into the building, watching the Latino boy out of the corner of his eye.

It was Alejandro who spoke first, when everyone but Matthew was inside, out of hearing. "Do you know what street you're moving in to?"

Matthew stopped and stared at him a moment before giving what he thought was the obvious answer. "Wilson Street."

The boy—Matthew didn't know his name yet—made a rude noise. He gestured at the doorway behind him. "This building has my family— the Varelas—and the Perezes living upstairs. *Your* building has the Riveras on the first floor and the Castillos on the third."

"So?"

"What's wrong with this picture?"

Matthew frowned at him and set the box he was carrying down on the walkway. "Nobody told my mom we had to be Hispanic to move in." What was obvious about the houses on the street was that they were all rundown and broken up into as many apartments as the landlords could fit. This was a poor neighborhood, and Matthew and his mom were poor. So why couldn't they live here too?

The boy shrugged. "You can live wherever you want."

"Fine," Matthew retorted. "I'll move into *your* place."

To his surprise, the boy burst out laughing. "You gonna sleep in my bed, *huero*?"

The word, Matthew would later learn, meant "blond boy." But all he could think about at the moment was the implication behind the question. He knew it was just teasing, but it still made his face feel hot. It was probably safest to just ignore it and go back to what he was doing, but he couldn't resist answering, "Only if I get to be on top."

Ugh. Did I just say that? He's gonna kick my ass!

Fortunately, the boy just laughed harder. Matthew quickly scooped up the box and hurried inside, dodging Frank on his way out the door. "Whoa, there, kid! Watch where you're going!"

Matthew ignored him. Frank was just some guy his mother had met at the diner she worked at. He'd be gone in a few months, just like all the boyfriends she'd had before him. Matthew only spoke to him when he had to.

MATTHEW'S PREDICTION about Frank came true even sooner than expected, when his mother caught one of the other waitresses at Frank's apartment a couple of weeks later. But the Latino boy next door stayed. For six years, they lived side by side while the neighbors on all sides of them came and went. Not surprisingly, almost all the new neighbors were Latino.

Matthew learned the boy's name was Alejandro Valera, and when he wasn't being a wiseass, he was a surprisingly cool guy. By the time they entered high school, they were best friends.

Alejandro was the first person Matthew came out to. Matthew had been a nervous wreck, but Alejandro was totally cool about it. About a year later, when they were both sixteen, Alejandro finally admitted *he* was gay too. Unfortunately, despite the fantasies that revelation stirred up in Matthew's lustful teenage mind, nothing happened between them. They remained friends, but Alejandro never showed any sexual interest in Matthew, so Matthew learned to accept that they would always just be friends.

Wilson Street wasn't strictly a Latino neighborhood, but it was close enough. If anyone had a problem with the huero and his mother living in their midst, however, it was never mentioned. Matthew suspected that might be due to his friendship with Alejandro and who the boy's grandmother was. Abuela, as Alejandro called her—as everybody called her, though it simply meant "grandmother" in Spanish—had lived in the neighborhood a very long time. More importantly, she ran St. Peter's Botanica a few blocks down, one of the few Santeria *botánicas* in the city.

Abuela was ancient—or at least she'd always seemed so to Matthew—tough, and generally cranky. She was also very tiny. Neither boy was particularly tall, but they'd towered over her since their second year of high school. She spoke very little English, and her face wore a perpetual scowl. Matthew had been convinced she hated him the first couple of years. But Alejandro began tutoring him informally in Spanish, starting with insults and obscenities and gradually moving on to more coherent phrases. Eventually, Matthew grew interested enough to take Spanish in school. Alejandro helped him with his homework, and once Abuela saw that he was putting some effort into learning the language, she began to talk to him too. Matthew didn't always understand the first, or even the second, time she said something, but she was more patient than he'd expected. By his senior year in high school, Abuela treated him like a second grandson. She still scowled at him and her manner was still curt, but now there was an undercurrent of humor in it.

And that's how he came to be working in the botanica. Abuela didn't like strangers working in her shop, so she refused to hire anyone she didn't know. And she didn't know anyone—not really. She was known in the neighborhood and people respected her, but Matthew got the impression she made a lot of people nervous. Some would come to St. Peter's for herbs or protection sprays, floor washes to drive out dark magic, holy water, powders for money or love, or Florida Water—a cheap cologne Abuela was fond of that used to be common in the eighteen hundreds and was now used for spiritual cleansing. Many people consulted the old woman for advice, both magical and otherwise—she read cards, cowry shells, and coffee beans. But few people came to her apartment for just a friendly chat. So she worked the botanica alone and drafted her grandson, when he was old enough. By the time he was eighteen, Matthew was allowed behind the counter to help out.

HE WAS there in the back room, unpacking some boxes sent from New York, with Abuela tallying up the day's receipts in the front, when Alejandro called his cell phone.

"Yo."

"Are you alone?"

Matthew laughed. "Why?"

"I don't want Abuelita to hear this," Alejandro replied. He sounded dead serious.

"What is it, amigo?" Matthew lowered his voice and added, "She's out front. I'm in the storeroom."

"Good. Listen, I'm sending some stuff back through FedEx. Three boxes from Abuelita's friend. But there's something I don't want her to see. Can I send it to your house?"

"What is it? Porn?"

Alejandro didn't laugh. "No. It's a book. A very old book."

"Uh… sure." Now he was really curious. Alejandro didn't keep many secrets from his grandmother. What, apart from porn, could he be so anxious to hide? "Is it a present or something?"

"No. It's hard to explain over the phone. Just don't let her see it. And don't open it!"

"Why not?"

"Just do what I say, huero. Don't make me kick your ass."

"Don't you mean *lick* my ass?" Sadly, Matthew already knew the answer to that. Alejandro had never shown the slightest interest in him.

"You wish, *cara de culo*."

Matthew laughed. "That just means you'll lick my face." The insult translated to "butt face."

"In your dreams."

ALEJANDRO DISCONNECTED and put his phone back in his pocket, thinking about how much he really would like to lick Matthew's face… and ass, for that matter. And anything else the handsome blond boy offered him. He'd been attracted to him since the day Matthew moved in next door. Matthew had just been a skinny little white kid back then, but when Alejandro gave him shit, he gave it right back. Alejandro didn't know it at the time, but he fell a little in love with Matthew that day. He'd been falling more and more in love with him every day since then.

Only now he knew it. But it was too late. They'd grown too close. And the thought of actually *dating* Matthew felt… weird. Like thinking about dating his brother or something.

He walked back to the desk at the FedEx office and handed the clerk the fourth package he'd addressed. "This one's going to a different address." He thought about paying for it all with the money Abuela had given him, but on second thought, he said, "I'll pay for it separately."

Alejandro stepped out of the French Quarter Postal Emporium—a much smaller building than its name suggested—into a bright July afternoon. He wandered lazily down Bourbon Street, whistling the tune to Sting's "Moon Over Bourbon Street." He was done rummaging through Grand-père Passebon's dusty shop, there was a full day left until his flight home, and he was in one of the coolest cities he'd ever visited.

Time to do some sightseeing.

Chapter Two

THE PACKAGE arrived the next morning. Matthew wasn't expected at
the botanica until after it arrived. He'd told Abuela he was waiting for a
delivery that morning, though he didn't tell her who it was from. She
didn't have a problem with him coming in late, because as far as she was
concerned, she was doing *him* a favor by allowing him to work some
hours there—not the other way around.

Matthew tossed the package onto his bed, kissed his mother good-bye,
scratched his dog on the head, and ran out to the botanica. There, he found
Abuela suspiciously eying three boxes the FedEx guy had dropped off.

"Alejandro sent these," she said in Spanish.

"He told me he was sending them yesterday. They're from the
botanica in New Orleans."

"Sí, I remember he went down there," she said with exaggerated
patience. "Do I look senile?"

"Sólo un poco."

"Mocoso!" ("Brat!") She pretended she was going to backhand
him, though she'd never laid a finger on either him or Alejandro. "I have
no idea where I'm going to find room for this much crap!"

It was a challenge. They spent the rest of the afternoon unpacking
the boxes and trying to wedge icons of the saints, candles, and other
things Alejandro had thought worth saving onto the overcrowded shelves
of the tiny shop. Some of the saints could go in the window, on the other
side of the heavy cloth that prevented curious outsiders from peering into
the inner depths of the botanica. There they presented a fairly innocuous
"front" for the shop that might pass for a Catholic religious display to
strangers walking by.

Only people who worshiped the saints knew the icons weren't
Catholic, or perhaps a devout Catholic might notice something off about
them—that some had darker skin than most Catholic saint figurines or
that the colors of the clothing seemed brighter. Some of the figurines
resembled dolls more than the Catholic icons found in churches. Because
these saints were really African gods—spirits would be more accurate—
in a European guise. Back when slaves were first being brought to the

Caribbean, they'd been forced to accept Catholicism, but they'd continued to honor the African spirits in secret. They'd simply hidden them behind the guises of the saints. St. Theresa became Oya, the queen of the dead. St. Barbara became Chango, the spirit of fire and thunder. Matthew's favorite was Eleggua, in the guise of St. Anthony. He was the patron of luck and destiny and something of a trickster, but Abuela had told him and Alejandro when they first came out to her that he was the guardian of gay men and women.

How, exactly, the worship of the saints found its way from Caribbean slaves brought to the United States to the Latino community, Matthew didn't know. Maybe he'd find the answer someday in the books on the botanica's shelves. For now, he was only mildly interested. His mother was more or less an atheist, which made his friendship with Alejandro and Abuela a little easier. At least she wasn't constantly freaking out about him losing his soul to the devil or anything like that. But that didn't mean Matthew was a believer himself. He just found it all kind of cool and interesting.

After they'd unpacked all the boxes and found places for everything, Abuela shooed him out of the shop. She always liked to be the last one there at night, so she could go around and make sure everything was in its place without the two boys "stumbling around like goats" and getting in her way. There were also a few altars set up in corners of the shop that needed to be tended.

Before he stepped out the door, the old woman insisted upon spritzing him with Florida Water, as she did every night. He hated the stuff. It smelled like cheap cologne—which, of course, it was. But he'd gotten used to the nightly ritual, just as Alejandro had. As always, Abuela muttered under her breath when she did it, "To keep you safe."

"Gracias, Abuelita."

Matthew went back to his apartment building and let himself in. Fifteen-year-old Gabriela Rojas was in the stairwell, making out with her boyfriend, but they ignored him as he climbed the stairs. His mother was working late, so it was just him and Spartacus. Spartacus was Matthew's pit bull, named after a character in a TV series his mother didn't like him watching. The dog was still kind of a puppy, though he was already massive. It was unlikely he'd be any good at protecting Matthew and his mom if a burglar broke in, since he was inclined to trust everybody, but Matthew had gotten him as a companion anyway. And he was great for that.

"Hey, pup!" Matthew laughed as he opened the door and the pit bull nearly knocked him back out onto the landing. "Hold on a second! Let me get the light."

He felt around for the light switch just inside the door, and a second later, the apartment lit up. The first thing Matthew saw was his muscular ball of puppy love making excited circles in front of him. The second thing he saw was the shredded paper and cardboard strewn across the living room carpet. It took him a moment to figure out what it was.

Then he remembered Alejandro's book.

"Oh shit!"

SPARTACUS HADN'T eaten the entire package. The external wrapping was pretty much destroyed, but once the dog had gotten through to the wooden box inside, he'd contented himself with gnawing on just one corner for a bit. Considering his powerful jaws could have made short work of the entire box, that was something, at least. But if the box was an antique, Alejandro was going to be furious.

Matthew sat on the couch, picking bits of the paper wrapping off the box, while Spartacus curled up beside him, happily gnawing on one of the immense rubber Kong toys he was *supposed* to chew on when he was bored, totally oblivious to how much distress he'd just caused his owner. The wooden box was damaged beyond repair. In addition to the corner, which simply wasn't there anymore, one side was splintered and there were several places where Spartacus's canines had punched holes all the way through the wood.

He's going to kill me.

Alejandro would never harm a hair on Spartacus's cast-iron head, of course. But Matthew would be in for it. He should have had the sense to put the package on the counter or a shelf out of the dog's reach.

The box had once had a carving on the lid. Matthew recognized it as a *veve*—a symbolic picture representing one of the African spirits. The elaborate crisscrossed veve on the cover represented Ogun, the smith, and was sometimes used for protection. But much of it had been chewed up, destroying any power it might have had. Matthew felt a slight chill of superstitious dread pass through him at the sight of it, as if whatever the lid had contained was now free to get out. The feeling wasn't helped by the bizarre chain wrapped around the box. It was fastened with a padlock, but thanks to the gnawed-off corner, the chain on that side was slipping off, so the entire thing could slide off the box without having to open the lock.

Matthew let the chain fall off and peered into the broken corner of the box. He could see what looked like a book in there, but he couldn't tell for certain that it hadn't been damaged. Alejandro had told him not to open it, but of course he hadn't anticipated this circumstance. It couldn't hurt to assess the damage, could it?

Matthew popped open the wooden cover of the box and looked at its contents.

It was a book, as Alejandro had told him. But it looked cheap, homemade, as if someone had written it by hand and then stitched the pages together. The cover was warped with age and apparently nothing more than cardboard with a hand-drawn paper cover glued to it. It was clearly old, though Matthew had no idea how old. The paper was yellowed and the edges were curled. The corners of the cover illustration were peeling away from the cardboard. The illustration itself was odd—an old man in a robe and a frankly silly-looking pointed hat, with skeletons and devils floating in the air around him. Maybe a hundred years ago, people would have thought it looked frightening, but in the light of modern horror movies, it was more goofy. Still, Matthew felt uneasy looking at the book, as if he was seeing something he shouldn't be.

El Gran Libro de San Cipriano. The Great Book of Saint.... *Cipriano*? He'd never heard of a saint by that name.

He glanced up and was startled to see Spartacus staring at the book too. It wasn't that the dog was growling or cowering or anything else particularly strange. He was just looking at it fixedly. But Matthew still found it unsettling.

He closed the wooden cover again and gathered the chain in one hand. "It's a good thing you didn't eat the book," Matthew told the pit bull, getting up off the couch. "Alejandro's gonna be pissed off enough when he sees the mess you made of the box. Don't expect me to take the blame."

Spartacus ignored him and went back to chewing on his Kong.

Matthew looked around for a place to put the box. For some reason he couldn't explain, he really didn't want the thing in his bedroom. He finally settled on the closet near the front door, hiding it behind the winter hats and mittens on the top shelf. Then he went back to the couch and put the DVD in for *Ip Man*, despite having watched it about twenty times already.

He thought about calling Alejandro about the damage done to the box, but he chickened out. It would be easier to explain when Alejandro got back. His flight was due in late that night, so Matthew would see him tomorrow.

Every once in a while as he watched the movie, and later, as he got up to bake himself a frozen pizza, he glanced at the closet. He didn't know why. It was stupid. Did he think the book was going to jump out of the closet and chase him around the room? The image that brought to mind, with the book flapping its covers through the air like a bat, made him laugh. But it didn't make him any less uneasy. He wasn't generally superstitious—at least, he didn't think so—but he'd feel better once the book was out of his apartment.

Chapter Three

THE DARK thing slithered down the wall and across the floor of the apartment, hugging the edge of the room, though all was still and dark. It avoided the splash of light near the wall, where some kind of cold blue flame flickered, but quickly returned to the comfort of the baseboard. It disliked being out in the open.

It was hungry.

It sensed food had been left for it on top of the counter, but when it climbed easily up the side to explore the surface on top, it found little to satisfy it—bread, cheese, and mashed tomato. Peasant food. It needed food with power—blood and flesh.

It sensed something... something nearby that could ease its hunger... and slithered back down to the floor. Following the contours of the room, it came to a closed door. There was a thin gap between the door and the floorboards, and the thing easily slipped through.

Inside, it found a bed, in which two warm bodies slept. The human was protected by a faint, lingering trace of magic—not much, but enough to make him unappealing. Yet the dog was not. The dark thing curled around the unsuspecting animal, which whimpered softly in its sleep, and then insinuated itself in through the nostrils, through the mouth, through the ears... claiming the animal with every breath, marking it as its own....

HIGH ABOVE the New England countryside, Alejandro started in his sleep and woke from the nightmare to the pilot announcing twenty minutes until landing at Manchester Airport. He shifted uncomfortably in his seat, wedged between an elderly woman who insisted on taking her smelly shoes off and a business man who kept eying Alejandro as if he might make a grab for the man's wallet.

Something was wrong. He'd never considered himself to be particularly psychic, but the dream had been too vivid, too disturbing to ignore. He took his cell phone out of his pocket and verified the time he'd heard from the flight attendant. Just past one in the morning.

It was possible Matthew would be awake. He sometimes stayed up late watching a movie. He'd been sleeping in the dream, but hopefully that's all it had been—a dream. Hopefully, Matthew and Spartacus were all right. They *had* to be all right.

Twenty minutes, at least, until he'd be allowed to use his phone. He wasn't sure how he'd be able to stand it.

MATTHEW WOKE in semidarkness, with only a street light coming through his second-floor bedroom window to cut across his ceiling in a broad band of orange-yellow, and found Spartacus standing over him, looking down into his face. It wasn't something the dog had ever done before, and it was unnerving.

"What's up, pup?"

In response, the dog that had never once shown any aggression to his owner—or *anyone*, for that matter—lowered his ears and growled deep in his throat.

"Spartacus—"

That merely caused the pit bull to draw his lips back and growl louder, his canines clearly visible. A drop of saliva fell onto Matthew's shoulder.

THE MOMENT they were on the ground and the captain announced passengers could use cell phones, Alejandro flipped his out of airplane mode and dialed Matthew's number. It rang a few times but went to voice mail.

Shit.

"If you're still awake, huero, call me back. I just landed in Manchester."

He left the phone on vibrate and slipped it into his pocket. Then he waited, fretting, while the plane taxied to the gate. Everything was probably fine. Nightmares were usually just that. None of his dreams had ever come true before, so there was no reason to think this one would. Besides, it hadn't even made sense. Just a vague sense of something menacing loose in Matthew's apartment. Matthew would probably laugh at him if he told him about it.

Still, Alejandro knew he wouldn't be able to rest tonight until he checked on his friend.

SOMETHING WAS very wrong with Spartacus. He didn't appear to recognize Matthew at all. Was it possible for dogs to sleepwalk? Should Matthew try shouting at him to see if it would shake him out of it? Matthew was afraid to even move, never mind make loud noises. For the first time since he'd met the lovable pit bull at the shelter and wrestled with him, he was frightened by those sharp fangs and powerful jaws.

Was he bitten by something? Is he rabid?

The thought filled him with dread. Matthew couldn't remember encountering any animals recently when he'd walked Spartacus. Nothing that could have bitten him, anyway. Just some squirrels and chipmunks. Besides, he would have noticed if the dog had bite marks on him.

The buzzing of Matthew's cell phone in his pants pocket halfway across the room set the pit bull off. As soon as the phone broke the silence, Spartacus started barking ferociously, as if Matthew was an intruder. Instinctively, Matthew grabbed the dog's collar with one hand, shoving him back just long enough to yank the pillow out from behind his head and shove it in Spartacus's face. He rolled off the bed as the pit bull savaged the pillow, tearing it to shreds.

There wasn't time to sort things out. Matthew scrambled to his feet and bolted for the bedroom door as Spartacus launched his muscular body through the air. The dog landed at the door just as Matthew went through and slammed it behind him. A hundred pounds of muscle smashed into the wood while Matthew braced it with his body. Spartacus tore at it with his claws, snarling savagely, causing the door to bang loosely in its frame. The stupid thing had been put on backward before Matthew and his mother moved in six years ago, so it opened out into the living room. It also had no lock. Only the short latch bolt, rattling loosely against the metal strike plate, kept it from flying open as the dog slammed his massive paws against it.

Matthew's heart pounded in his chest, and his breath came in painful gasps. *This isn't happening!* He was terrified, but not so much for himself as for Spartacus. Why had the dog suddenly snapped like this? Maybe it *was* rabies. Or a brain tumor or encephalitis. Unfortunately, it didn't matter. Because if Spartacus didn't calm down soon, somebody would take him away and have him put down. And that scared Matthew more than anything.

In between the barking and the slashing of claws against the wooden door, Matthew could faintly hear the phone buzzing insistently.

Damn it!

He'd left it in the room, along with all his clothes. It had to be Alejandro calling. His mother had already called before he went to bed, saying she'd be spending the night at her boyfriend's apartment, so it wasn't likely to be her. But Alejandro's plane was supposed to be landing tonight. Since he was coming in so late, the plan had been for him to get a taxi home, instead of pestering Matthew for a ride. But nobody else would call him at this hour, unless it was a wrong number.

It took a minute for Matthew to realize some of the pounding he was hearing was coming from the apartment door, rather than the bedroom door. *Terrific.* One of the neighbors had heard the noise, and the knocking was starting to get insistent.

"Quién es?" he shouted.

"Señor Rojas! Qué demonios estás haciendo ahí?" ("What the hell is going on in there?")

Matthew groaned. "Un minuto!"

The couch was nearby, so he took a chance that the door would hold for a moment against Spartacus's assault and ran across the small room. Putting his weight against the opposite end, he slid the couch across the wooden floor until the other arm was wedged firmly against the bedroom door. That would hopefully keep the damned thing closed for a few minutes.

When he opened the door to the second floor landing, Mr. Rojas was standing there in his bathrobe, arms across his chest, glaring. Matthew himself was dressed in nothing but red-and-black checkered boxers. "I'm sorry if we woke you—" he began in Spanish. The man spoke English, Matthew knew, but it was rare to hear it in the apartment building.

"It's nearly two in the fucking morning!" Mr. Rojas snarled. His eyes were puffy, and his thinning black hair was sticking up in all directions. "Some of us have to work in the morning, you know! What the hell is going on in here?"

The sound of his voice seemed to rile Spartacus up even further, and the dog increased his attack against the bedroom door. Matthew knew the cheap pressed wood wouldn't hold up for much longer.

Mr. Rojas looked past the boy in horror. "What is that?"

Matthew didn't want to stand there chatting while there was a chance the dog could break out and come after him again. Or worse, get out of the apartment. He had no idea what to do, but he knew he needed to get out of there. At least until he could figure out a plan. Maybe the dog would calm down if nobody was in the apartment with him.

And he needed to call Alejandro. He couldn't think of anyone else. His mother would probably want to put Spartacus to sleep. It had taken her a long time to get over her fear of big dogs, but Spartacus's affectionate nature had gradually won her over. Her fragile trust in him wouldn't last long if she saw him like he was now. And the police would just shoot him. Matthew saw stories in the news all the time about police shooting big dogs at the slightest sign of aggression. Maybe not all police were like that, but he was too afraid to take the chance.

Alejandro loved Spartacus as much as Matthew did. He'd want to save him too. And maybe between the two of them, they could think of something.

"Mr. Rojas, can I use your phone?"

ALEJANDRO TRIED calling three times and then gave up. If Matthew was sleeping and the phone woke him up, he'd be pissed. Alejandro had left messages, but now he just needed to catch a cab and get home. He could poke his head in at Matthew's when he got there.

His phone vibrated while he was in the cab, and he anxiously fished it out of his pocket. To his surprise, it wasn't Matthew. The display read "Fernando Rojas."

"Sí, Señor Rojas?"

"It's Matthew," his friend said in English, sounding frantic. "I'm using Mr. Rojas's phone."

Alejandro wasn't sure whether he should feel relieved or not. Something was obviously off. "Why?"

"Where are you?" Matthew demanded, ignoring his question.

"I'm in a cab."

"You're heading home?"

"Yes."

"Come next door as soon as you get in. It's urgent!"

"What the hell?"

"I'll explain when you get here."

Chapter Four

MATTHEW FELT ridiculous, sitting in the Rojas's kitchen wrapped in a blanket like a victim of hypothermia. It was July and about eighty degrees out. But Mr. Rojas had insisted he cover up rather than sit there in his underwear. The man didn't want his daughters to wake up and see Matthew half naked.

So fine. At least he'd let Matthew call Alejandro. "Thank you," Matthew told him, handing the phone back.

"De nada," Rojas grunted. "I have to get some sleep. I have work in the morning. You can stay here until Alejandro comes, but don't make any noise."

"Gracias."

ALEJANDRO DIDN'T bother going to his own apartment when the cab dropped him off. All he had with him was a laptop case and a carry-on bag with wheels and an extendable handle. So he just wheeled it up to Matthew's apartment building. Before he could ring the buzzer, the front door swung open, and there was Matthew, standing there in nothing but a blanket.

"Don't ring the buzzer!" he hissed under his breath. "And keep your voice down. If I wake Mr. Rojas again, he'll kill me."

Alejandro struggled to keep his gaze from searching the gaps in the blanket, trying to see whether his friend was really naked under there. He knew Matthew slept in his underwear, so it seemed unlikely. But it was hard not to speculate. "What's going on?"

"Come into the stairwell."

Matthew stepped back so Alejandro could enter. He helped lift the luggage over the doorstep so it wouldn't bang against the wood, and while his hands were occupied, the blanket slipped off. Alejandro wasn't surprised to see the familiar red-and-black checked boxers, but he was certainly disappointed. He'd seen Matthew naked on occasion, changing clothes, but… not enough.

Once they were safely inside, Matthew wrapped the blanket around himself again, though he was sweating in the summer heat. "There's something wrong with Spartacus."

That snapped Alejandro back to reality and away from thoughts of Matthew's smooth butt. "What? What happened to him?" He remembered his bizarre dream on the plane. Had it been some kind of premonition, after all?

"I don't know. Suddenly he's acting like Cujo. I barely escaped from him without getting my face torn off." He was talking calmly, but his voice sounded strained, and Alejandro could tell he was close to tears. "I don't think he got bitten by anything...."

Alejandro felt a chill go through him. If Spartacus was rabid, that would be it. The poor pup would be put down. The thought horrified him—he'd never known a more awesome dog—and he knew it would kill Matthew. "When did it start?" He had no idea what that would tell them, but it seemed like a good question to ask.

"He was fine before bed...." Matthew hesitated a moment before adding, "Oh, he chewed up your package. I'm sorry."

"What?"

"He didn't destroy the book. But he chewed up the box pretty bad."

"The book?" It finally dawned on him what Matthew meant. *Oh shit.* Well, so much for owning his own copy of *El Gran Libro*. It hardly seemed important at the moment. "He attacked you, then chewed up the book?"

"No, the other way around," Matthew replied, clearly growing frustrated.

It took a few minutes, but Alejandro finally got the complete story. And the more he learned, the more he was disturbed by it. Not only because of what was happening to Spartacus, but because he was becoming more and more convinced it might have something to do with the book. Matthew often poked fun at him for being too superstitious—it was hard not to be, living with Abuela—but Alejandro knew the reputation of the book, and he knew how it had felt when he touched it. The way Matthew had described Spartacus staring intently at it, the way he'd felt about keeping it out of his bedroom... it seemed possible, at least.

Of course, when he explained his theory to Matthew, it didn't go over well. "Oh please! I said he was acting like Cujo. I didn't say we were actually living in a Stephen King novel."

"I had a dream," Alejandro said quickly, "when I was on the plane." He described seeing something coming out of the closet where Matthew had admitted hiding the book, slithering through the apartment, and then honing in on Spartacus.

Matthew stared at him openmouthed for a long time after that. At last he gasped, "You *fucker!*" He glanced at the door to the Rojas's apartment quickly and lowered his voice. "You sent me a cursed book!"

MATTHEW WAS furious. At least, at first. Alejandro was supposed to be the expert in this kind of thing. He was the one who'd grown up surrounded by all this stuff. He should have known better! True, Matthew had, by now, been around saints and floor washes and Florida Water nearly as much, but still....

Gradually, something occurred to him—something that caused his anger to evaporate. Or, nearly. "Wait a minute. If this is... possession or something... then it isn't permanent, right? All we have to do is force the spirit to leave Spartacus, and he'll be just like he was before!"

Alejandro looked uncertain. "Maybe. But I'm not sure how we can do that."

"There has to be something!" Matthew insisted.

His friend frowned and glanced up the staircase. "What's he doing now?"

"I don't know. It's been quiet for the last hour or so, but I think he got out of the bedroom. I thought I heard him pacing around up there while I was in the Rojas's kitchen. I'm afraid if I go up, he'll go nuts again. Even if he doesn't rip me to shreds, someone might hear him and call the police."

"Okay," Alejandro said, surprising Matthew by placing a hand over his. It was an unusually affectionate gesture, coming from him. "Let's go to the botanica. There are things there we can use."

Matthew nodded, his gaze still locked on his hand, held in Alejandro's. Then he recalled, "I need clothes. I can't walk across town in a blanket." Technically he could, but he didn't need the police harassing him.

Alejandro opened his suitcase and dug down past several shirts to a pair of shorts. "These are... well, I've worn them. But they're not that bad."

"You were wearing underwear, right?" Matthew asked, eying them dubiously.

"Yes. Don't be an idiot."

Matthew took them and slipped into them. They fit, as he'd known they would. He and his friend had worn each other's clothes more than once.

The shirts, however, were a lost cause. Alejandro sniffed them and grimaced. "You don't want these, huero. They reek."

"There's nothing clean?"

"No," Alejandro replied. "I just brought enough clothes for the trip."

"Fine." Matthew was happy with the shorts. It was hot enough to go shirtless, and he was relieved to get out from under the blanket. He folded it and quietly slipped it back into the Rojas's kitchen. Then he rejoined Alejandro in the stairwell and said, "Let's go."

Chapter Five

ALEJANDRO KNEW his grandmother wouldn't appreciate him raiding the supplies in the botanica. She wasn't a wealthy woman, and everything he took had come out of her own pocket—at least, the reserves she had in the business bank account. If she didn't sell it, she lost money. So he'd have to replace everything he took out of his salary.

But he was convinced what had happened to Spartacus was his fault. Or perhaps, like Matthew, he was *hoping* it was his fault... and that it could be undone. In any case, he had to try.

He started with the books on the shelves. He'd read about "duppies" in Jamaican voodoo—their word for malicious ghosts—but he didn't know if what had possessed Spartacus was one. Could a ghost be bound to a book the way this spirit seemed to have been? Some practitioners of voodoo and Santeria believed in demons, but the difference between demons and ghosts seemed vague in the books. And he was having trouble finding anything useful for getting rid of them, apart from prayers and offerings to the saints.

He really needed to talk to Abuela, but he was frankly more frightened of her than of the spirit, at the moment. She'd kill him for sending that book to Matthew's apartment. At any rate, he wasn't going to wake her up at three in the morning—not until he'd tried some things on his own.

The botanica had incense, sprays, and floor washes for cleansing a house of evil. Those seemed like a good place to start. He grabbed some of the ones he'd seen his grandmother pushing at customers and a couple of others that looked good.

But when he said, "Okay, let's go," Matthew stopped him.

"We can't! If we go into the apartment, he'll flip out again!" Matthew was still sounding like someone on the edge of a nervous breakdown. "They'll call the police and take him away!"

"Okay, okay," Alejandro said, caressing his back to soothe him. "We'll wait until Mr. Rojas goes to work. Then we'll tell Mrs. Rojas and the girls not to call the police if they hear Spartacus barking."

"That's not going to work!" Matthew protested.

It might not. But Alejandro was counting on the fact that few people in their neighborhood really liked dealing with the police. As long as they weren't keeping everyone awake in the middle of the night, the other people in the building might be more prone to look the other way. Or listen the other way, as the case may be. "We'll talk to the Torres's too."

"Don't you know a spell or something to put him to sleep? You know, without harming him?"

Alejandro waved his arm in a gesture that took in the whole shop. "You've been working here too. Do any of these powders and sprays claim they can do that?"

"I don't think so."

"I don't think so either. And the only spell I can remember is putting your nightie over your husband's face when he's asleep to keep him from waking up. I don't think that applies. Besides, you don't own a nightie, so you'd have to use your underwear." An image of Matthew stripping out of his underwear flashed into Alejandro's mind, making his mouth go dry, but he deliberately shoved it away.

Matthew frowned and said sullenly, "Fine."

"When does your mother get home?"

"She has to go directly to work from her boyfriend's house," Matthew replied. "She won't be back 'til tonight."

"Perfect! We'll just wait until about nine." That was five hours away.

It was Matthew who found the potential flaw in that plan. "We probably don't want to be here when Abuela opens the shop." He glanced at the small stack of supplies they'd "borrowed." It was going to be difficult to explain all of this.

"Why don't we go to my apartment?" Alejandro suggested. "Abuela's asleep now. We can sneak in and crash in my room until morning." They'd slept over at each other's apartments plenty of times over the years. Even if his grandmother saw them, she wouldn't think twice about it.

"Okay."

THEY SNUCK into Alejandro's apartment to avoid waking his grandmother. Matthew felt completely at home there, just as Alejandro felt in Matthew's apartment, so he quietly used the bathroom and grabbed a glass of orange juice from the kitchen while his friend stashed their ill-gotten booty in his bedroom. Matthew entered the room, juice in hand, to find Alejandro already stripped to his boxers and pulling down the blankets on his bed. The sight of so much smooth, warm beige skin was distracting enough to make Matthew hesitate a moment, the desire he'd been feeling for years welling up in him again. But he forced himself to ignore it, as he always did.

He sat in the chair next to Alejandro's desk and attempted to take another sip of juice. But his hand was shaking, and Alejandro noticed it.

"He'll be okay," Alejandro said softly.

Matthew wasn't convinced. All they had to work with was an assortment of powders and sprays he didn't have a lot of faith in. But he tried to smile as he set the glass down on the desk.

"I'll be right back," Alejandro said. He slipped out of the room for a moment—probably to use the bathroom.

Normally, when he stayed over, Matthew slept on the floor, on a mat and sleeping bag Alejandro had stowed in his closet. So he got up and went to the closet to fish those out. He unrolled the mat and then laid the sleeping bag down on top of it.

But when Alejandro returned, he glanced at the sleeping bag and asked, "Do you want to share the bed?" When Matthew's eyebrows shot up in surprise, Alejandro quickly added, "I'm not gonna make a pass at you. I just thought… you know… you might want to be… near someone tonight."

It was awkwardly phrased, and Alejandro seemed too embarrassed to look him in the eye as he climbed onto the bed. It wasn't something either of them would have been brave enough to say normally—they were too prone to teasing each other. Matthew couldn't even acknowledge the suggestion in words. He turned off the desk lamp, plunging the room into near darkness except for the faint light coming in the through the window blinds. Then he stepped out of the shorts he'd borrowed and slid under the sheet.

The moment Alejandro's arms wrapped around him, pulling him close, he felt as if he'd been so, so thirsty… dying of thirst… and Alejandro's embrace was pure, cool water, the only thing that could quench it. But he would only have a few hours to drink his fill.

When Alejandro kissed him gently on the back of the neck, Matthew felt a flood of warmth spread from the spot to fill his entire body. "I'll make it better," his friend whispered. "I promise."

Chapter Six

ALEJANDRO WASN'T sure if he slept or not. Maybe he did, because it seemed like Matthew had only just settled into his arms when the alarm clock went off. Matthew moaned softly in protest, and Alejandro quickly reached across him to silence the alarm. He was still stretched out half on top when Matthew snickered. "What?"

"Somebody has a boner."

It was true. Alejandro realized he'd been mashing it into Matthew's hip. He quickly rolled away. "Shut up. You probably do too."

Matthew didn't confirm the accusation... but he didn't deny it either. Instead, he turned red and glanced away. "Is Abuela still here?"

Alejandro forced his mind away from thoughts of Matthew's hard-on and glanced at the clock. It was just past nine. "She should be at the botanica by now."

Matthew slipped out of the bed, muttering something about needing to piss, and quickly left the room. Alejandro couldn't help but notice that he made sure to keep his front hidden while he did so. A short time later, he could hear his friend taking a leak in the bathroom.

Frustrated, Alejandro got up and dressed, thankful Matthew wasn't there to see how much his boxers were jutting out in front of him. It wasn't the first time they'd awoken with morning hard-ons and teased each other about it, but it was the first time they'd cuddled the night before. Everything felt different now—weird.

Did I actually kiss him? It wasn't that he minded the thought. Not at all. But.... Christ, where had he gotten the courage to do that?

By the time Matthew came back into the room, Alejandro was deflated enough to pretend there hadn't been any sexual overtones to sharing the bed. After all, it wasn't like anyone had done any groping in the night. It had just been one friend consoling another.

Yeah, that's all.

At any rate, they had more important things to worry about. "Get dressed," Alejandro said. He didn't bother suggesting Matthew borrow his clothes, because of course he would. "Then I have something I want you to do before we go over there."

The "something" was totally revolting, and he knew Matthew would give him shit over it.

"You're fucking kidding me," Matthew said, his face screwed up in disgust as Alejandro held out the raw meat from the fridge. It had been thawing in there last night. Alejandro had been happy to find it just before they went to sleep. But he had no idea how he'd explain to Abuela where a big chunk of it had gone.

"It's a very old spell," Alejandro explained again. "It will turn a dog away from its master and make him loyal to you."

"I *am* his master!"

"Not at the moment."

"Raw meat," Matthew said. "In my armpit."

"You have to hold it there for an hour."

"While it drips blood down my side. What the *fuck*, Alejandro? We don't have time for this!"

Alejandro shrugged. "I'm going to talk to the neighbors and try to convince them to ignore any noises coming from your apartment. Spartacus still has a crate in the living room, right?"

"Yeah. We never use it anymore, but it's there."

"Then we need to try to throw the meat into it so we can lock him up."

MATTHEW STOOD outside his apartment building as the morning grew hotter, feeling the squishy, raw steak slipping around under his armpit every time he moved. *He cursed my dog, and now he's making me do this. Why haven't I killed him yet?*

Matthew was shirtless, thank God. Wearing a shirt would have just made it worse. Alejandro had tucked a plastic grocery bag into the waistband of the shorts he was wearing—Alejandro's shorts, since there had seemed little point in putting on something clean—and although that kept some of the blood off the *outside* of the shorts, it caused it to pool in places along the waistband and dribble down the *inside*. The whole experience was beyond disgusting.

He thought back to Alejandro spooning him the night before. If he hadn't been falling apart, it might have been one of the best moments of his life. He'd fantasized about Alejandro holding him like that more times than he could remember. Though in his fantasies, the cuddling had just been the beginning, moving on to kissing and caressing and hot man-on-man action. But things would probably go back to normal when this was over—hopefully with Spartacus safely restored to his old self—back to just being good friends, horsing around, teasing each other. Caring about each other, but not... *loving* each other.

While he was wallowing in these dismal thoughts, Alejandro came out the front door of the building. "I've talked to everyone. I told them to stay inside until I give the all clear. I don't want one of their kids opening their apartment door and getting mauled by Spartacus if he gets out. And it sounds to me like he's still pacing back and forth in the living room. I listened at the door for a minute, and he growled at me."

"Terrific," Matthew muttered.

"I also called Abuelita to let her know I got back last night. But I told her I need to help you with something this morning." Alejandro checked his cell phone for the time. "We'll go in, in about fifteen minutes. Stay here a minute—I have to get dressed."

Matthew wasn't sure what he meant by that, since he was already wearing a T-shirt, pants, and sneakers, which was more than Matthew had on. But he waited while Alejandro went back into his apartment. A few minutes later, he returned in the most ridiculous getup Matthew could have imagined. Despite the fact that it was almost eighty degrees, Alejandro had put on his leather jacket and leather gloves. Most absurdly, he was wearing the hockey mask he'd worn in high school when he was on the team for a while. Matthew had to laugh. "How the hell can you breathe in that thing?"

"I'm dying," Alejandro admitted. He lifted the mask up to gasp in some air. "Jesus! We've gotta get this done fast or I'll pass out. Here's the plan. Do you have your key handy?"

"The apartment isn't locked," Matthew said. "There wasn't time to grab my pants, and that's where my keys are." He hadn't wanted to lock himself out.

Alejandro nodded. "All right. Fine. I'll throw open the door and rush in first. I'm gonna try to grab Spartacus by the collar. Once I've got him restrained, I need you to run to his crate and toss that delicious, underarm-sweat-soaked meat inside. Then get the fuck out of the room before he takes a bite out of your ass."

"And go where, exactly?"

"I don't know. Lock yourself in the bathroom if you have to. Once I get the crate closed, you can come back into the room."

It didn't sound like a brilliant plan, but Matthew didn't have a better one, so he agreed to it. By the time they'd gone into the building and climbed the stairs to the apartment, Alejandro's jet-black hair was plastered to his face and dripping rivulets of sweat. He slipped the mask into place as he crept up to the door. They were afraid of alerting Spartacus, so Alejandro counted down silently with his fingers: three… two… one….

He burst into the apartment, and almost immediately Spartacus was upon him, barking ferociously. Then Alejandro cried out in pain. From his place on the landing, Matthew couldn't see clearly, but it looked as if the pit bull had sunk his teeth into Alejandro's arm. Matthew wondered fearfully whether the leather was tough enough to prevent the dog from ripping an enormous chunk of flesh out of his friend's forearm.

Then Alejandro shouted, "Matthew! Now!"

Matthew ran into the apartment and slammed the door behind him. Alejandro had Spartacus by the collar as he'd planned, holding it tightly in his left hand, but the dog hadn't released his death grip on his right arm. Blood was dripping out the end of the jacket sleeve.

Fuck!

The living room couch was still kitty-corner to the room, one end pressed up against Matthew's bedroom door. The door, surprisingly enough, wasn't smashed through, but Spartacus had apparently broken the latch and shoved the couch back far enough to make his escape. Matthew ran around the other end of the couch to where the dog's crate lay open in the far corner of the living room, but when he moved to toss the meat into it, he glanced back and realized Spartacus wasn't paying any attention to him at all. He was holding fast on to Alejandro's arm, despite the boy trying to pull him off. Alejandro was managing not to scream, but he was grunting in obvious pain and swearing in a steady stream of Spanish.

"Spartacus!" Matthew tried waving the piece of meat in the air, but the dog didn't pay any attention.

This was a stupid plan!

Matthew scrambled over the top of the couch until he was close enough to shove the meat directly in front of the dog's nose. "Come on, you dumb dog! It's meat!"

"Matthew! Get away—"

Spartacus released Alejandro's arm and lunged for the chunk of steak faster than Matthew was prepared for. He came close to losing a finger as the pit bull sank his teeth into the meat.

"Fuck me!" Matthew had just enough presence of mind to keep a hold of his end of the steak. It tore in two, and Spartacus wolfed down his chunk in a single gulp. Then he lunged for the other half, still in Matthew's hand.

If he'd thought for two seconds, Matthew would have jumped back over the couch—it was the shortest route to the crate and might have slowed Spartacus down, since the dog was relatively short and squat. But he didn't think. He ran. Somewhere in the back of his mind, he saw a flash of an old silent movie where people were running at high speed with silly piano music playing, as he scrambled around the far end of the couch and looped around the coffee table before he remembered where he was supposed to be going. In one motion, he tossed the scrap of raw meat into the crate and jumped up on top of the thing.

He wasn't exactly safe there. It was strong, but nothing more than a wire mesh. His fingers and toes were sticking down into the crate, where Spartacus could easily bite them. But the dog took a minute to pounce on the meat and scarf it down. In that tiny interval, Matthew jumped down to close the door and throw the bolt.

Spartacus was trapped.

He didn't like it. The dog threw himself against the crate, but it was strong enough to hold him. While he clawed at it and snarled, Matthew scrambled out of reach. He turned back to Alejandro, who was still standing near the door, clutching his arm.

"I'm sorry," Alejandro said. "I was supposed to do that."

And then he collapsed.

Chapter Seven

ALEJANDRO WOKE to find himself lying on the floor with a pillow under his head and all his clothing gone. Well, he figured out after a second that his boxers were still on. But otherwise, he was naked. Matthew was wiping his chest and stomach down with a cool, damp washcloth.

"Um… where are my clothes?"

"In the bathtub," Matthew replied, looking a bit embarrassed. "They were all covered in blood."

"You had to take my pants off too?"

Matthew turned red, which Alejandro thought was adorable. "You bled all down your leg. Besides, you were sweating like a pig. I was afraid you'd get heatstroke or something, all bundled up like that in this weather. So I thought it was a good idea to cool you off."

Truthfully, Alejandro was incredibly relieved to be out of the leather jacket, gloves, and hockey mask. The rest… well, who was he to complain if Matthew wanted to undress him? "Did you at least have your way with me?" he asked. "It's been a while since I've gotten laid."

Matthew snorted. "Don't forget who you're talking to. Unless you had a really good time in New Orleans, I know you've never gotten laid—ever."

"Jose Garcia gave me a blowjob."

"I know. I was there, and he gave me a blowjob too. But that's not the same as getting laid."

Alejandro didn't argue. If he did, he might have to admit that Jose had come on to him a few days later, offering a lot more than just a blowjob. And Alejandro had turned him down, because he hadn't wanted his first time to be with someone he didn't feel anything for.

He'd wanted it to be with Matthew.

"Your arm is all chewed to shit," Matthew said, frowning. "I've been waiting to see if you turned into some kind of were-pit bull or something."

Alejandro rolled his eyes. "Don't be an idiot."

"I see," Matthew said, frowning at him. "Possession by evil spirits is totally realistic, but were-animals are silly. Got it."

"Fuck you, huero. I don't have the energy to argue. And my arm hurts."

Matthew didn't bother responding to the "fuck you" part—they said that to each other all the time, anyway—but he looked concerned about the rest of it. "We should probably get you to a doctor."

Alejandro lifted his arm to look at it, but Matthew had cleaned it and wrapped his entire forearm in bandaging. He couldn't see how bad the damage was. It was throbbing painfully, but not nearly as bad as it had felt when Spartacus had his teeth embedded in it. "Later. We have to do what we came to do." If he did go to a doctor, he'd have to lie about some "strange dog" biting him. If he mentioned Spartacus, someone might insist the dog be put down, regardless.

Alejandro struggled to sit up and Matthew helped him. For the first time, he noticed Matthew had cleaned the blood off himself and changed into some fresh shorts. "How is he?"

"He's gone kind of quiet," Matthew said, glancing in the general direction of the dog crate. They couldn't actually see it from down here on the floor because the couch was in the way. "But he's sure as hell not back to normal."

"Get the bag of stuff from the hall," Alejandro said. "Then we'll cleanse the apartment."

THE APARTMENT would have needed cleansing even if there hadn't been an evil spirit in it. Spartacus had crapped on the floor in a couple of spots and urinated God knew where. He'd also managed to get under the sink and drag the garbage out onto the floor. In eighty-degree weather, it wasn't surprising that the place reeked.

Matthew scooped up the poop with paper towels and flushed it down the toilet, while Alejandro did his best to clean up the garbage in the kitchen. Although he wasn't complaining, he was deathly slow at it, and Matthew could tell he was in a lot of pain. Matthew did most of the cleaning and then left his friend to fill the mop bucket with water and one of the cleansing washes from the botanica. He went around the apartment with a small black light that illuminated urine spots. He'd bought it when Spartacus was a puppy. He hadn't had to use it in a while, but he found a few spots now on the floor and furniture and cleaned them with an enzyme spray specifically designed for animal urine. Apparently, evil spirits weren't house-trained.

Matthew was having a hard time keeping it together. Every time he allowed himself to glance at the dog crate, he was shocked at how little the animal inside resembled his sweet puppy. Spartacus panted and watched him intently—perhaps suspiciously—with eyes that seemed glazed over, ears flattened against his head, drool mixed with blood from the raw steak hanging in ropes from his mouth....

Matthew focused on cleaning and prayed the washes and sprays Alejandro had brought would somehow bring Spartacus back from wherever he was.

The floor of the apartment was wood in all the rooms, including the living room, which made things a little easier. The wash had to be mixed with water and then used to mop the floor throughout the entire apartment. Since Alejandro couldn't do that effectively one-handed, Matthew did it. Alejandro opened a window and sprayed the place with Eleggua spray.

Eleggua spray was exactly what it sounded like—a spray to encourage the spirit Eleggua to manifest himself and chase away evil. The first time Matthew had seen that, and aerosols dedicated to other spirits, on the shelves of the botanica, he'd been flabbergasted. Spirit summoning in a can? The idea seemed beyond laughable. But Abuela had glared at him, and Alejandro had explained that it wasn't all that different from lighting incense at the beginning of a religious ritual. This particular scent—which frankly smelled a bit like Florida Water to Matthew, but sharper, more masculine—was pleasing to Eleggua, so the spirit was more likely to make his presence known where it had been sprayed.

Matthew still wasn't sure how much he believed, but he knew Abuela took these things very seriously, and her grandson... well, he suspected Alejandro took it more seriously than he let on. He might act dismissive of it when he was just talking to Matthew, but deep down he believed in it. And right now, if it would get Spartacus back, Matthew wanted to believe in it too.

While he sprayed the apartment, Alejandro was muttering under his breath in Spanish. Matthew couldn't hear him clearly, but he was pretty sure it was a prayer to Eleggua or his Santeria equivalent, St. Anthony.

Between the wash and the spray, it was getting hard to breathe in there, open window or not.

When Matthew had finished mopping, Alejandro approached him and dabbed some Florida Water on his neck and the middle of his forehead. Then he handed him a small plastic bottle of clear liquid. "Splash this on Spartacus."

Matthew looked at the label. "Holy water? This is *real*?" He'd seen it on the shelves at the shop but dismissed it, convinced it was... well, if not a joke, then at least something only gullible people believed in. He'd only ever seen people using holy water in horror movies to kill vampires.

Or... exorcisms. There was that.

"Of course it's real," Alejandro said impatiently. "It's water that's been blessed by a priest."

"It won't hurt him, will it?"

Alejandro hesitated. "Well... it's just water, so it's not like you have to worry about it getting in his eyes like Florida Water or something." Florida Water was highly alcoholic. They'd put some in a bowl and lit it on fire once. "But the spirit's not gonna like it."

Matthew nodded. He'd seen *The Exorcist*. He knew what that could mean. But that made him think of something else. "Do I have to say something? Like 'the power of Christ compels you,' or something like that?"

Alejandro clearly tried not to laugh, but he couldn't stop himself from snorting.

"Fuck you," Matthew said. He stalked off, holy water in hand, though he couldn't go far, since the living room was only about twenty feet across.

He approached Spartacus's crate and looked down at his beloved dog. The pit bull looked up at him expectantly, not growling but panting heavily. Maybe the stupid meat "spell" had worked, at least a little, because every time Alejandro had walked near him over the past hour, the dog had growled at him. But he hadn't been doing that with Matthew. He just watched his master, panting and... waiting.

"Dipshit over there tells me this won't hurt," Matthew told him in a quiet, soothing voice. "I don't want to hurt you. You know that, don't you, Spartacus? I just want you to come back to me."

With that, he opened the bottle and shook it back and forth over the crate, so that its contents rained down upon the dog. Whatever he'd hoped would happen, what he got was definitely not it. Spartacus threw himself against the door of the crate, barking and snarling in rage.

Matthew jumped back in terror, only to discover Alejandro standing there, blocking his retreat.

"It's not working!" Matthew said, feeling the sting of tears behind his eyes. "Nothing's working."

To his surprise, Alejandro wrapped his arms around his waist from behind, as if to comfort him. He pressed his cheek against Matthews neck and murmured, "It's okay. It's okay. We'll think of something else."

WHAT ELSE they could try, Alejandro had no idea. He'd brought some more things from the store, such as a small bottle of Cast Away Evil powder, a can of Go Away Evil spray, and a perfume called *Alcalado Kitamal* for chasing away evil. But he no longer had much confidence that they'd do any good. Perhaps sprinkling some Florida Water on Spartacus wouldn't be a bad idea after all....

"When you left the shop last night," he asked, "did Abuela spritz you with Florida Water?"

"Yes, of course. She always does."

In his dream, Alejandro had seen the spirit shy away from Matthew. Perhaps it had been the Florida Water. They could try it on Spartacus. But what if that just angered the spirit and made the situation worse? He simply didn't know what he was doing.

His thoughts were interrupted by his cell phone going off somewhere in the apartment. Since he was in his underwear, the phone wasn't on him, and he was busy anyway, so he was tempted to ignore it. But that ring tone was for his grandmother, and he didn't like to ignore her calls. "Is my phone still in my pants?"

"Yes."

Reluctantly, Alejandro withdrew his arms from around Matthew's waist and went into the bathroom. There he found his pants piled on top of the rest of his clothing in the bathtub. Matthew had been right—the right side of his jeans had a lot of blood dribbled down it. He couldn't get his phone out of the pocket without getting it on his hands, but he ignored it. "Sí."

"Alejandro! I've been robbed!"

"What?" he asked, alarmed. "What happened?" He was picturing some thug with a gun going into the botanica.

"I noticed that there were fewer bottles of Florida Water since last night," Abuela went on nervously. "One's missing! So I looked around the shop. A lot of things are missing! Some *pinche cabrón* broke in and robbed a poor old woman who can barely scrape by!"

Alejandro was simultaneously relieved and terrified to realize that the pinche cabrón was him. He'd intended to present her with a list of items he'd taken after this whole mess was over, along with a promise to pay for all of it. Now he was going to have to come clean when she was already worked up. Not exactly ideal.

"It's okay, Abuelita! Nobody stole anything. I took those things, and I'm going to pay for them."

There was shocked silence on the end of the line. Then she gasped, "You? *Idiota! Baboso!* You steal from your own grandmother! Scare me half to death! Didn't I raise you to have more respect?" The tirade went on for a considerable time before Alejandro was able to get a word in.

"Abuelita! I told you I'd pay for them!"

"What, in the name of all that is holy, could you possibly need that stuff for? Alcalado Kitamal? Eleggua spray?"

There was no way around it. He wasn't clever enough to come up with a lie that would make sense. So he told her the whole story, from finding the book all the way up to his and Matthew's failed attempt to cleanse the apartment and douse Spartacus with holy water.

"Estupido!" she spat out. "Just where did you expect the spirit to go, if you managed to chase it out? Downstairs to one of those sweet little girls?"

She normally had a somewhat harsher view of the "sweet" teenaged Rojas daughters, but Alejandro got her point. The spirit could easily have attempted to possess the next unprotected animal or person it came into contact with. "We were trying to chase it out the window," he said, realizing how lame that sounded.

"Tu eres un idiota!" Abuela told him. "Don't do anything more! You'll just make it worse. I'm coming over."

Chapter Eight

MATTHEW FOUND a pair of shorts for Alejandro so he wouldn't have to face the Wrath of Abuela in his boxers, and the two of them spent the next few minutes straightening up the rest of the living room. It didn't take Abuela long to get there, considering she normally walked pretty slow and the botanica was a few blocks away. When she knocked, the boys exchanged worried glances before Alejandro opened the door.

She stood on the landing, a tiny old Latina in a cerulean-blue blouse and pink slacks, clutching a worn, woven handbag, and scowling enough to wither the houseplants. She ignored her grandson, marching past him and directly into the living room, where she peered down at Spartacus.

The pit bull had quieted again, but he was still panting heavily and salivating. He looked ill.

"Poor boy," she told him, her voice surprisingly soft. "We'll make you well again, sí?"

Then she turned to Matthew, the stern mask falling back into place. "Close the window and draw the shades. It must be dark."

While he hurried to obey, the old woman ordered Alejandro to bring her a wooden chair from the kitchen so she wouldn't have to strain her bad knee kneeling on the floor. Then she handed him several black candles in small jars and some old-fashioned wooden matches. "Light these and place them on the floor in a circle."

Alejandro did so, forming the circle between his grandmother and the dog crate. Spartacus growled low in his throat whenever Alejandro got too close, but otherwise he remained quiet, as if fascinated by what Abuela might be up to.

Maybe he is, thought Matthew. *Or at least, maybe the spirit is.* The thought of something sinister watching them from behind Spartacus's eyes made him shiver.

Under Abuela's direction, Alejandro drew a pattern on the floor inside the circle of light created by the candles. He used white cornmeal to create the lines, and the pattern was one Matthew didn't recognize, though it looked similar to veves he was familiar with. When it was done, Abuela pulled a small glass bottle from her bag. It had a wide mouth and was filled with brand-new shiny nails, dried leaves of some thorny plant, and some gray-green spidery substance that might have been Spanish moss. The bottom had some kind of powder in it.

"What is that?" Alejandro asked quietly, but his grandmother shushed him with a curt gesture.

"Put this in the middle," she said, handing him the bottle. Then she took a small bottle of Jack Daniels and a cigar out of her handbag and set the bag on the floor. "Now help me up."

When she was standing, Abuela lit the cigar and began to sing, stopping now and then to puff on the cigar and lean down to blow the smoke at the bottle on the floor. Matthew could only hear bits of the song, since she was singing softly, half under her breath. It was in Spanish, of course, and what little bits he could catch seemed to be cajoling, calling the spirit to come drink and smoke with her. Once in a while, she would take a sip of the Jack Daniels—which shocked him, since Abuela never drank, as far as he knew—and then she would sprinkle some of the whiskey down onto the bottle.

Matthew crouched off to the side of the ritual circle, opposite Alejandro, and kept silent. He had no idea what was going on, but he knew interrupting would probably be extremely bad. In the flickering candlelight, Alejandro seemed to be watching his grandmother with rapt attention, and when Matthew dared to look at Spartacus, he was surprised to find the dog lying with his massive head on his paws, looking at the candles through half-closed lids, as if he were falling asleep.

Suddenly the room seemed to darken, and Matthew felt as if he was having trouble breathing. He looked at Alejandro in alarm and saw fear flicker across his face. Was something going wrong? The candle flames sputtered and appeared to be about to blow out. The smoke in the room was so thick, Matthew thought he was going to suffocate or vomit or both.

But Abuela remained calm. She continued to sing, slowly bending down to get close to the circle. Then with a single, swift motion, she reached out and shoved a broad cork into the opening of the bottle. She smiled slyly and said with a chuckle, "Got you!"

The air immediately felt lighter. It was still full of cigar smoke, but Matthew no longer felt as if he was suffocating. Nevertheless, he was relieved when Abuela told Alejandro, "Open the windows and let some light in. It is done."

A whimper came from Spartacus's crate, and Matthew turned to see his dog pawing at the floor and whining, the way he always did when he wanted to be let out. Matthew leaned closer, not yet daring to hope the ordeal was over. Spartacus looked up at him, tired and bedraggled, but his eyes finally clear. He barked once—not a ferocious sound, but the sound of a dog greeting his master—and wagged his tail.

"Spartacus!"

"I think he wants to come out," Abuela said behind him, her voice full of warm humor.

Matthew fumbled with the bolt on the crate, and Spartacus came charging out at him. But there was nothing savage in his "attack" as he bowled Matthew over onto the floor and began licking his face. "Ugh! You're drenched in spit! It's disgusting!"

But Matthew couldn't stop laughing, even though his eyes were brimming with tears.

TO ALEJANDRO, the sight of Matthew rolling on the floor with Spartacus, laughing after a night and morning of pure hell, was the most beautiful thing he'd ever seen. He wanted to join in their roughhousing, but his grandmother had other ideas.

"Where is the book?" she asked him, tapping the cigar out on the side of the whiskey bottle. She was scowling again.

Alejandro wasn't sure, but Matthew had said it was in the closet by the front door. He didn't feel like disturbing the happy reunion going on at the moment, so he walked over to the closet and peered inside. Up on the top shelf, he could see a spot in the corner where some packaging was half buried underneath hats and mittens, so he reached up to pull it out. Before he touched it, he asked his grandmother, "Is it safe now?"

"Sí."

He could tell that the moment he touched it. The sense of foreboding was gone, and when he removed the box from the shredded packaging and opened it to touch the book, the pages no longer felt greasy. They felt like dry, brittle paper.

He brought the book to his grandmother and held it out to her, but she made no move to take it. "Burn it," she said, her voice dripping with contempt. When Alejandro hesitated, some part of him still reluctant to destroy something so old, so rare, she added, "You can read parts of it, if you absolutely have to. It won't do you any harm now. But I won't have it in my house, and I doubt Matthew wants anything more to do with it."

"No!" Matthew affirmed from his spot on the floor. He was scratching Spartacus behind the ears, the pit bull lying against his leg, half asleep from exhaustion but moaning contentedly at his master's touch. "I don't ever want to see that fucking thing again."

"Okay," Alejandro said.

He took it outside to the barbeque grill in the tiny backyard of the apartment building, intending to set it on top of the grill. But he changed his mind. Abuela was probably right about it being harmless—she would know, if anyone would—but the thought of putting it on a grill used for cooking hamburgers and hotdogs bothered him. He pictured the building being plagued by an outbreak of cursed cheeseburgers. So he laid it on the dirt in a corner of the yard instead, digging a small pit for it.

He flipped through the pages one last time, seeing invocations to the devil, curses for enemies, spells for forcing someone to love you or forcing them to leave their lovers, and then he closed it and doused it with charcoal starter. He lit a match, tossed it onto the book, and watched it go up in a ball of fire. He sat there for a long time watching it burn, dousing it with more charcoal lighter whenever the flames seemed about to go out. He made sure not a single scrap of paper was left unburned.

Then he buried it.

Chapter Nine

IT WASN'T easy to get into a cemetery in Manchester undetected at midnight. There were lights everywhere and cop cars patrolling the streets that bordered the low walls, on the lookout for vandals. But Matthew and Alejandro were teenagers living in one of the low-rent neighborhoods of the city. They were used to being regarded with suspicion, especially at night. And they were experts at dodging patrol cars.

Abuela had sent them on this mission. "Someone, a long time ago, bound this spirit to the book. Maybe to guard it—to keep fools like you two from messing with it. The spirit was a dead man with a troubled conscience. A criminal. Maybe a murderer. I lured it into the bottle, but now you must finish the job. Take it to the cemetery and bury it. And give the spirit some peace."

Matthew didn't really care much for giving the spirit some "peace." As far as he was concerned, the spirit could damn well suffer for what it did to Spartacus. But if this would get the goddamned thing out of his life forever, he'd go along with it.

They'd gone to the Elliot at River's Edge, the new urgent care center, to get Alejandro's arm seen to that afternoon. He wasn't going to die, but he'd definitely have some scars. The doctor had forced him to take a rabies shot, since Alejandro couldn't exactly tell her he knew the dog that'd bitten him wasn't infected. Matthew knew he wouldn't go back for the remaining four she wanted to give him.

He was still in pain, so Matthew had to do most of the work that night, digging the hole with a garden trowel. It wasn't actually in somebody's grave, but at the base of a tree, and Abuela had insisted it be three feet deep. The bottle was still corked, of course, and she'd threatened to kill both boys with her bare hands if they let the cork slip out. Matthew placed the bottle in the hole and buried it while Alejandro kept lookout.

When it was done, Alejandro recited some prayers his grandmother had taught him and placed a coin on the makeshift grave for the watcher of the cemetery, payment to keep the spirit there.

On their way out, a patrol car drove by, forcing them to duck down behind the stone wall at the boundary of the cemetery. While they were crouched, their heads close together, Alejandro whispered, "I'm sorry."

"You already said that. About ten times."

"I'll never be able to say it enough."

"Oh, stop it," Matthew said, reaching one hand up to cup behind Alejandro's neck. The affectionate gesture wasn't something Matthew would normally have done, but the past twenty-four hours seemed to have changed the boundaries a bit. "I shouldn't have left the package on the bed for Spartacus to tear apart. If it had just been a rare book, I'd be the one apologizing."

He moved to take his hand away, but Alejandro reached up to hold his wrist. Their faces were incredibly close together, and in the moonlight, Matthew could see the pain in his friend's eyes. Alejandro wasn't able to accept forgiveness this way—not through mere words. So Matthew leaned forward and forgave him with a kiss.

He would never have done it if he'd allowed a moment's thought before acting. There were a million reasons why kissing Alejandro could be the worst idea ever. A surge of panic rose up in him, and he tried to pull back, but it was too late. Alejandro enveloped him in his arms and practically devoured his mouth. The feeling of panic gave way to shock, and then slowly, tentatively, to joy. The feel of Alejandro's lips was softer than Matthew had imagined they would be, and so wonderfully warm. With their faces pressed together, the familiar scent of Alejandro's skin—musky, and smelling faintly of Ivory soap and the inescapable spice of Florida Water—overwhelmed him and filled him with a sense of coming home.

There was an odd light, somehow growing brighter, until Matthew realized someone was shining a flashlight down at them. A man's voice said gruffly, "All right, you two. Get up here where I can see you. I hope, for your sake, you've got pants on."

Shit.

They broke the clinch and stood awkwardly, blinking into the flashlight. The policeman was standing on the other side of the wall. If they'd really wanted, they probably could have made a break for it into the cemetery. It would have taken him a few seconds to get over the wall and come after them. They'd probably have been able to outrun him.

But when he said, "Come out here onto the sidewalk," they obeyed. The wall was only waist high, so it wasn't hard to just climb over it. The policeman turned the flashlight off once they were on the sidewalk in front of him, and Matthew could see that he was young—probably in his twenties. He didn't look threatening. More amused.

"Okay, I know doing it in a cemetery is a turn-on for some people, but it's public property. It's also locked up after dark, so you shouldn't be in there anyway."

"We weren't 'doing it,'" Alejandro said sullenly.

He had a tendency to mouth off to cops, teachers, anyone in authority—except for Abuela—and Matthew was afraid he'd get them into even more trouble than they were already in. But the policeman just nodded, as if conceding the point.

"Tell you what," he said. "If you promise to find someplace where you're not trespassing before you get back to whatever you *were* doing… we'll just call it good."

Alejandro looked like he was about to say something unpleasant, so Matthew jumped in. "Sure. Okay."

"All right," the policeman said, smiling and turning away. He didn't even bother asking their names. "You two have a nice night."

ALEJANDRO FUMED the entire walk home. The best moment of his entire life! Ruined by a cop! *Figures.* Gradually, though, it dawned on him that Matthew was still there, walking beside him. Maybe the best moment of his life wasn't *entirely* ruined.

"So…," he said, not sure if talking about it was a good idea. But he kind of had to. "Do you want to be my boyfriend now?"

"I guess so."

Alejandro stopped walking, unsure whether to feel elated or crushed. "You don't sound very enthusiastic."

Matthew turned back to him. They were in the shadows between streetlights, so it was hard to see his face. "We've been best friends for so long, it feels like my entire life. And I've been in love with you for just as long. You have no idea how desperate I've been to tell you I love you—"

"I think I know."

Matthew stopped for a second, as if he had to absorb that. Then he continued. "What if it all falls apart now? What if we break up and can't stand the sight of each other? I don't know if I could deal with not having you around anymore."

Alejandro stepped forward and put his hands on Matthew's waist, feeling the heat of his skin through the thin T-shirt he was wearing. "I'm scared of that too. But I know I love you—"

"I love *you!*"

"—and right now it's feeling like a good thing."

Matthew leaned closer until their foreheads bumped together and Alejandro could feel his soft breath on his face. "Yeah."

MATTHEW'S MOTHER had come back to the apartment earlier in the evening, after she'd gotten off work. She'd immediately insisted upon opening all the windows, saying, "What on earth happened while I was gone? It smells like a whorehouse in here! And were you *smoking?*"

Matthew had told her Abuela had come over and smoked a cigar, which killed any further discussion about it. Nobody told Abuela she couldn't smoke a cigar, if she wanted to.

Now, as the boys let themselves into the apartment, everything was quiet. Mrs. Shaw had long ago gone to bed. Of course, the moment he noticed the door opening, Spartacus launched himself at Matthew.

Spartacus was still a bit worn out from his ordeal, so rather than a full-on assault, Matthew merely had to deal with being circled and licked to death. Alejandro received the same treatment, and both boys ended up on the floor for a few minutes, nuzzling the beast. Matthew had cleaned him up that afternoon, so Spartacus was more or less back to normal now.

He would have nothing of being locked out of the bedroom, however, so Matthew had no choice but to let him in. Spartacus immediately jumped on the bed and curled up in his usual position at the foot of it.

"So much for a night of hot sex," Matthew muttered as he closed the door behind him.

Alejandro stood by the bed as he slipped out of his shirt, revealing the same lean, muscular chest Matthew had seen a million times before… though somehow it seemed much, much sexier now. "I suppose we can wait on that," he said, laughing. "As long as I get to hold you tonight."

Matthew approached him and ran a hand down his sternum, following the faint trail of dark hair that started there, down over the contours of his taut abdomen to hook his fingers into the waistband of his jeans. "Naked?"

Alejandro growled quietly, a low, lustful sound that made Matthew's cock swell. "Naked would be good."

JAMIE FESSENDEN set out to be a writer in junior high school. He published a couple short pieces in his high school's literary magazine and had another story place in the top 100 in a national contest, but it wasn't until he met his partner, Erich, almost twenty years later, that he began writing again in earnest. With Erich alternately inspiring and goading him, Jamie wrote several screenplays and directed a few of them as micro-budget independent films. He then began writing novels and published his first novella in 2010.

After nine years together, Jamie and Erich have married and purchased a house together in the wilds of Raymond, New Hampshire, where there are no street lights, turkeys and deer wander through their yard, and coyotes serenade them on a nightly basis. Jamie recently left his "day job" as a tech support analyst to be a full-time writer.

Visit Jamie: http://jamiefessenden.wordpress.com/

Facebook: https://www.facebook.com/pages/Jamie-Fessenden-Author/ 102004836534286

Twitter: https://twitter.com/JamieFessenden1

By JAMIE FESSENDEN

Billy's Bones
Bones (with B.G. Thomas, Kim Fielding, and Eli Easton)
By That Sin Fell the Angels
The Christmas Wager
Dogs of Cyberwar
The Healing Power of Eggnog
The Meaning of Vengeance
Murder on the Mountain
Murderous Requiem
Saturn in Retrograde
Screwups
Stitch (with Sue Brown, Kim Fielding, and Eli Easton)
We're Both Straight, Right?

Published by DREAMSPINNER PRESS
http://www.dreamspinnerpress.com

UNINVITED

B.G. THOMAS

IT WAS bad. It was really bad. It made me wish the cop had ignored my press badge (like they often did) and refused to let me go in.

He'd grinned at me—"Ah, what the hell. Go on."—and motioned me past.

That's weird, I thought.

That's when I saw why.

Fuck! I looked away, felt my Egg McMuffin try to return to the open air, and forced it to stay down. I would have been a laughing stock—the cops would *never* forget it.

Remember the Hindenburg, I said to myself. *Remember the Hindenburg.* My mantra.

I took a deep breath, stepped closer to the nightmare. An officer moved to block my way—

"It's okay," said the first cop to his buddies.

—and I raised my cell phone and took a picture. Took several. I wasn't much of a photographer and had to make sure I had some good ones.

Good ones! Ha!

I shuddered and turned away. That was when I saw the words, written in blood, on one white wall. "TO SERVE BARON MANGE KEY," it said in big, bold capital letters. *Fuck!*

The victim had been laid out over some kind of large, low table, his limbs tied to the legs. His face had been painted with a skull and his chest cut open from throat to navel. I knew because the dude was naked. There was... *something* on the man's penis. I hadn't wanted to look too close. The blood had been enough. There was a lot of it. Everywhere.

"Jesus," I muttered and once more ordered my breakfast sandwich to stay put. *Remember the Hindenburg,* followed immediately by the thought, *Thanks loads for the tip, Brookhart.* Brookhart being the cop who had called me and told me to get my "cute butt down to the Heritage Hotel right *now!*" It was okay for her to say that because she's a lesbian and I'm gay—part of the reason we'd connected about a year before. I'd been bashed, and she and her partner had shown up, and I'd gotten far more sympathy than a friend of mine who had once had the same thing happen. Luckily *I* hadn't had to go to the hospital.

"Taylor! There you are."

I jumped as if I'd been goosed, spun around, and looked up, and up, to see Dt. Brookhart looking down at me with those big dark eyes of hers. She was tall at, well, any height compared to my five five. "You're letting your hair grow, Daphne."

She reached up and touched her short, natural waves as if surprised they were there. "Not really." They weren't much longer than a few inches.

"Where's Detective Asshole?"

She gave me an amused smile and an arch of one of her wondrous brows. She swore she didn't pluck them. I didn't believe it. "He's looking for something." She pointed at the body. "Nice, huh?"

I shook my head and saw the open chest in my mind's eye. The McMuffin gave me a cheery wave and let me know it would still be glad to let me taste it a second time. *Just as good the second time*, it told me.

Stay! I ordered. "No," I told her. "Not nice at all."

She smirked.

"What's it about?"

Brookhart shrugged, always sure not to commit. I was a reporter, after all. Sort of.

"Not for me to say. But if I were asked off record...."

I rolled my eyes. "Off record."

"*Then* I would say it looks like a ritual killing of some kind. Witches, Satanists, I don't fucking know. Did you see the chicken head?"

"Chicken head?" *Chicken head?*

"Tied to his willy."

Willy. Oh my God. The *some*thing on the man's penis.

"Rooster head, actually," she replied matter-of-factly, like it was an everyday occurrence. "Cock on a cock."

"Cute," I said.

"I don't ever think they're cute. But hey, what do I know?"

"What can you tell me about the vic?" I asked, trying to sound cool and televisiony.

Brookhart turned and looked back at the bloody disaster. "His ID says he's Douglas Brightwell—*don't* use his name."

"Daph!"

Those lovely brows of hers came together in a dark slash. She hated it when I called her "Daph."

"Daph is too cute," she had told me more than once. She wasn't "cute."

I thought she was okay, but hey, what did I know?

"*No name!*"

I sighed. "Fine."

She nodded. "Married, father of three. He's in town for a business convention. Or he was. Six two, two hundred fifty pounds, more or less, most of that muscle. Whoever cut him open was determined."

God, I thought, looking away. *That* was an image.

"And they cut out his heart."

"Heart?" I snapped my eyes back in her direction.

She nodded, expression totally neutral. "Yup. We haven't found it yet either. But there's a lot of other shit. Feathers everywhere. Chicken bones. Bottle of rum, most of it gone."

"Drunk killer?"

She shrugged again. "Oh. And there's a bucket. Full. Of blood."

"With *blood?*" I actually *felt* my own draining from my face.

"Like in *Carrie*, but they left it behind. No prom queens need worry."

"Funny," I said. God. Chicken bones. Bucket of blood. Missing heart. "*Why* did you call *me?*"

"Are you tired of covering pet parades and gay pride, or not?"

"Yeah." I sighed, then nodded. "Tired."

"Then I suggest you get another couple of pictures before the chief gets here—which should be in about thirty seconds—and get the story to your boss before Chadrick or Rockower get a whiff of this." She cocked a thumb over her shoulder in the direction of the corpse.

Chadrick and Rockower were two of the *Chronicle's* "star reporters." And they would get a "whiff" of this soon—and try to steal the story. *My* story, if I had any say. I nodded, swallowed *hard*, and darted back to the body to take more pictures. There was a coroner there now, peering down at the man's face. And Brookhart's partner, Dt. Asshole, was there as well, arms crossed over his chest, the scowl on his ugly face making him even less attractive than usual.

"Well fuck me," the coroner said suddenly.

"What?" said Dt. Asshole (aka Townsend).

"There's a statue in this guy's mouth."

"A statue?"

"It's a goddamned Virgin Mary," the man said, apparently totally unaware of the blasphemy in his choice of words.

I gulped and keyed that info and a few more sentences into my phone, attached the pictures, and hit the send button.

Twenty minutes later, I was sitting in my boss's office.

LOOKING AT my pictures on Mencken's computer wasn't quite as bad as seeing the real thing. That's when me and the boss saw that, yes indeed, there was a rooster's head tied to the man's impressive genitalia—

"Not that that's going to do him any good any longer," Mencken said and took a gulp from his mug of coffee.

—and that yes, there was a bucket filled to overflowing with what *appeared* to be blood.

"Never assume anything," the boss liked to say, and then he'd finish the cliché with, "It makes an ass out of you and me."

"You" in this case meaning the reporter, and "Me" meaning the *Chronicle*. Making the *Kansas City Chronicle* look asinine was verboten.

Besides the chicken head and the blood, there were feathers—lots of them—more blood—even more of that—and more Catholic statues— a Saint Francis and a couple I didn't recognize, having grown up in a household where my mother told me that all Catholics were going to hell for "worshipping idols." I knew that wasn't true because I dated a guy briefly who liked to describe himself as a "recovering Catholic." He was a sexy Irish guy who assured me that "Nah. We don't worship Mary. *Really.*"

Speaking of the Virgin Mother: "And you say there was a Mary statue in his *mouth?* I'm just trying to picture that. Since there *is* no effing picture." The word "effing" was Mencken's way of not swearing. He was a big man who looked a lot like Lou Grant, but not quite as heavy, and he had a full head of dark, badly styled hair. His tie had been pulled loose, and one of the duties of his secretary was to remind him to tighten it whenever he had to meet with someone important. Apparently I wasn't important.

"Look, I was lucky to get the pictures I did," I told him. "The Chief came in just as I was leaving, and the coroner wasn't letting me any closer than I already was."

Mencken made a raspberry. "It couldn't have been very goddamned big, then. I mean. In his mouth?" He was toggling back and forth between two of the better—read: focused and bloody—pictures.

"Well... it was...." The image came to mind again, and I was thinking that, if I was lucky, my breakfast was well past being able to make a personal appearance. "It was lodged down his throat." And when the guy pulled it out, it made the most horrible squelching noise. "It was about six inches long."

"They measured it or something?" Mencken asked, giving me "the eye."

"I *know* six inches," I said before I could stop myself.

Mencken's brows shot up, and then he shook his head and let out a half laugh. "I suppose you might." He looked at the pictures once more. Shook his head again. "I guess you think I should give you the story."

"I think you should," I said. "It was my contact that got me those pictures. Does anyone else have them?"

"I don't know if we're going to be able to effing use them! I mean, can you see this on the front page?" he asked, pointing to the rooster and dick photograph.

I shrugged. That was his decision to make.

"I'll give you till tomorrow morning to come up with something good. Otherwise, you turn over all you got to Chadrick."

No. He was not giving *my* story—my first *real* story *ever*—to fucking Chadrick! "You'll have something."

"Something *good.*" Mencken slapped his coffee mug down on his desk, and coffee swilled out. He didn't seem to notice.

I jumped up and headed for the door.

"Dunton!"

I spun around.

Mencken was leaning forward onto his desk with an intent look on his face.

"Yeah?" I managed.

"I know you can do this. You can write. You've wanted your chance. This is it. Let's see if you can write murder instead of bake sales."

I nodded and ran out the door.

WHICH IS why it made no sense that I met Gay for cocktails later that afternoon. Hey, I could stay up all night if I needed to, I reasoned. And martinis helped me write. As long as I stopped at two, three at the most, that is. Four is where I always forgot the end of the evening.

And yes, "Gay" is her real name. We laugh about that sometimes.

We met at The Corner Bistro, which was about ten blocks east of The Male Box, my usual hangout. It's not that Gay didn't like The Male Box—*au contraire*, she liked it a lot, and if it was karaoke night, her competition fled the bar. Or at least the stage. She was that good. But The Male Box was always one of two ways: dead and boring or loud and packed. There seemed to be no in-between. The Corner Bistro, on the other hand, was Kansas City's answer to a classy gay bar. And it was. Classy. Quieter. The waiters even had matching shirts, and ain't *that* special? The drinks were good too. They even had food—chichi stuff like calamari and crab cakes and stuffed artichokes. A little pricey, but always good. Gay was in the mood for chichi.

To my surprise she beat me there. Gay almost never beat me *any*where. It takes time to look fabulous, after all, and she was looking fabulous that afternoon, as usual.

Gay could have been anywhere from forty to sixty—it was impossible to tell. Her skin was all but flawless, there were only the tiniest lines around her eyes, and to look at her would put her on the younger end of that age range. But she would say things, mention events in her life, that would place her on the other end.

She was wearing a black-and-gray Chanel sweater dress that fell to just above her knees and a huge black hat with a white band that was straight out of *Breakfast at Tiffany's*. She wore black-and-white pumps, and, of course, there was her jewelry. When was Gay ever without her jewelry? Today it was gray freshwater pearls. Two long strings around her neck and matching bracelets and earrings. And then a huge crystal doorknob ring. Ostentatious, and yet she always got away with it. I asked her once why she wore such large stones, and she said, "Well, because most people are afraid of them, and I'm not at all. The bigger, the better." She wagged her eyebrows. "Wouldn't you agree, Taylor?"

She smiled her huge, perfect, white smile the minute I walked in the door, and her big brown eyes went wide, as if she wouldn't or couldn't be happier if I were Matthew McConaughey or Bradley Cooper instead of plain old short Taylor Dunton.

If I were a woman, she is the woman I would want to be. What's more, even though I'm not flashy like she is, she says I'm the man she would want to be. Not sure why, but she always says it's so.

"Hey, darlin'," she said without a trace of a drawl.

I went to her table, where she was perched on a high stool as if modeling for a magazine ad. I kissed her cheek. "You look gorgeous."

"Oh stop," she said with a girlish smile and a tone that meant she didn't want me to stop at all.

"Let me see that ring," I said and held out my hand.

She placed hers in mine. "You mean *this* old thing?" She giggled.

The stone wasn't quite the size of a doorknob, but it looked just like one of those old-fashioned ones like my grandmother had in her house in West Virginia. It had to be the size of a golf ball cut in half.

"Damn, girl." It was all I could think to say.

She dropped her head back, exposing a lovely white throat, and let out a long and delightful laugh. Heads turned. She laughed loudly, and there was nothing she could do about it. Gay was who she was.

A waiter arrived like quicksilver. "Good afternoon," he said with a flamboyant hand gesture.

He was very cute and *very* gay—he could not have passed for straight for love or money. Not that he needed to. I was just generally more attracted to men who were a little more, well, masculine. Please note I did *not* say "straight acting." God I hate that. Straight acting. What bullshit.

"I'm Dart," said our waiter, "and I'll be serving you today. May I interest you in a cocktail? Something to eat?"

Gay's eyes flashed. "Martinis?" she asked me.

"Of course."

She turned to the waiter. "Why, yes, Dart. You *may* interest us in cocktails. We'll have two martinis, *very* clean, three olives."

"Gin or vodka?" Dart asked.

Gay rolled her eyes. "*Please.* We want *real* martinis. Gin." She looked at me. "Tanqueray? Bombay? Do you have a preference?"

I raised my hands. "Whatever Gay wants."

"Gay wants *lots* of juniper." She turned back to the waiter. "Bombay Sapphire, please. And don't do more than wave the bottle of vermouth in the general direction of the glasses."

"Ah… okay," our cutie replied, and I could tell by the expression on his adorable face that he had missed the Winston Churchill reference completely.

She opened the little menu and pointed. "We'll have the hummus b'tahini as well and"—she glanced at me—"the steamed mussels?"

"Ummm, not today," I said. Not on a stomach that had been witness to what I'd seen. "How about their vegetarian spring rolls." Something without meat.

Gay sighed dramatically and nodded, and the waiter scurried off.

"Did he really say his name is Dart?" Gay asked. "*Really?*"

We laughed and then we talked. About life and jobs and her husband and my lack of one. We talked about the waiter's ass and how round it was and about the bartender who made our cocktails and what a hunk he was.

"I wouldn't kick him out of bed," Gay said and giggled.

"Not even if I had to listen to country and western," I added.

I waited for the second round of martinis before bringing up the dead body. We needed a bracer for that.

Gay's eyes went wide and wild. It was hard to tell if she'd gone pale—that's how creamy-white her complexion is. "Gee whiz," she said, never taking her Lord's name in vain. "How did you do it?"

"I remembered the Hindenburg," I said, and took a healthy swallow of gin with more gin.

"Ah," she said with a nod. She knew the reference and partook of a generous amount of her martini as well.

On May 6th, 1937, Herbert "Herb" Morrison was the reporter who covered the famous Hindenburg disaster. Everyone's heard it—or at least a version—at one time or another. "It burst into flames!"—"It's crashing terrible!"—"This is one of the worst catastrophes in the world." And of course him signing off the air because of "the humanity" of it all.

As the story goes, Herb was fired that day. Never go off the air!

Turns out, it's an urban legend. Herb left WLS on his own a year or so later and pursued a long and distinguished career. But the point is still there nonetheless. Cover the news. As a reporter for the *Chronicle*, it's my job to observe and report and *not* to look away. Of course, I had looked away, hadn't I? I guess pet parades and gay pride events hadn't prepared me for the sight of that man cut open from stem to stern. Could anything have prepared me for that?

I hadn't signed up for that.

But hadn't I?

Wasn't reporting the news what I wanted to do? Didn't I want to be the next Woodward and Bernstein? The new Judith Miller? One who doesn't go to jail, of course.

Would Chadrick or motherfucking Rockower have looked away?

I don't think so.

"Next time, I won't look away."

"You think the killer is going to strike again?" Gay asked.

I looked at her in surprise. Had I said that out loud?

But it was right then that I realized I *did* think there was going to be another killing, just like in the movies. I don't know how I knew, but I did. I was sure of it. Did I have a reporter's instincts after all?

"Yeah," I said. "I do think they're going to strike again." I downed the rest of my cocktail.

Gay waved the waiter over and held up two fingers, so I quickly grabbed the pick with the olives so he could take the glasses away. I popped one in my mouth.

"Brookhart seems to think it was witches or Satanists," I said through a mouthful of olive, staring into the nothingness over my friend's shoulder. I could see that body still. Horror movie special effects had nothing on the real thing.

"Oh, heavens no," Gay said and made a clicking sound with her tongue. Was she *tsking* me? "Not witches. I don't know about Satanists, but certainly *not* witches."

I opened my mouth to ask her how she might "certainly" know any such thing, when I remembered. She had a friend who was a witch. Gay might consider herself a Christian, but she had a very eclectic circle of friends. Hey, I was her gay best friend, after all.

"I knew her back in college when she was called Party Patty," Gay had told me one evening while we were soaking in her hot tub and drinking G&Ts. "*Now* she's *Patricia* the *Prairie* Witch." She made quotes with her fingers in the air over that last part. "I couldn't *believe* it when I saw her at Greta's little soiree." Greta was another of Gay's friends and a rival for who threw the best parties. "It was actually kind of funny. Apparently it was some kind of coup getting Patricia the 'Prairie Witch' to give a little talk at her party and perform a little *Beltane* ritual. So when Patty and I took *one* look at each other, screamed like college girls, and threw ourselves into each other's arms, I thought Greta was going to *shit*."

Gay wouldn't say "Jesus Christ," but she had no compunctions about using the word "shit."

"So I can tell you right now," Gay said as Dart delivered out fresh martinis and our noms, "that witches do *not* believe in human sacrifice."

Dart's eyebrows shot up and disappeared in his gel-coated bangs— I sighed and gave him a "don't ask me" expression—and he swiveled on one heel and flew away. Gay and I burst into laughter. And remember, Gay's laugh was not a quiet one.

When we settled down, she leaned across the little table, and in a conspiratorial tone, said, "Sounds a little closer to voodoo to me."

"Voodoo?" I snapped.

She tossed a shoulder. "The skull face. The chickens. Doesn't that sound all very *Serpent and the Rainbow* to you?"

I sat up straight in my chair. "Well, damn. It does, doesn't it?"

She nodded, delicately picked up a crab cake that was no bigger than a KFC biscuit, and took a bite.

Voodoo? Really? "In Kansas City? I mean, whoever heard of voodoo in Kansas City?"

Those eyes of hers got wide again. "Oh, darlin'. There's a shop and everything."

"Huh? A *voodoo* shop?" I couldn't believe it. KC was hardly New Orleans. "Where?"

She laughed. "Baby, walk out the front door, turn right, walk ten feet, turn right at the corner—walk, maybe twenty feet? Look to your left, and there it is. Right across the street."

"You're shitting me!" I looked at her, eyes agog.

"I shit thee not! I went in there one day to buy stuff for my little St. Patrick's Day party and got the surprise of my life!" She laughed nervously and rolled her eyes. "It's called Lucky Charms, so what did I know? I mean, it's got a four-leaf clover painted on the front of it. I walked in and saw not one *bit* of green! It was all candles and skulls and creepy little altars on every wall. My hair stood on end! It did!"

Voodoo? Here? In Kansas City? I couldn't be more surprised if it had been a church dedicated to the worship of Lovecraft's Cthulhu.

"Maybe you should talk to them." She nodded enthusiastically. "Yes! Of course you should. There's no 'maybe' about it."

Voodoo? I gulped.

"I'll go with!" She grinned.

"I thought it spooked you," I said.

"Oh, it did. It *does*. Quite a bit in fact. But I'll have you with me this time."

"I don't know...."

"Quick," she said. "Down your drinkie. We'll get a third round, and that should give us the courage to enter the lion's den!"

Good God. Was I going to do it again? Was it Lucy and Ethel on another ill-advised adventure?

Of course, if she was right—if the murder was some kind of voodoo sacrifice—what better place to get information?

But then again, it might also be a place to get noticed by a group of voodoo killers.

The gin won out in the end, and armed with liquid courage, we marched out the door of The Corner Bistro, ready to take on a zombie army.

BUT THE little shop, set back from the side street and looking ridiculously innocuous, would not get a visit from us that day.

Marching back and forth in front of the little cement block building was a small mob carrying signs and sandwich boards. Protestors. "God Will Prevail," and, "On Your Belly You Will Go." "Drive Out the Serpents," blared another, and, "Suffer the Witches to Burn!"

There was even a man standing on a folding chair and yelling to all who would listen. "And the great dragon was thrown down," he cried. "And the great dragon was thrown down, that ancient serpent who is called the devil and *Satan*, the deceiver of the whole world—he was thrown down to the earth, and his angels were thrown down with him!"

The man was incredibly handsome, as such evangelical types are wont to be. He reminded me of Aaron Eckhart, the actor who played

Harvey Dent in one of the Christopher Nolan *Batman* movies—I'm not sure which one. I mix the titles all up in my head. He was wearing a gray suit, of course, with a dark blue tie—I could tell that even from across the street—and I found myself hoping he was sweating his balls off. Not that he was. Preachers who knew they spoke *the* Word of God didn't seem to sweat, not even in a revival tent on a morning when it was already topping a hundred degrees, even in the shade.

I shook my head. I knew people like this. I'd seen them outside gay pride events.

I took pictures. I even recorded a bit of it.

And then Gay and I went home.

I was tempted to stop for one more martini. But four *is* where I always forget the end of the evening, after all, and I had a story to write.

I spent the rest of the afternoon and early evening researching voodoo online.

The information was conflicting. Different essayists and bloggers couldn't even agree on the spelling of the word. Besides "voodoo," there was also "vodou," "voudou," "vodun," "vudun," "Vudu," and hell, so many others. Even "hoodoo."

And yeah, Vudu was some kind of Internet service, wasn't it?

There was general finger-pointing as well, plus lots of "my-version-of-voodoo-is-better-than-your-version," just like with every denomination of Christianity I'd ever seen. The Haitians said the New Orleans version was a bastardization of real voodoo, and the New Orleans "vodouisants" seemed to stick out their tongue and bang their assons all the louder—assons meaning ceremonial rattles. There was Santería as well, and apparently it was very different, and practitioners of either didn't appreciate being lumped together with the other.

I couldn't find any real information on a Baron Mange Key, although there *was* a reference to a Baron Manjè Kè. I could only wonder if he was the same guy. There was almost nothing on him at all except that he was a part of the whole voodoo thing. He seemed to be someone you didn't want to mess with.

I found out that the serpent shouter was quoting from Revelation 12:9. It had nothing to do with voodoo or snakes or anything creepy like that. It was a total out-of-context rant that in reality had to do with the Roman Empire being the devil or some such thing. But hey, taking verses out of context seemed to be commonplace. My mother had certainly done a lot of it in her time. I don't like to read the Bible. Far too much of it had been pressed on me—read: shoved down my throat—when I was growing up. And Revelation had always been the most confusing and scary part of the whole damned book.

After reading all I could read about voodoo online, I headed over to Video Obsession and rented everything I could find. Luckily, Blockbuster hadn't killed the independent store—due mainly to the gay porn and movies like I was renting. *Voodoo Island. The Zombie King. The Skeleton Key. Isle of the Snake People. I Walked With a Zombie.* And yup, even *The Serpent and the Rainbow*, which was supposedly based on a true story. I watched them all night, drinking lots of coffee from The Shepherd's Bean, often with my finger on the fast-forward button. I only had to watch a small part of *The Believers* because it turned out that movie was all about Santería, and yeah, that was something different.

There *was* one powerful line from the movie though: "Name me one religion where atrocities have not been committed in the name of a god."

It made me think. What religion, indeed.

But still. Human sacrifice?

The Internet said *vodouisants* didn't practice human sacrifice. Of course, it also said Herb Morrison was fired for going off the air when he was covering the crash of the Hindenburg. So, what to believe?

Or maybe this murder wasn't voodoo, vodou, Vudu—whatever—at all? Maybe it *was* Santería after all?

I guess I was going to have to go to Lucky Charms.

So early in the morning, exhausted but pumped up on caffeine, I put together a story I hoped Mencken could tolerate and sent it off, along with an e-mail that said I'd talk to the owner of Lucky Charms.

"You read that right," I wrote. "Kansas City has a voodoo shop, and the only reason I haven't talked to the owner yet is because the protestors wouldn't let me by." It was a bald-faced lie, of course, but I had to say something he might accept.

Lucky Charms had a website—who doesn't these days?—and I knew they would be open at 11:00 a.m., and I planned to be there with bells and rattles.

After I got some sleep, that is. Although that turned out to be sleep filled with dreams of zombies and a strange-looking black man with a crow on his shoulder and a bright red heart painted on his face.

THERE WAS nothing about Lucky Charms that was anything like I expected. Even the building, which I could see, now that the protestors were gone, was rather uninteresting. It was a simple cinderblock, shoebox-shaped structure, the front a pale butter yellow color along with the store's name in large green letters that stretched from one side to the other. Someone had also painted a large four-leaf clover (the easier to fool Gay into looking for St. Patrick's Day decorations), what I *think* was supposed to be a rabbit's foot, a horseshoe (end's facing upward, of course), a lady bug (I wasn't sure why), a rainbow (gay friendly?) and a penny on the facade.

It looked nothing like Marie Laveau's shop in New Orleans. I'd stopped in front of it once when I had gone to Southern Decadence—the big gay version of Mardi Gras that often attracted as many as 125,000 people. I even peeked inside the place but hadn't gone in like some of my friends. The small, white, weatherworn building with the black shutters had creeped me out a little bit.

Lucky Charms, on the other hand, looked harmless. I could see how Gay hadn't realized what lay within. How many times had I passed it and not even noticed it was there?

The inside was nothing like the Voodoo (Vodou?) Queen's store either. Hers was small, almost tiny, and crammed to the rafters with all kinds of crap. Dolls, skulls, bags, candles, hats, oils and liquids, bones and herbs, and strings of beads, cowrie shells, and necklaces. The ceiling dripped with the stuff. But Lucky Charms? While it had some of the same stuff, it looked positively empty compared to Marie Laveau's House of Voodoo. It was two or three times as big, quite spacious inside, full of the light that came in through the big plate-glass window, and the interior walls painted even brighter than the outer. There were banners on the walls that reminded me a bit of those in the meeting hall of any church—nothing sinister about them. Common saints, it appeared, but with names like Ezili Danto, Legba, Marassa Dosou Dosa and La Sirene (although this last looked more like a mermaid than a saint).

The first third or so of the shop had some long tables and tiered displays with books, tarot decks, candles (including some shaped like men, women, penises, and female genitalia), soaps, and other novelties. On one wall was a set of shelves lined with tiny bottles of oil with labels such as Stop Gossip, Lavender Love Drops, Return to Me, Clarity (I could use some of that!), Cast Off Evil, Bend Over (I was dying to know what that was), Jinx Breaker, and my favorite, Bitch Be Gone.

Oh. And there were statues. Statues of Catholic saints. I still found that weird. The hair on my arms moved as I remembered the hotel room and the ceramic Virgin Mary figurine lodged in a dead man's throat.

I had just noticed a cabinet with little baskets filled with Charms! Only $5.99! when a man spoke. "Good morning!"

I jumped as if someone had snuck up behind me and shouted, "Boo!" and all but pissed myself. I spun around—

"May I help you?"

—and nearly gasped at the sight of the man walking toward me.

He was *that* guy.

He looked like he was in his late twenties, around my age. He was taller than me (of course), with a perfect olive complexion and short ringlets of jet-black hair that framed a breathtakingly beautiful face. His eyes were sparkling black, and my friend Gay would have killed for his dark, thick lashes. ("Boys aren't supposed to have such beautiful eyelashes! It's not fair!") His nose was large but not overly so—strong, I would say—and those lips. Christ! So full. *What must it be like to kiss lips like those?* I wondered.

I could see he had an athletic build, even in his baggy white islander shirt, and with the top buttons undone, it was apparent he had a smooth, probably hairless, chest. He was wearing what looked like a shark's tooth on a leather thong around his neck, and it seemed to point downward—or maybe that was just me grabbing an excuse to *look* downward. I had to force my eyes to stay on his beautiful face, those dark eyes, wide nose, and full lips.

He was gorgeous.

He was *fucking* gorgeous.

He was "that guy." That type I see at a bar and can't stop looking at and desperately want to approach, even buy him a drink, but never, ever actually have the nerve to do so. That guy I try not to stare at, but I can't stop.

Everyone knows "that guy."

And then, "that guy" spoke to me....

"Are you all right?"

Could it have been a worse question? What kind of total doofus was I in his eyes? And dammit, even his voice was beautiful.

He was looking at me with those eyes like polished obsidian, waiting—I could see he was waiting for me to say something—but the goddamned words wouldn't come out of my mouth. It was as if there were some kind of misfiring going on in my brain, and the thoughts weren't getting translated into actions.

Finally: "I-I, yes?" I felt a rush of heat travel up my face. *Jeez! Get your act together. He's just some dude.* "I'm sorry, but it's just…. You're…." *Watch what you're saying.* "Ah. You're… not what I was expecting."

"You were expecting Angela Basset, maybe?"

"Huh?" I so intellectually asked.

"You know. As Marie Laveau? From *American Horror Story*?"

"I've never watched it," I replied, finally able to speak. *American Horror Story* had apparently not been an offering at the video store.

"You should. It's *great*. Nothing like real life, of course—they got a lot mixed up. People got all bent out of shape about what they did with Papa Legba. Seemed to mix him up a bit with Bawon Samedi."

Bawon Samedi? Could he be any relation to Baron Manjè Kè, I wondered.

"Papa Legba would *never* kill babies. But I still *love* the show. Can't help it. I love to be scared." He grinned, and sure enough, he had perfect teeth, and those eyes of his flashed like summer lightning.

This is ridiculous. I mentally slapped myself. I was acting like a fool. "I think maybe I was expecting a crazy little old black lady."

"Well, I've certainly been called crazy," he said. "But I'm not a little old lady—although there is some African a few generations back."

That explained his lovely complexion. I would have to lie out in the sun all summer long to get that color.

"It was my great-grandmother. She married my Italian great-grandfather. It was *scandalous*, I guess." He waggled thick brows.

I nodded, at a loss for words once more. What did you say to that? That's nice? I'm sorry? Cheers?

"So you've never been in the shop before," said the pretty man. It was a statement and not a question.

I shook my head.

"I would remember if you had," he added.

He would? "Why?"

"Why what?"

"Why would you remember me?"

He laughed. Music. "I think the way you blush is adorable, for one thing. I would remember *that*."

My face blazed all the more. Was he shitting me? This guy was a salesman!

"You don't believe me, do you?" He winked, but with both eyes. Now *that* was adorable. Would that be more a blink than a wink? "Let me guess. You're in here looking for a *love* charm." The way he said *love* sent a jolt right to my crotch. "You want to find the *perfect* man."

He knew I was gay?

Well, of course he knew. He had to see I was practically drooling over him!

"Wow. You just blushed even more."

He did that blink/wink thing again, and I felt the heat rise up even more. I felt like my face was on fire.

"Look, ah...." My words started to tangle again, and I *forced* myself to talk—started by pulling my press badge out. My shield. "I'm with the *Chronicle* and—"

His expression transformed. I couldn't believe how quickly. Like a marionette with its strings cut, his shoulders slumped and his whole face seemed to fall. Those bright eyes stopped flashing, as if a light switch and been turned off. "Oh," he said quietly.

Even the warmth in his voice was gone. It was all business now. I was surprised how much I missed it.

He turned that intent gaze away from me and glanced around the room, put hands on hips, then visibly forced himself to look back. "How may I help you, Mr....?"

"Taylor. Taylor Dunton." I groaned inside. Had I really said that? Who *says* that? Except for maybe James Bond.

"Mr. Dunton."

Mister. Shit.

"I'm sorry to bother you. I just hoped... well... I...."

For Christ's sake, Mencken said in my mind (he wouldn't say "fuck," but had no compunctions with Gay's Lord's name). *Act like an effing professional! Are you a reporter or not? Stop thinking about how hot he is and do your job!*

I gulped. "I'm sorry Mr....." I trailed off as he had done.

"Parry," he replied. There were actors auditioning for the role of a Vulcan in a *Star Trek* movie with more emotion in their voices. And he'd given me one name, not two. Was it his first name or last?

"Mr. Parry"—he didn't correct me, so it must have been his last name—"there was a murder yesterday that looked suspiciously like—"

"Yes. I know. The police have already questioned me." His tone went from neutral to cold, if not hostile.

Really? Brookhart? But she'd said witches or Satanists. She hadn't mentioned voodoo at all.

Ah well. In for a penny. "I'm sorry about that. But it *does* look a lot like a—"

"What it looks like is another case of people not having a single clue what my religion is all about." He shook his head. "Prejudice. You people watch movies like *The Skeleton Key* and *The Serpent and the Rainbow*, and you think you know what we're all about. Hollywood bullshit."

I grimaced. That's exactly what I had done. "Along with *Isle of the Snake People* and *I Walked With a Zombie*," I admitted. "I'm sorry." I shrugged. "It wasn't just movies, though. I got online and—"

He rolled his (beautiful) eyes. "Let me guess. Wikipedia?"

I bit my lip, embarrassed. What kind of reporter was I? "Not *just* Wikipedia. I read a bunch of blogs...."

"We don't sacrifice people," he said quietly.

"*Vodouisants?*"

He closed his eyes and shook his head. Sighed. "I don't know *any*one who uses that word. *I* don't."

"Oh." I thought maybe at least *that* had been good. "Wh-what word *do* you use?"

"I am a practitioner of my religion."

"I—To be fair there's a lot of contradictory stuff out there," I said. "Even with the—" I almost said "*vodouisants.*" I cleared my throat. "Even among practitioners of voodoo. I didn't know what to believe. Hell. I don't know how to spell it. V-o-o-d-o-o. Or V-o—"

"In my house it is spelled V-o-d-o-u."

"Your house?"

"House. It's.... I suppose you could say it's like a denomination. Mine is out of New Orleans."

"Like Marie Laveau."

"Yes." Parry gave me one quick nod. So this guy believed in this stuff. He didn't look crazy. Normal clothes. No bones in his nose or ears, no doo-rag over his hair. There was nothing creepy about him at all. If I saw him on the street—or in a bar!—I would never take him for anything but a normal guy. A normal *gorgeous* guy.

"Some people don't like my denomination because I was not initiated in Haiti."

Really? "Is that a big deal?"

"Some people say so. Some say only Haitian vodou is real. That you have to go to Haiti to take your asson."

Asson. I knew that! "A ceremonial rattle?"

There was a flicker in his eyes. Was that a slight nod?

"It was given to you when you were, what? Brought into...." I shrugged, not wanting to say the wrong thing. "When you became a...."

"Houngan. *Ounsi*—a first-level priest."

I'd seen the word "houngan" as well. "So in *The Believers*, the human sacrifices...."

"*The Believers* is *not* vodou, it's—"

"Yes. Santería. Sorry."

Another flicker. This time he gave me a nod.

"Not all online research is useless," I said. "It points the way. It gave me background and then made me see I had to go to a source. So I came here. My boss sure isn't flying me off to New Orleans, let alone Haiti."

"Too bad. Because I was thinking of closing the store for a few days. Flying home myself."

"Home?" I asked. "Is that New Orleans or—"

"Yes. Remember, I wasn't initiated in Haiti."

"That doesn't mean Haiti isn't your home."

Parry smiled. Not that big smile that had sent lightning to my crotch, but it did make my heart flutter. "True. I meant New Orleans. I want to see my manbo. And when there's another killing, I'll be out of town—"

"And have an alibi. Smart." *And when there's another killing....* "So you think there's going to be another?"

"Of course I do," Parry said. "So do you. Isn't that why you're here?"

"I suppose it is," I replied. "If I found the killer, it would make my career."

"Well, it's not me." He put his hands back on his hips.

"Good."

"Good?" he asked. "Why 'good?'"

Because I like you, I thought—and very suddenly he was smiling again. Shit! Had I said that out loud?

"I'm sorry," Parry said. "It's just...."

"Just what?"

He sighed, relaxing. "You know how people watch the coverage of a gay pride parade and all the news shows is NAMBLA and men in leather chaps with their asses hanging out? And then straight people think that's all we're about?"

We're. So he was gay. I fought back a grin. "Yeah...." I did know. I surely did.

"It's like that. And I thought maybe you were doing the same thing."

I shrugged, gave a nod. "Sure. And maybe I am guilty. But now I want to know. Explain it to me?"

The left corner of his mouth turned up. "Over coffee?"

My heart sped up. "Sure." Coffee with this guy? You bet!

"I'm closing at five. Be here or be square."

"I can talk now."

He glanced out the big front window, and when I turned to look, I saw two vans pulling into the parking lot. "Thought you might want to avoid *them*. The protesters are back."

Shit. "I'm not afraid." I looked back up into those eyes of his. *Wow.*

"Thanks," Parry said. "But still. It'll be easier."

"All right." If he insisted. "Five."

I offered my hand, being sure to wipe my palm casually up my jeans leg on the way, the way Mencken had taught me—"Never offer a sweaty hand!"—and when he took it, a shock traveled up my arm. Our eyes locked, and it felt like he was looking right into my head. Who knew? Maybe he was. Could *vodouisants*—no, *practitioners* of vodou— do that? Vodou-do? I laughed and he joined me.

God! *Could* he read my mind? I trembled. It felt delicious.

You better get the hell out of here before you make a complete fool of yourself! Like I hadn't done that already.

I made myself turn toward the door—and my eyes caught on the baskets of charms. They had little signs next to them. Love & Passion, Blessings, Peaceful Sleep, Court Case. And.... Well, I'll be damned. Same-Sex Love. I reached in and pulled one out. It was a small ball of something tied up in a little piece of rainbow fabric. For something so small, it felt surprisingly heavy. "So, does this work, Mr. Parry?"

"Myles," he said. "I look over my shoulder when someone calls me Mr. Parry. And, yes. It works. Why else would I sell them?"

"Gotta keep the doors open," I answered. "This is vodou?"

"Hoodoo." Myles grinned. "We'll talk about it over coffee."

"It's a date," I said, and felt the heat travel up my face once again. *Date? Did you really say "date?"*

"It's a date," Myles echoed, and his eyes were flashing in that way of his.

I nodded, once more unable to talk. I held out the charm.

"On the house," he said. "I'll tell you how to take care of it tonight."

"O-okay." I shoved it in my pocket and fled before I really *did* make a fool of myself.

THE FIRST call was to Gay. I had to tell someone, and who else?

"You're kidding me!" she squealed.

"I kid thee not," I said, using one of her favorite phrases.

"You're going on a date with a witch doctor? Isn't that a little scary?"

"He's not scary." *Although there is a part of me wondering if he really can read my mind.*

"I don't know, baby. I don't think I could go on a date with a vodou-guy. I don't care how *hot* he is."

"And he *is* hot."

"Gee whiz" came her quick response. "This isn't all about you getting laid, is it?"

"Not *all* about," I answered. "Besides, he's not interested in me like that." *How could he be?* After all, he was *that* guy.

"Well, is it a date or not?"

"It's an interview."

"Over coffee?"

"Over coffee." Was that weird?

She harrumphed into the phone. "Well, just be careful, okay? I don't want to have to try and find you an exorcist. I wouldn't even know where to look for one. Nazarenes don't believe in exorcists."

"But they *do* believe in demon possession," I said. I knew. My childhood was filled with stories of Jesus casting demons into swine. I was—to paraphrase that long-ago-date's words—a recovering Baptist.

"They do," she said. "I'll be thinking about it. *You* be thinking about me not needing to think about it!"

"I promise."

The second call was from Dt Brookhart.

There had been another killing.

I jumped into my excuse for a car and made it there in record time. The chief of police beat me there, so I had to do my best to look invisible.

This one was at an old abandoned theater downtown, and I tried to figure out why that was tickling some back part of my brain.

She was laid out on the stage, and there were lots of candles and lots of feathers and lots and lots of blood.

Like the first guy, she was cut open, her chest wide, and it was all I could do not to faint. There was something horrible about her breasts, splayed to either side. I wanted to puke. *Remember the Hindenburg!* I tried and failed to convince myself. *Don't puke! Don't puke! Don't puke!* That worked. Barely.

And like the first time, there, on the wall, were the words: TO SERVE BARON MANGE KEY. Baron Mange Key? Who the fuck was that? Was he the mysterious Baron Manjè Kè?

Brookhart materialized at my side. "Stay in the background," she commanded. "I'll get you what I can." She held out her hand. When I looked at her, puzzled, she told me to give her my phone, and she used it to get me some photographs.

Wow, I thought. She really *did* like me, didn't she?

The information on the VIC turned out to be: Karen Overcamp, thirty-six years old, five six, one hundred forty-five pounds (which apparently is heavy, for God's sake), single. Her ID said she was from Weeping Water, Nebraska.

"Ever heard of it?" Brookhart asked, returning my phone.

"Never," I said. "Sounds small." I checked. "Yup. Population 1,050, according to the 2010 census. Looking for her on Facebook now...." What *did* we do before smartphones?

"Are you fucking kidding me?" she snapped.

"Here she is. And guess what?" I gave her a smirk. "She's in town for a convention."

Up shot one of her perfect eyebrows. "Interesting."

I glanced toward the victim, trying to hide behind the detective so the chief wouldn't see me. He hated reporters. "Is her heart gone?" I shuddered.

"You bet your cute butt it is."

I thought of Myles. Would he be brought in again? "You wouldn't be the one who questioned the owner of Lucky Charms, would you?"

Her other brow joined its twin. "What would you know about him?"

"Not much. Only that he was questioned. I was hoping it was you. He'd get half a chance that way."

She nodded. "Yeah. It was me."

"Witchcraft," I said with a huff.

"Witchcraft. Voodoo. It's all the same."

"No, it isn't," I said, as if I hadn't lumped a bunch of shit together only hours before. As if I had a vested interest. "You were throwing me off."

"I wouldn't do that. Didn't I just sneak some fucking pictures for you?"

So she had.

"So, like I said. What would you know about him?" When I didn't say anything, she rolled her eyes. "Oh, for Christ's sake. Are you *fucking* him?"

I laughed. "I just met him earlier today." Oh, and what I would do to fuck him!

"But you wanna."

Of course I did! "Think I've got a shot?"

Brookhart shrugged in that way of hers: with one shoulder. She ran a hand through her short waves. "I'm not really a good judge of that kind of thing. Gold-star lesbian, here. Still. I think you're cute. If I was a gay man, I'd do you."

And that was dedicated homosexuality if she could only think of having sex with me if she were a man. I laughed. Couldn't help it. The chief snapped his head in our direction, and I ducked. For once my height was an advantage.

"Is there a statue in her throat again?"

Brookhart grimaced. Shook her head. "No. Somewhere else."

"Where," I asked. She just locked eyes with me, then darted her glance downward, then back up. It took me a second. "God."

"God didn't have shit to do with it," she said with a scowl.

"Virgin Mary again?"

"It was a guy this time."

I supposed it made some kind of weird, freaky, hetero version of sense.

"I don't know saints any more than I know dick," she continued. "But I'll try and find out, if it makes any difference."

"It might."

She nodded. "I'll call you."

"I guess I can't use the victim's name?" I asked, forgoing the word VIC.

Brookhart shook her head. "But I'll call you when you can. Now amscray."

"You gonna haul Myles in again?"

"Probably."

"Can you be done with him by five?"

Those brows arched upward again, and she smirked at me. "I'll do my best."

"Thanks, Daph."

I amscrayed.

I couldn't amscray fast enough.

But I called Myles and warned him. It was the least I could do.

HE WAS waiting for me at five. Brookhart was good to her word, if she in fact had hauled him in. At least the protestors were gone.

"She took care of that," Myles told me when I asked.

"She?"

"Detective Brookhart. She even questioned me in the shop this time, while her partner went around and touched things. Even the altar. Can you believe it? The Lwa don't like their things bothered with."

I didn't know how to respond to that. There had been a lot of that the last two days, not knowing what to say.

Was I really cut out for this?

"I'm sorry about that. Townsend. I call him Detective Asshole."

"Good name for him. Of course, the police *do* like to play good cop, bad cop. Is she a lesbian?"

"You have to ask?"

"I never assume."

Mencken would approve.

"How about we go to The Shepherd's Bean?" I asked. "It's my favorite and they're open late tonight. We can even walk over."

"Sure," Myles answered. He checked the door of the shop to make sure it was locked. "Let's do it."

Oh, I could take those words wrong, I thought.

"So about your gris-gris," Myles said. He pronounced it "gree-gree."

"My what?" The word sounded familiar.

"Your charm," he replied, just as I was figuring it out.

I pulled it out of my pocket.

"You need to feed it if you want it to work."

I looked over at him and saw he was completely serious. No smile—no flashing eyes. "Feed it?" It sounded a little creepy. I suddenly remembered an old Karen Black movie that was made before I was born but was creepy as shit. She'd been chased around her house by a little doll with huge sharp teeth. The babysitter had shown it to me, and it was weeks before I could get in or out of my bed without leaping. The boom when I landed on the bare wood floor pissed Mom off every time. That babysitter never came back.

"Feed it," Myles said. "A tiny bit of rum—just a few drops will do. And some oil. I'll give you that. The Lavender Love Drops would be good. Then keep it on you, a different part of you depending on the kind of man you're looking for. Shirt pocket near your heart for love. Your underwear if all you're looking for is sex."

I looked at him again. Seriously? I waited for him to burst into laughter, but he didn't. "You believe in this stuff."

"Of course I do."

"Where do you get these things?" I held it up.

"I make them, silly."

Really? "Really?"

"You sound surprised."

What's in it? I wondered. "What's in it?"

"Mostly sand," he explained. "But herbs too. Sacred herbs. I grind them into the sand, then bag them up."

"And the gay Lwa like the rainbow flag?"

"That's mostly for you. If *you* feel the gris-gris is gay, the power is *gay*, then it is. It attracts a gay man to you."

"Hmmmm…." I looked at it. "Why rum?"

"The Lwa *love* rum," Myles said. "Maybe because Haitians love rum, and the Lwa are Haitian spirits."

"I see." I looked at the gris-gris, then stuffed it back in my pants pocket.

"Sex, then?"

I looked at him startled. Had he just asked me for sex?

"For your gris-gris. The man you want? You put it in your pants pocket. Next to your dick."

My eyes went wide, and *now* his eyes were flashing. "I—I…." Once more I was stuttering, and he burst into laughter.

Music.

"No, ah, no shirt pocket," I managed and pointed to my T-shirt.

"Ah!" A beatific smile spread across his face. "Then you are looking for *love*…." He drew that last word out a seeming lifetime, and I felt my dick stir.

"Actually, I'd like both," I replied. "Love *and* sex."

"*Very* good." Summer lightning in his eyes. "Then trade off. Next to your heart one day, underwear the next. And sleep with it under your pillow."

"What if I don't wear underwear?" I asked before my filter switched on.

He gave me that double blink, laughed again, and now there *was* a shifting in my underwearless jeans. "Me either," he said in a whisper. As if anyone were listening!

We'd turned onto the street for The Shepherd's Bean, and fifty or so feet later, we were there. There was a little courtyard of sorts out front, paved in old red brick, and lots of lights inside. Quite the crowd as well. Someone was singing—the entertainer with his back to the big plate-glass window, the audience in a set of chairs before him. We went in.

The man sitting on the barstool had a blond Mohawk of sorts, although nothing emo or punk. It was just fairly long on top and very short on the sides. He was really cute. I realized I was standing in front of someone, and I motioned for Myles to follow me to the counter. There was a Finca La Nube from La Perla, Ecuador, on the menu. "Cherry, lime, and subtle almond character," it explained. "Browned-butter thing going on too." It was a little pricey, four fifty a cup, but I'd pay at least that much for a cocktail, twice that for a martini at the Bistro, and the coffee would last longer. I ordered two from the barista with the big black plastic glasses. She was even shorter than me.

"I can pay," Myles said.

"Not this time," I told him. "It's the least I can do."

"Why's that?"

"Because I watched *I Walked With a Zombie*. And for calling you a *vodouisant*."

Myles grinned. "It's a *terrible* movie."

I gaped at him. "You've *seen* it?"

"Of course I have," he said and laughed that lovely laugh, like wind chimes.

Wind chimes, I thought. *Damn, I've got it bad. This is stupid!*

"My favorite part is when the woman in the white robe shows up. Scared the shit out of me when I was a kid. I laughed my ass off when I saw it all grown up. The things that scare us when we're little."

"Like the doll in that Karen Black movie."

Myles's dark eyes went wide. "*Trilogy of Terror?* No! *That* really *was* a scary movie!"

We got our coffee and went outside to sit at one of the tables under the shade trees. The entertainer was good, but we wanted to talk. Besides, the door was propped open, so we could hear him in the background.

It was a lovely October afternoon. Still warm enough that we didn't need jackets. I wasn't ready for winter. Of course, I never was.

We tasted our coffee. Excellent, as always. The Shepherd's Bean had turned me into a coffee snob. I went in there once to feast my eyes on the guy who owned the place, and upon finding out he was partnered, stayed for the coffee. At least he was gay. I liked spending my gay dollars on the community.

"So what did you want to ask me?" Myles leaned forward on the little round table. "I mean, besides, 'Did you do it?'"

"I don't think you did," I replied and took a sip of joe.

He tilted his head and gave me a shy look. "I'm glad. That could make things awkward. Later."

My heart bounced. Was he flirting with me? Hot damn! "Awkward?"

"Going on a date with a man who might be a vodou killer could be a mood-messer-upper."

"Date?" I squeaked.

"I thought we established that already," Myles said, and it was all I could do to keep from falling off my stool.

"I-I thought that was just a figure of speech."

He rested his chin in his upturned palm. "Why don't you ask me one of your questions?"

I gulped. Questions? Besides, *Are you a bottom or a top?*

I tried to make my mind work again. Stupid. *Ask him a question!* "Look. Why don't you tell me what vodou *is*, if it's not all that Hollywood stuff. If there aren't zombies."

"Oh," he said. "There *are* zombies—"

I felt a little shiver. I couldn't help it.

"—they're just not like what you see in *The Walking Dead* or anything like that. They're…. No. Let me back up. You want to know what vodou is."

"Yeah." I looked around me to see if anyone was listening. No. They were talking. If they were listening to anyone but each other, it was the singer inside the café. "Backing up sounds like a good idea."

Myles smiled that lovely smile. "There is nothing that *isn't* vodou. Vodou is the rhythm of life itself. It flows through and in and around every single act in the Universe."

"Like the Force?" I asked, and tried not to laugh.

He laughed for me. "Yes. A *lot* like that. Vodou *informs* all of life. It is the Divine nature within us all."

"I… I see," I said, not seeing at all.

"In vodou, we believe that there is only one God—Bondje, the Good God. But he is distant from his creation. So it is the Lwa that we turn to."

"The, low-ah?" I'd heard of them. Even before my online crash course. Wasn't that word used in every "voodoo" movie ever made?

"Yes. They're like saints, in a way. We call them the Mystères, or the Invisibles, and like saints, they are the intermediaries between Bondje and us. Like Catholics pray to the saints, we go to the Lwa for help, as well as to our ancestors. We worship God, and not the devil like Hollywood would like you to believe. There are no orgies, sorry, blood-soaked or otherwise. We serve the spirits—the *mistè*—and treat them with honor and respect, just as we would any elder in any home. Any family. And they help us. They *want* to help us."

I nodded. Okay. "Ah.... How does one become a voo*oo*—a practitioner of vodou?"

He looked off into space, got quiet. Took a drink of his coffee. "Well, in my case, the spirits called to me."

Called to him?

"First in my dreams."

"Your dreams?"

He looked at me, those black eyes now thoughtful. "Yes. It was Papa Legba who came calling—although I didn't know it at the time."

"Papa.... Leg-ba?"

That faraway look came back to Myles's face again. "In my dream I was walking along a road. It was night. There was this full moon, and up ahead, I saw that there was this man wearing this large, wide-brimmed straw hat, smoking a pipe, and leaning on a crutch."

My heart sped up, and not in a sexy way. "Was it scary?"

"No. Not at all. I suppose it would have been normal if I was—scared, that is. But I wasn't. Even when I got closer, could see him better. He was black, and there was this little cloud of smoke around his face, sort of hanging under the brim of that hat, like it was caught there before floating away...."

A slight tremble went through me. "So detailed...."

"It was *very* real. I woke when I felt this wet something hit my hand, and I looked down to see this mangy old dog nudging me to be petted, and when I opened my eyes, it was *my* old dog, Boo." Myles laughed. "I thought it was just a dream."

"Sure," I said. I'd had lots of weird dreams. Who hasn't? "When was this?"

"I was about twenty or so. I was in college. I'd been dating this hot little bear cub and I found out he was cheating on me, and it was all very *tragique*, *very* theatrical. God, that was ten years now. Losing our first love is *so* dramatic, isn't it?"

I nodded, remembering a beautiful, tanned boy at summer camp when I was in high school. The way he looked standing naked in the sun when he took me to the far side of the lake, away from everyone else. "Yeah. It was." God, I thought I would love him forever.

"Anyway, I drank a lot of rum the night I first had the dream. Didn't think a lot about it at first, but that image…. It kept coming back to my mind—that little cloud of smoke around the black man's face… the dog…." Myles took a drink of his coffee. "This is very good."

"I love their coffee," I agreed, happy for a respite so I could absorb all I'd heard. "I used to use sugar in my coffee, but you would have thought I'd asked them for rat poison the first time I asked for it here. The girl with the big glasses? She told me they didn't *have* any sugar. I couldn't believe it. She told me to trust her. I'm glad I did."

"Have you ever had New Orleans coffee?" Myles smiled. "With chicory?"

I shook my head.

"Now *that's* coffee where you use sugar. *Lots* of it, and tons of cream—real cream and not that powered nondairy stuff either. I'll have to fix you some next time."

Next time? My heart danced a little. I forced myself back to Myles's story. "So I take it there was more to your dream?"

"Yes!" Myles leaned back. It pushed his chest out against his shirt. It was a big chest. "Papa Legba came to me again. The next time I saw him, he was standing at this four-way corner and the street signs said weird things. Like 'awake' and 'living' and 'death.'"

"Death?" My voice cracked.

"But I wasn't freaked at all. I felt very safe. I told a couple friends, and they reacted so bad I stopped talking about it. Then one night I broke down and told a cousin—we'd been drinking, rum of course—and just as calm and collected as can be, he said, 'Well, it sounds like Papa Legba is trying to talk to you.' And I was like, 'Who is Papa Legba?'"

"Yeah?" *Exactly. Who is Papa Legba,* I wondered.

"Papa Legba is the guardian of the crossroads," Myles told me. "In Vodou, Papa Legba is always the first spirit invoked in any ceremony, because he is the go-between, the liaison, between the Lwa and us. He is the one who gives or denies permission to speak with the spirits of

Ghede. He opens and closes the doorway between this world and the world of the dead."

I froze. Dead. *Dead?*

He reached out and touched my hand. I felt a little chill. "It's not crazy," he said. "You just don't understand."

I shook my head. "No. I don't."

He shook his head. "When we die, we don't end."

"We don't?" Did he really believe that? "Because *I* kind of think we *do*. That when we die, it's all over."

"No, it's not."

I shrugged. "I used to believe that. But not anymore. My mom thinks there's going to be this big bad Judgment Day, and we're all going to go single file before God and he's going to check in this big book, like Santa Claus checking his list, to see who's naughty and who's nice. And if we're naughty, we're going to hell. Mom thinks *I'm* going to hell. And those people who are nice get to go to heaven and walk in the garden and talk to Jesus and finally find out what this—" I waved to the everything around us. "—what this was all about."

"She believes that because she's afraid."

"Afraid?" I couldn't think of a time where my mother had ever seemed afraid.

"Of dying," Myles said. "Because isn't that what most people are afraid of? That we all just end when we die?"

"Yes," I said. That was exactly what I thought. "And people like my mother are so afraid of dying that they find a religion that assures them that there is some kind of life after death."

"I take it your mother thinks you're going to hell because you're gay?"

I nodded.

"Vodou welcomes homosexuals. We make the prettiest altars." He laughed.

My eyes went wide.

"In fact, some say the Lwa Ezili Danto is a lesbian."

"So in your case, you just found a religion that says it's okay to be gay," I said, my filter once more failing to activate. "It's all the same thing."

"Maybe. But I've *experienced* things, Taylor. Things I can't explain. I've *seen* things. I've seen people ridden by the Lwa."

"Ridden?"

"Possessed. I've seen them do things that people can't do. I saw a man take hot peppers and rub them in his eyes and they didn't even water. He yanked his pants down and rubbed them all over his cock and balls. And when he came out of it an hour later, he was perfectly fine. Had no idea anything had happened."

I looked away. *Crazy.* It sounded crazy. It opened up too many possibilities. The least being that the peace I had made with myself by throwing out the possibilities of a "God" might have been hasty.

"And what about my cousin?" Myles held up a finger. "A guy I thought was Catholic, pointing me to Papa Legba? Here my cousin had been practicing vodou all these years, and I had no idea."

"Well, it isn't exactly a religion people have bumper stickers for," I said.

"W.W.P.L.D?" he asked.

I looked at him confused.

"What Would Papa Legba Do?"

I laughed despite myself. "Yes."

Myles leaned on the table again and stared into my eyes.

I felt my dick stir. I forced myself to look away.

"It could just be coincidence, you know," I said. "Your cousin being into voodoo."

"And my dreams?"

"You just read about this Papa dude once and forgot about it. Then you broke up with your first love and got drunk and had a weird dream."

"And the guy with the hot peppers?"

I turned back to him. "You *know* they were hot peppers? They could have been any kind of pepper. Did you touch them? Did you try one?"

"I smelled them," he said. "No way was I going to try one. I don't have the taste for hot and spicy like my grandmother. Her *étouffée* set my tongue on fire even when I was a kid."

"The guy could have switched them. Used sleight of hand."

Myles sighed. "Yes. I suppose."

"And the human mind is capable of some pretty weird stuff. There have been religious fanatics doing all kinds of wild things since religion was invented. Walking on hot coals, lying down on beds made of nails. And those Catholics who manifested the stigmata. Hands and feet bleeding. Hysteria. It doesn't mean that there is a God or that there is anything after we die."

I wound to a stop. Shit. *Why did I do that?* I wondered. Mr. Hottie was looking at me with sex in his eyes, and I had gone and acted like a fool. Talk about a mood-messer-upper.

"Well, Taylor. *I* do believe there *is* life after death. I know what I know. I know that through vodou. The other religions? They never interested me. My mom sent me to Sunday school when I was little, but she never went to church. She didn't care when I stopped going. And then... well then, Papa Legba. Less than a week later, I found a teacher—right out of the blue. I never looked back. It was like I had no real life before vodou. It was like before then, I was only waiting for my life to begin...."

Myles drew in a long, deep breath, smiled, and took a drink of his coffee. After what seemed like an hour, he turned back to me. "Above all, Taylor, vodou is about the spirits of your ancestors. Not only the Lwa, but our *personal* family dead. They're *there*. They see us and want to help us. The vodou religion is about keeping family *with* you, in your thoughts and in your heart. It's about preserving the love of family. Public ceremonies are for the Lwa, but for me, for practitioners, the most important spirits are always those of our family."

I bit the insides of my mouth. Closed my eyes. Forced them back open and looked at the sexy man sitting across the table from me. There was such passion in his eyes, in his expression. But a peace as well.

Had I ever seen my mother look peaceful?

Boy! What would she think if she saw me sitting here today? *Ha!* Not only with a man, but a practitioner of vodou! She would roll in her grave. Or in the grass of paradise, or wherever she was.

I sighed. Religious crap. "Have you ever been ridden?"

"Not by the Lwa," he said, and wagged his eyebrows.

I grinned.

"So the evil stuff. That's *all* Hollywood?"

He sighed. "Well...."

"Well, what?"

"Well, I'd be lying if I said that. It's like that thing about the news only covering NAMBLA—the North American Man/Boy Love Association. There *are* Lwa who run hot."

"Hot?"

"There are Lwa that are more forceful and ready to do violence. I don't have anything to do with them. Only the most trained should approach them. There is just no reason to call upon Bawon Kriminel, or Bakalou Baka, or especially Linglessou Basin-Sang. *His* name means Bucket-of-Blood."

I froze. *Bucket-of-Blood?* I thought about the buckets at the murder sites. "What about Baron Manjè Kè?"

Myles eyes went wide. "What do you know about *Baron Manjè Kè?*" He pronounced the name much more exotically than I had.

I gulped. "Just wondering?"

Myles shook his head. "I *wouldn't* wonder about the Heart Eater, if I were you."

Heart eater? Should I tell him about the missing hearts? Wait. He should know, right? It was in the papers. In my stories. Surely he'd read them?

"Are you hungry?" Myles asked.

"What?"

"I've got a lasagna I made last night. I could throw it in the oven—only take about an hour or so."

"Lasagna?" I asked stupidly.

"You were expecting maybe jambalaya?"

I grinned, suddenly feeling more at ease. "Maybe."

"My jambalaya's not bad. But my lasagna is better. And it's ready."

"Okay." I said. "And maybe I can have some of that New Orleans coffee?"

"That's for next time," Myles said with a flashing grin.

Next time? I returned his grin.

And with that thought in my head, and all too happy to stop thinking about a Baron who eats hearts, we amscrayed to Myles's apartment.

IT WAS a nice little place, a six-unit brick building a few blocks from Troost. The kitchen was tiny, as it was in most of the old apartment buildings built at the turn of the last century, mine included. But whereas mine was a disaster, his was an organized miracle. That he'd made something that I found as complicated and messy as lasagna in such a small area was a wonder to me.

"The secret is you don't cook the pasta ahead of time," Myles said. "You prepare everything the night before—layering like usual, meat, cheese, lasagna pasta—but you use the pasta dry. During the night, the pasta absorbs moisture from the sauce. None of it gets broken or shredded that way."

"Hmmm...," I said. "Of course, it's not a secret now."

"It is if you don't tell," he said and then shocked the shit out of me by kissing me. Not on the mouth, on the tip of the nose, but it was a kiss! *That* guy had kissed me.

While the lasagna cooked, and after he cut up some bread and slathered it with garlic butter and set it aside to pop in the oven at the last minute, he poured us a couple of cocktails—rum, of course—and we went out onto his balcony.

"You know, I'd never guess you were into vodou. You. Your apartment. It doesn't look the least... ah...."

"Vodou-ie?" Myles asked, giving me a goofy grin.

I shook my head. "Not the least bit."

"But you saw the saints?"

I stopped, turned around, and looked back through the glass doors. Had I?

"There's one right here," Myles said, and pointed to a small figurine on the ledge of the balcony. It looked a lot like a statue of the Virgin Mary, except she was black. "Our Lady of Czestochowa, the Polish black Madonna, represents Ezili Danto."

"The lesbian Lwa," I said.

"Exactly." His smile got bigger. "You remembered. Some people think of her as an evil spirit, all rage and anger. When she was alive, it is said she was instrumental in the Haitian revolution and that slavers cut out her tongue for what she did. But she is a loving mother and gives her children the strength to face any obstacle. She can be a fierce warrior, but she is a faithful protector and fights hard for her devotees. She is one of my patrons, and I've been praying to her a lot these last few days."

"I—I see."

"I can show you my altar if you want."

"That's up to you."

He looked thoughtful for a moment. "Maybe tomorrow," he said. "I have my reasons."

I didn't care what his reasons were. I just knew he'd used the word "tomorrow," and I was kind of hoping he was thinking what I was thinking.

We sat and chatted, about things vodou and non-vodou, and watched people walking their dogs—Kansas City was a very dog-friendly city. A man across the street worked on his glorious garden. Most of the flowers were done for the year, but he had some rose bushes that were going full guns and some tall purple daisy-like flowers that were a cool splendor.

I told Myles that the job at the *Chronicle* had brought me to Kansas City. After my mother died, I had to get out of Chicago. I'd been working at a small city paper in the suburbs, doing mostly human-interest stories, the feel-good kind. The ones that made you smile or cry happy tears.

"Not vodou-sacrifice stories," Myles said.

"People who practice vodou don't *sacrifice* people," I informed him.

His eyes flashed. "Really? That's good to know. I wouldn't want to sleep with a guy who might try to cut my heart out."

My heart pounded—in my chest (where it belonged).

I forced myself not to think about what he'd said and thought about something he'd said before instead. "Earlier. You were talking about being... ridden? By the Lwa?"

He nodded.

"But you never have been?"

"No," he said, a sad tone to his voice. "I've come close, I think. A couple of times. I was in a fete, a vodou ritual, and I was walking back and forth, and then my foot, my right foot, just suddenly *stuck* to the ground. I almost tripped. And I felt this... this tingling running up my leg, and I knew, *knew* it was about to happen, and I...."

"What?" I asked, gooseflesh running up my arms.

"I panicked." He sighed. "And it stopped."

"And you *want* that to happen? You want to be ridden by a Lwa?"

"Of course I do. I live for it. Wait for it. What a way to serve the spirits!" He went silent, and I had no fucking clue what to say to that. I was pretty creeped out, to tell the truth. "When they come through, when they ride someone, then they are able to talk to us, help us, give us advice."

"I see." God. It was starting to become more than I could take.

"So what made you want to do the crime stuff?" Myles asked me, suddenly changing the subject. "Why are you interested in vodou killers and all that stuff?"

"I'm tired of the bake sales and turtle races and stories about cops rescuing Chihuahuas off busy freeway medians. No one reads that stuff."

"*I* do," Myles said, leaning back and putting his feet up on the balcony ledge. He'd kicked off his shoes, and by Christ, even his feet were sexy. I'd never really been into toes before, but damn. There is an exception to everything. They were long, but not too long, and deep tan color, with just a bit of hair on each knuckle—nothing apelike. I found myself imagining all kinds of things I could do to them.

"Earth to Taylor?"

"Huh?" I jumped and looked into his face. Myles was grinning mischievously. "I'm sorry. What did you say?"

"I said I *like* those kinds of stories. I don't even *read* the news anymore because all it's about is war, and school shootings, and vodou serial killers." He shook his head. "I found the minute I stopped reading that stuff, my spirit lifted, and I was better able to face even the worst of days—like going in to work and finding protestors outside my shop."

"Don't you think we need to know about war and school shootings?" I said defensively.

Myles leaned backed and put his arms back over his head. "I don't seem to. I get through my day just *fine* without hearing about the horrible things human beings do to one another. Why doesn't the news cover more stories about cops rescuing Chihuahuas off busy freeway medians? *That's* the stories I would read."

"You know you're basically telling me that what I want to do is a waste of time, right?" I couldn't help but feel a little attacked.

Myles looked over at me. "Well, one good thing about your job...."

"What's that?"

"It brought you to me." And he leaned forward and kissed me. Not on the tip of the nose either. Right on the mouth.

And oh, those lips. Gentle at first, then quickly demanding my full participation, tongue asking for entrance into my mouth. I gave it and answered with tongue of my own. My cock shifted to full hardness, throbbing in my pants. By then his hand was cupping my face, and I was all but dizzy.

Myles pulled back. Then he kissed the end of my nose. And then the son of a gun leaned back in his seat again, head resting in his crossed arms, as casual as could be. As if he hadn't just given me about the hottest kiss of my life. He flashed me an innocent look. Except there was a decided bulge in the crotch of his pants as well.

I'm going to get laid, I thought. *With one of the most beautiful men I've ever seen.* For some reason, I flashed on that boy in summer camp—so dark brown from the sun. How his high, round ass was so white against the rest of his tan, tan skin, and how it was red by the time we had taken each other's virginity. How funny it was that he couldn't sit down that night (for more than one reason) and how fun it was when we snuck out of our cabin and down to the shower house, and I rubbed burn cream all over those solid, round mounds of flesh.

I wanted Myles. I wanted him that *minute*. Fuck the lasagna. It could burn to ash. And I'm not even the kind who jumps into bed with just any guy at the drop of a—no, who am I kidding? I *am* that kind of man. I am a *man*, after all. Men think with our dicks, even if we don't always do what they tell us to do.

And then there is the fact that I am a *gay* man. So no hetero flowers are required.

Plus, I'm thirty and fucking never had a boyfriend last longer than a few months, and goddamned if I know why. I'm a nice guy. *I'd* date me. And I'm not exactly a "ten," but I'm not ugly. Men don't pound on my door, but I don't exactly have to wait until closing time to get lucky either.

So if I can't get a man who wants to marry me, I've learned to settle for one-night stands. Forget about movies and popcorn. If I didn't pounce on opportunities, I'd never have sex. And isn't sex better than nothing? At least it's some human contact.

Yes. I wanted Myles. And I wanted him now.

"Later," Myles said with a knowing grin. "We have all night."

"Why?" I blurted, that echo still in my head.

Myles turned those dark eyes on me. "Why wait? Why, because you're adorable."

"Me?" I squeaked. Oh, he could say that all night!

He sat up and turned in his chair. "Yes, you. What do you think?"

"I think your gris-gris are worth a hundred times what you charge for them," I said happily.

"Does that mean I get you?" Those eyes were summer lightning again. I could hardly breathe.

"You had me at 'May I help you,'" I managed.

Myles chuckled. "I wanted you the second you walked in the door of my shop." He leaned in and kissed me again. Not like the last time, but not a kiss on the nose either. Then again, with just a touch of tongue. "I think you are so hot," he whispered. "I'm kinda hoping you have a hairy chest. I keep thinking I see a bit peeking out of the top of your shirt."

"Hairy chest," I whispered.

"What?" he asked.

"I—I have a hairy chest."

"Oh good," Myles said.

Somehow we made it through dinner.

And the loving was good.

I KNEW it was a dream. I don't know if I have ever actually been aware I was dreaming before, but this time I did. It was night and there was a clear sky and a full moon shining down on the road where I was walking. The air was full of night sounds. The *reeeeeeee*-reeeeee of crickets, the *chir*-up, *chir*-up of frogs, and even a deep echoing *hoo! hoo!* of an owl (which, if you have ever heard one, you would never think it sounds like the supposed questioning *who?* of children's stories).

Then, up ahead, I thought I could make out two people. There was a flash of fear, and then I knew who one of them was, and the fear went away. Myles. He was too far away to tell from sight—especially under the silver-blue light of the moon—but I knew anyway, the way we know such things in dreams. And as I walked, I realized who was with him. The man had a wide-brimmed hat and a wreath of smoke around his face. It was Papa Legba. They were standing at a crossroads (with street signs that said weird things, like "awake" and "living" and "death") and I found myself speeding up, not slowing down, compelled to get to them as quickly as possible.

Suddenly, I was afraid, but it was not of the two men waiting ahead—one of them my now-lover and the other a vodou saint. No. The fear was because of the something I suddenly knew was behind me. *Right* behind me. Close and getting closer. I wanted to turn, to look back, but I was too frightened. What if it was close enough to touch me? What if I tripped and fell?

Then the hand dropped on my shoulder, and I screamed and spun around....

It was the man with the heart-painted face. The heart was the bright red of the exposed chests of the victims I'd been forced to witness, over a face as black as a crow. In fact, as I watched, a crow landed on his shoulder—a shoulder heaped with a great lion's mane of dark dreadlocks. My heart was pounding so hard I thought it would explode out of my chest. The whites of his eyes were almost glowing in the moonlight, and his dark coat was open, revealing a massive, muscular chest.

That was when he smiled.

His teeth were huge and sharp. Like that horrible little doll in that movie. Like shark's teeth. I screamed again and…

…woke to the simultaneous buzzing of Myles's Intercom and the ringing of my cell phone. I watched him get out of bed and let out an involuntary sigh. His ass, which was amazing by candlelight, was pure athletic poetry in the morning sunlight that streamed through his bedroom window. This butt was the color of the rest of him, though. No white patches and no worries about sunburn. I'd have to find another reason to rub something on those cheeks. And there was a tattoo across his upper back and shoulders, which had looked like nothing but lines and a heart in the light from the candles last night, and now I could see was definitely a design—familiar but unique. A heart checker-boarded with lines and a knife or sword running through it the way lovers had carved hearts with arrows in the bark of trees all over the world since time out of mind. Was that snakes on either side or tildes, that wonderful little mark on my laptop's keyboard I loved to use instead of a dash?

Myles pulled on a robe, and I found my phone under the bed, and while I struggled to answer it—shit, it was Brookhart, I saw on the screen. Another killing?—he shrugged into a short robe and left the room.

"*What?*" I all but screamed into the phone.

"Hey!" Brookhart said. "*Easy!* I thought you'd want to be the first on site for the third killing. And you can take your time. The chief went to New-fucking-Orleans to track down a lead. Wants his picture in all the papers."

"I—I was… *busy*," I said, trying to remember where my jeans were. They weren't on the floor with my polo shirt. I reached for it. "Or was hoping to get busy again." My morning wood was wilting in disappointment.

"Did Taylor-Waylor actually get *laid* last night?" She chuckled. "Well, well, well."

Myles appeared in the doorway. The look on his face was awful. Part anger, part panic, part I didn't know what. "It's your friends," he said. "Brookhart and Asshole. They're coming up."

"Here?" I did a double take. "Brookhart," I said into the phone. "You're *here?*"

"I don't know where you're fucking talking about," she said, "but I'm about to find out if there is any reason why I shouldn't arrest the vodou guy for murder."

"Shit!" I exclaimed and jumped out of bed to find my jeans. I didn't have to. Myles handed them to me.

While I struggled into them, he almost magically slipped into shorts and a T-shirt. There was a pounding from the other room, but Myles was moving a folding screen from the corner of the room. My eyes widened at the sight of an elaborate but small altar as he picked up a figurine—a black Madonna like the one on his balcony—and kissed it. "Protect me, Ezili Danto," he whispered. He looked at me. "They like their privacy," he said, touching the screen. "It's disrespectful to have sex in front of them."

"Disrespectful?"

"Would you have sex in front of your grandmother?" And then he left the room.

I remembered him talking about his altar the night before. How he said he'd wait to show me, that he had his reasons. Was this what he meant?

Maybe making love to a man and knowing there was a vodou altar just on the other side of the room could have been a mood-messer-upper...?

I walked into the other room only to find Detective Townsend, known in some circles as Dt. Asshole, slamming Myles against a wall. "All right, motherfucker," he shouted. "*You* are under arrest!"

"Hey!" I shouted and saw Brookhart right behind him, reaching for her partner's shoulder.

"Townsend! Watch it!" That's when she saw me. Her eyes went wide. Her eyes said, *I don't fucking believe this!*

"Stop it," I said, dashing up to the big cop.

Townsend now had Myles's arm behind his back. Then, to my surprise—I wasn't sure if it was Brookhart pulling the detective back or Myles's strength—Myles yanked himself free and spun around to face his assailant, breathing hard.

"What are you doing?" Myles growled.

Townsend surged forward, and Brookhart pulled him back.

"As if you didn't fucking know!" Townsend snarled.

"*Townsend!* Calm *down*," Brookhart cried.

He turned to face his partner, his ugly face even uglier. "What? You want us to wait for him to kill someone else?"

She reached out and laid a hand on his forearm. "I think our suspect might have an alibi." She nodded her head in my direction.

Townsend's head snapped in my direction. We locked eyes. Then: "Well, fuck me!"

Brookhart stepped between us. "Taylor. Is this who you spent the night with?"

Myles got a surprised look on his face.

"Yea-huh," I said.

"*All* night? What time did you two... ah, hook up?"

"Around five yesterday evening," I told her. "I picked him up and we went for coffee."

"At?" she asked.

"The Shepherd's Bean, just around—"

"I know where it is," she said. "How long were you there?"

I shrugged. "Hour? Less?" I looked past her to Myles.

"Something like that," Myles said, still breathing hard.

"Then what?" She looked almost like she didn't want to know.

"We came back here for dinner."

Townsend snorted. "I'll bet! Sausage?"

"Lasagna," I replied. "Really *good* lasagna. No torn pasta. The secret is—"

"And then?" Brookhart asked.

Myles answered. "Is that really any of your business?"

"It is if it clears you for the third murder," she said, her voice calm, yet like steel. Townsend was shaking his head, all but snarling.

"Then we went to bed," I replied and felt myself blush. For some reason that pissed me off. "All night."

Brookhart nodded. Turned to her partner. "Okay?"

"How do we fucking know *he* wasn't in on it?" Dt. Asshole barked, pointing at me.

Brookhart snorted. "*Taylor?*" She laughed. "He almost threw up on his shoes trying to take some pictures of the bodies. I don't think cutting people's hearts out is a part of his repertoire."

"Goddammit!" Asshole shouted.

"It would still be nice if you two could answer some questions," she said calmly.

I looked over at Myles. He was still clearly upset. Could I blame him? *I* was upset. "Myles?"

He sighed and his shoulders fell, tension at least easing a bit. "Fine," Myles said. "But I'm making coffee."

"Chicory?" I asked.

"Hell, no," he said. "*They* get Taster's Choice."

I DIDN'T want to leave, but I knew I had to go get pictures. I didn't *want* to get pictures. Far from it. Taking pictures of people with their chests split open was not getting easier. But so far Mencken hadn't taken my story away, and that was good. Right? He was sprucing them up, or someone was (please don't let it be Chadrick or Rockower), but not changing the byline. That *is* good, right?

But as I looked at the grisly remains of the older man, I couldn't help but feel like a fraud. I found I didn't want to be here, looking at a dead man. A dead man named Ramon Martínez, aged fifty-five, five eight, one hundred ninety-five pounds, married, father of two, and yes, in town for a convention. A human-resources convention, and could there be anything much more *boring* than that? He'd been found at the Just Off Broadway Theatre, which for nearly a century had served as offices for the Parks Department, a barn for the horses for the mounted police of Kansas City, and finally for storage for parks equipment before becoming a theater. I always thought of it as a little lost castle, because that's what it looked like. Something right out of England that had somehow mysteriously transported itself to Kansas City.

But then, looking at that dead man splayed out, surrounded by candles and dead chickens and face-painted with a skull, I got that shuddering little feeling of familiarity. Like I had seen something like this before. Before a few days ago, that is.

Then something clicked in my head. The murders. Several of them.... Why they reminded me a hell of a lot of that movie *The*

Believers. It was almost like they were inspired by that movie—which wasn't about vodou to begin with. Could it be...?

And if it were true, that would mean Myles really wasn't involved at all! Not that I thought that for a moment. At least not any more.

I looked but didn't find any words in blood about serving "Baron Mange Key." Of course there really wasn't anyplace to do that in this case. The big tan stone blocks wouldn't make a good easel.

So I took my pictures, and I took them fast. I wanted to go to the VIC's hotel room, and wonderfully, Daph had told me where to go. She was turning into my hero. Turning? Hell. She *was* my hero! Wasn't she the one who had caught one of the guys who beat the stuffing out of me the year before?

Stunningly, I was able to do something that showed me miracles do happen. There was a laptop open on a desk in his hotel room, and while the cops milled about, no one paid me the least bit of attention when I checked Mr. Martínez's recent browser history. I thought it was completely weird—how could they not notice me? But not one to look a gift horse in the mouth (and oh, what did *that* make me think of?) I checked that damned computer.

And what do you know? Craigslist, M4M. Interesting. While that cat's away, that cat had been playing. Apparently, playing was the last thing he did. I wasn't able to open his e-mail, not casually, but I did see the ad he'd answered said, "Sex in a Castle? Blow Me Now!"

Sex in a castle, huh?

I amscrayed and called Brookhart. "Hey, Daph," I said when she answered.

She growled.

"Any chance the previous VICs might have used Craigslist the night they died?"

There was a long pause. Then: "Yes. How did you know that?"

"I have my ways."

Another pause. "The first guy"—pause and the sound of shuffling pages—"Brightwell. He apparently *placed* an ad for hotel sex. I guess that's pretty common for married men on the down-low? Business man away from the wifey—"

"Where he can get away with all kinds of stuff and not get caught because he doesn't have to worry about running into them at Walmart when he and said wifey are shopping. Tale as old as time. Why do you think so many conventions are in Las Vegas? And in Martinez's case, what's the chance that anyone will recognize him? Especially if he's far from home? Where *was* Brightwell from?"

"San Marcos, Texas," she said after a moment.

"Yeah. See, he doesn't have to worry that someone will figure out who he is when he's out of town—and who knows, some married couples even have an it's-okay-if-you're-out-of-town rule."

Brookhart sniffed.

"And the girl. She was from… Nebraska?" I asked.

Shuffling paper. "Weeping Water. She met a guy from a dating service, though."

"Not a woman."

"Not a woman," Brookhart said.

"And this last guy answered an ad for someone who wanted public sex at the Just Off Broadway Theatre."

"What are you thinking?"

"I don't *know* that I am *thinking* anything. Only that these were people who kept their romances on the road and away from home. Anonymous. No way to really track down where they found their love."

"We're working on that."

"You are?" I asked, surprised. Could they do that?

"Most of what you see on TV cop shows is pure bullshit," she said. "But not all of it."

"Okay," I said, and hung up before she could tell me I couldn't use the information for my next story. I got it to Mencken right away. He hooted and said that was "effing great, kiddo!" I smiled. Maybe I *could* do this.

Then I headed to Lucky Charms. I wanted to see Myles.

The protestors were back. I started to turn away, then to cut through the crowd, and finally decided to do my job. I went to the preacher, the one who looked like Two Face in that *Batman* movie, but before the acid bath.

"Do not turn to mediums or necromancers," he was bellowing. "Do not seek them out, and so make yourselves unclean by them: I am the Lord, your *God*."

"Excuse me," I said, pulling out my press badge. "I'm from the *Chronicle*. I was wondering if I could ask you a few questions, Mister…."

He looked down at me, finger still pointed at the sky. *"Reverend,"* he barked, and then seeming to be just as surprised that he yelled at me as I was, shook himself and stepped off his folding metal chair.

Couldn't he find a soap box? I wondered.

"Reverend *Doctor* Royle Van Young."

I bit the insides of my mouth to keep from laughing. *Royle? Really?* "Reverend," I said instead.

"How may I help you, young man?" he asked, and once more I had to fight not to laugh. Was he *maybe* ten years older than me? Maybe? And calling me "young man?"

"I was wondering if you might tell me what this is all about?" I waved to indicate the protestors, then gestured to Lucky Charms.

"We are here to drive out the serpent," he said in a tone that indicated I must be an idiot.

"The serpent?"

"The *serpent.* The Devil. *Satan.* Lucifer *himself!"* Van Young pointed to the ground with a downward thrust finger.

"I see…."

"This place of evil must go. The proprietors of this den of sin—devil worshippers—have brought the fallen angel to Kansas City."

"Proprietors? I was only aware of one."

"His partner," the rev-doc said, and pumped his finger to the storefront of Lucky Charms, "has already fled, gone back to New Orleans from where she rose up—tail between forked feet."

"Ah," I managed. "I didn't know Mr. Parry had a partner."

"One down and one to go," the Aaron Eckhart look-alike said.

I nodded in what I hoped looked like sympathy. "And you're glad she's gone because they brought Lucifer to town." Somehow I managed to keep myself from grinning. I thought of open chests and blood and winced. It had the desired effect on the preacher.

"Yes, young man. By driving out this other sorcerer, we can save our children from the Devil's influence. By marching outside this evil place, we are driving away those who would seek his aid. Aid which the proprietor of this evil place receives from the Prince of Hell!" The reverend pointed once more to Myles's shop. "'And he burned his son as an offering and used fortune-telling and omens and dealt with mediums and with necromancers. He did much evil in the sight of the *Lord,* provoking him to anger.'"

"Son?" I asked. Myles had a son?

"Human sacrifice," Rev Royle said. "Surely you know about this, *if* you're a reporter."

"Well, I know there have been killings," I replied. "But I don't know that it was human sacrifice."

"How can you know it not?"

Know it not? Really?

"Their hearts were cut out! No doubt eaten by he who did it."

Eaten? "Now that's a considerable jump in a train of thought, isn't it?" I asked. "From human sacrifice to eating hearts?" I shuddered. For some reason I thought of the man with the heart painted on his face from my dreams.

"Leviticus 19:26: 'You shall not eat any flesh with the blood in it,'" he said. "'You shall not interpret omens or tell fortunes.' That man in there tells fortunes."

"But that doesn't mean he eats hearts."

Van Young's eyes narrowed. "He has already poisoned your mind, hasn't he, my son? Get down on your knees and pray with me. For as it says in James 4:7, 'Submit yourselves therefore to God. Resist the devil, and he will flee from you.'"

"Look," I said, stepping back. I had no intention of getting on my knees. Not for Van Young, anyway. "I'm fine, really."

"That man in there. The *beautiful* man." The reverend pointed once more at Lucky Charms. "He has ensorcelled you, hasn't he? My son! Make no mistake! Vodou is nothing more than witchcraft! It is the summoning of demonic forces! It is the raising of demons to perform evil tasks. These '*vodouisants*' pretend to help people, to heal, to mend relationships. But they are summoning evil with their words and rituals. They are making a deal with *the* Enemy, himself! And make no mistake about it, Satan does not do anything for free. He does not do favors in return for cigars and bottles of rum, does not care about sacrificing chickens and pigs! I have *seen* it! I have the discerning eye. Mr. Parry practices witchcraft!"

It was then that the police arrived. Finally.

It turned out the Reverend Doctor had no permit. He'd been told twice before to get one.

"I'll be back," he shouted as he was ushered to his van. "The Lord will *not* be silenced! Evil will *not* be permitted to thrive here in this city. It *will* be driven out!"

Thankfully I didn't have to listen anymore. I went into Lucky Charms. I went there for a little sanity.

WE HAD dinner at my apartment that night. It wasn't lasagna, but I had a little hibachi grill, and I cooked hamburgers out on *my* balcony this time. I liked the fact that almost all the tenants in my building—the Oscar Wilde, and wasn't that a great name?—were gay and lesbian. Both apartments next to mine belonged to gay men. The couple to the right were nudists and were often right out there naked. We were on the sixth floor, and since there were only houses across the street, no one could see anything. I had to admit the situation and my neighbors had given me the freedom to sit out naked myself.

I was clothed tonight.

While I flipped burgers and traveled back and forth to the kitchen, cutting tomatoes (and opting against onions tonight—I was hoping for much kissing) and lettuce and such, Myles found my scrapbook from my Chicago-suburb days.

"Oh, God, Myles! Don't look at that?"

"Why not?"

I swallowed hard. "It's embarrassing."

He looked at me, concern in his dark eyes. "Why embarrassing?"

"It's—it's just it's all such sappy stuff. You know, 'Kid With Autism Confronts His Bullies with Forgiveness,' and 'Old Man Turns His Garage Into a Shelter For Strays.' That kind of bullshit."

"It doesn't sound like bullshit to me."

I gave up and let him read.

Which surprised me all the more when I came out on the balcony with cheese for the burgers—I mean, who eats burgers without cheese?—and found him with tears running down his face. "Myles!" I said, alarmed. "Are you okay?"

"This story," he started to reply and then his voice broke. "Th-this story about the twins...." His voice broke again and he pointed. I looked.

"Twin Carries Injured Brother Across The Finish Line At 800-Meter Race." My breath caught. I remembered that day. It had been a spring morning, a Saturday, and I'd been planning on going to the Rocks on Lake Michigan to sun myself and maybe get lucky when my boss called and asked me, as a favor, to cover the sporting event at the high school. I didn't do sporting events. Not even high-school sporting events. Maybe *especially* high-school events. But I went. As a special favor. I'd been there in the bleachers, trying not to kill myself from boredom, when I saw the kid fall down. Saw another kid, who had been in the lead, stop, go back, and pick him up and carry him the rest of the way. "They came in dead last," I said quietly.

"...but for the very best reason." Myles read, "'I couldn't leave him there,' said fourteen-year-old Julian. 'He's my brother. And I'm my brother's keeper.'"

Myles sighed and wiped his face, and I was surprised myself when I realized there were tears gathering in my eyes as well.

"Oh, Taylor. You're ashamed of stories like these?"

"Not—not ashamed," I said.

"But embarrassed."

I shrugged, suddenly at a loss for words. It had been a powerful day. Imagine if more people stopped to help their brothers.

"Taylor, I *would* read the paper if there were more stories like these." He pointed at the article, carefully cut from the *Daily Herald* and glued on the scrapbook page. "Imagine," Myles said, "if more people stopped to help those in need. Not caring if they come in first place, only in making sure everyone crosses the finish line."

And once more I had to entertain the idea of wondering if Myles could read my mind.

"This reminds me of the Marassa."

"The Marassa?" I asked.

Myles smiled. "The Lwa twins. They are always the second to be honored in any vodou ceremony, after Papa Legba. Some say they were one soul born into two separate bodies. They bring good fortune. But watch them!" Myles chuckled. "They *are* children, after all, and they *can* be impish! Kids will be kids."

"Even... on the other side?" I asked. "When they became saints?"

"Of course!" Myles exclaimed. "How else can they help us if they don't *feel* like we do? That is why I always had trouble with Jesus. We are supposed to follow His example, but how can we? He was *God* on earth. Christians say He knew what He was, even as a child. So how could He have been tempted in the wilderness? I mean, *really*? He knew the devil couldn't give Him anything because everything already belonged to Him, right? How could He have been afraid of death? He already knew He was going to rise on the third day, right? According to the Christian stories. But we humans have only faith. So how can we live up to Christ's example? We aren't God!"

I nodded slowly. It's something I hadn't thought of in a long, long time. Part of why I had let my mother's religion slip out of my life. How *could* I possibly follow the example of a perfect being who knew He was God?

"Now the Lwa on the other hand," Myles continued "And the spirits of our ancestors? *They* were *human*, and sometimes, even though they are powerful, they are *still* human. If you have a relative that was always trying to set you up on a date because she never realized or couldn't figure out you were gay—then don't ask her to help you find a mate. She'll still be looking for a woman. Unless you finally let her know. Tell her. And in vodou, you *can* tell her. Then with the wisdom she has with the Ghede, she will do what she can to help."

"What are the Ghede?" I asked.

"They are the recently dead. They know all about human suffering. They *remember* it clearly. The altar at the store, the one covered in purple? That is *their* altar. I go to them for healing. They can be pranksters, though. Like Dasou and Dasa, the Marassa."

I closed my eyes and took a deep breath. "You really believe this stuff, don't you?"

"Stuff?"

"I don't mean stuff. I…." I didn't know what I meant. It was hard to believe. It sounded like wishful thinking. Like just another religion created from man's fear that when we die, there is nothing.

I jumped when Myles pulled me into his arms. "I *do* believe in this stuff. I have proof. I don't have to take it by faith. I have *seen* it." He kissed the top of my head. "Shit."

"What?"

"I'm so sorry, Taylor."

Sorry? "For what?"

"Oh, Taylor. We—people who believe in vodou—there is something that we do *not* do. We don't evangelize. We *don't* try and bring people into the fold. That's what I've been doing to you, isn't it?"

"I—I...." Had he? "No, Myles. I've been asking you—"

"My own monbo," he said. "The priestess who taught me vodou, she tried to talk me out of it at first. A good teacher always does. She asked me, 'Why vodou?' and I surprised myself when I said, 'Why *not* vodou?' It must have been the right answer, because then she was willing to teach me. And most practitioners stay at the lowest levels—believing but never becoming monbo or houngan, priestess or priest. Never ounsi, first level like me, let alone surr pwen, second level, or asogwe, the highest level. But I knew I had been called for more. Papa Legba called me."

I looked up into his dark eyes, filled with emotions. This wasn't religious crap to him. It was real. And when he talked of vodou, I could hear the love in his voice. It wasn't about the hellfire and brimstone from my childhood. It was so different. And what had he said? Something about how before he found vodou—before it found him—he was only waiting for his life to begin.... "It's okay, Myles," I said quietly. "I was curious. I *asked*...."

"Then maybe you should stop."

"Stop what?" I asked him.

"Stop asking. Because you need to know *this*. Asking will bring you to their attention. In fact, you probably already have. Unless you stop, they might start calling to you...."

"Me?" Gooseflesh ran up my arms. I closed my eyes again. So much to take in. And did I really want to take all this in?

God. What was I doing? This was all crazy! I was seeing a man who believed in Haitian saints! He had an altar in his home. He ran a vodou shop. There were religious fanatics trying to drive him out of the city. Did I want that in my life?

"Look," Myles said. "I know how this all sounds. I know how it sounded to me. But it is who I am. The Lwa know me. They called to me. And I serve them. It is the most important thing in my life. You might as well sleep with a Catholic priest, except he would have to keep it a secret. Taylor... I like you. I like you a *lot*. I want to see you. But I come with... with *this*."

I opened my eyes and he raised his hands above him.

"I am ounsi. I am a vodou houngan. I will always be a part of the *société*."

Very abruptly, he pulled his shirt off over his head, revealing the well-muscled chest I remembered so well from the night before. Kissing it. Sucking on those dark-chocolate nipples. But then he turned and showed me his back. He pointed at his huge tattoo. "This is the vévé—the ceremonial drawing to Ezili Danto, my patron." He turned around. "I *am* vodou. If you can't deal with that, we should stop now."

"The hamburgers are going to burn."

"What?"

"I said the hamburgers are burning. Let me put the cheese on them. Let's deal with that first, okay? Hamburgers? Then the rest of our lives?"

"S-sure." He backed up.

I flipped the meat patties once more and placed the cheese slices over top. A minute later, they were done, and I took them off the fire and back to the kitchen, where we fixed our burgers and heaped our plates with the potato salad and chips we'd picked up from the local Thriftway. We watched TV and we cuddled on the couch and then we kissed.

Oh, it was such good kissing.

We could just sleep on this, right?

But then I saw the man in my dreams again. The man with the red heart painted on his face. Suddenly a chill ran through me, and I shuddered and pulled away from Myles.

"Are you okay?" he asked.

"I'm not sure," I said. "I've been having this dream. And I thought about you and your dreams, and it made me wonder."

"Well, if you've been having some weird dreams, it's pretty normal. The last few days have *been* pretty weird."

I nodded. "Yes. But…."

"But?"

"This man—he's come to me twice now. And he seemed *very* real. Scared me half to death." I scooted closer to Myles.

He nodded.

"He was a black man and he had this huge mane of dreadlocks, and painted on his face with this bright red heart."

Myles eyes went wide. It was only for one second. Not even that. He tried to hide it, but I saw.

"And he had very sharp teeth. Like shark's teeth." I took the tooth that was hanging around Myles neck. "Bigger than this. And much sharper."

I saw him swallow, saw his Adam's apple bob. It meant something. I saw it. He was still trying to hide it, but I saw. "He's real, isn't he?" I shivered. Moments ago, I had tried to tell myself it was all crap. Just more religious crap. And now? Now I was entertaining the idea that this vodou stuff could be real. Wasn't I dreaming about something I couldn't know anything about? In all my research, there hadn't been anything about a man with a heart on his face—a man with shark's teeth.

"Tell me," I said.

There was a moment then that seemed to stretch forever. I was just about to ask again when Myles told me. "You saw Bawon Manjè Kè. The eater of hearts."

I shuddered.

"In life he was a plantation slave, and he helped with the Haitian revolution. He led the revolt on his own master and killed him and ate his heart. It is said in the days before the revolt, he sharpened his teeth into daggers. He killed many men in the days to come. He ate more hearts. And when they caught him, they actually burned him at the stake. Now fire is his symbol and it obeys him. He is a *very* dark, *very* hot Lwa. He is fierce. He is not to be taken lightly."

I began to shake. God. Myles believed this!

What's more, I was beginning to believe it myself.

"Is this what you meant? When you said the Lwa were probably already noticing me. Why this one? Why Bawon.... Man...."

"Bawon Manjè Kè," Myles said. "I don't know. I've never called on such hot Lwa. I steer clear of them. Even Mama Gloria, my monbo, *she* stays clear. I don't know why he would have noticed you."

"But you think he has."

Myles paused. Then he said, "I think he might have, and...." His eyes went wide. "Oh, God. The killings. They're calling on *him*."

"What?"

"Whoever is killing those people. They must be calling on him! They want power and fame and fortune. Something. They don't want to wait. They don't want their fair share. So they went to *him*. And he would demand hearts."

I shuddered. "Then—why *me?* I don't want *any* of those things."

Myles turned to me. "Don't you? You want this story. You want to be a big-time reporter. Isn't fame exactly what you desire?"

I began to shake harder. "But I didn't call on *him!* I didn't even know who he was. I didn't know anything about any of this until a few days ago!"

Myles nodded. "No. But you were there. At the murder sites. And he could have noticed you. Noticed your ambition. Maybe he thought it was you who killed those people. And now he is calling to you."

"No!" I cried. "No. This is *bullshit.* This isn't *real.* I don't believe it! You hear me? And I've read it over and over the last few days. If you don't believe, then it can't hurt you. I *don't* believe it."

Myles pulled me into his arms again. I tried to fight it at first. I was scared. I was damned scared. But resisting his muscles was like resisting coils made of steel. I didn't have a chance. And when I stopped fighting, I let myself melt against him, melt into his strength.

"Is he after me?" I asked.

"I don't know," Myles said. "But we can try and find out."

"How?"

"Tomorrow night. We will call on the Lwa."

IT WAS all quite complicated. Candle and cornmeal and incense.

We were at Lucky Charms. We stood before the altar to the far left of the room, the one set into a nook, the one that had been roped off. Myles's private altar and not the one to be stared at by customers (or touched, as Dt. Asshole had done).

There was an image hanging on the wall above it—Ezili Danto. I recognized her now. The Black Madonna.

Myles lifted a conch shell from the altar and blew into it. A long, haunting note filled the air.

"*Annoncé, annoncé, annoncé…,*" he sang. "*Annoncé, annoncé, annoncé….*"

He picked up a machete next and began to dance around me. "*Annoncé, annoncé, annoncé…. Annoncé, annoncé, annoncé….*"

The libations had already been poured. The vévé already formed in cornmeal on the floor.

The ritual went on for seeming hours. This was different, he had explained to me. We were doing this alone, he—nothing but first level—and me—not even a believer. But I was starting to believe, wasn't I?

This was different, because normally there would be drummers and laplas dancers and mock battles.

"We'll have to improvise," Myles said. "Luckily vodou allows for this. We'll make do. If only my partner hadn't gone back to New Orleans. She could have helped…."

Myles danced on. "*Pou Legba, kap véyé pot'la!*" he sang. "To Legba, who guards the door."

Ah, I thought and felt a chill run through me. Papa Legba—the first to be honored. The gatekeeper. Only through him could Myles reach the Ghede and the Lwa. Only with his approval.

Myles went to his knees, placed the machete on the floor, took up a bowl of cornmeal, and made a big *X* before him—between us.

"*Lé nou fé sa, nap man sid!*," he cried. "In doing this, we touch Ginen!"

Ginen, the underwater world of the Dead, Myles had explained. The homeland where the Lwa lived.

More cornmeal.

"*Fanmi Manman'm, Fanmi Papam'ap, manyin Ginen-yo.* My mother's family, my father's family, touch Ginen."

Something began to happen to Myles voice. It was like… like he was taking on an accent. An accent that reminded me of almost every vodou movie I had watched. Damn. Was it really only days ago? It seemed like weeks at least.

Myles dipped his fingers back into the bowl. Brought a pinch of the meal up before him. "*Isit' nap dancé, nan Ginen yap dansé.* We are dancing here, and in Ginen, they dance!"

It went on and on, and often I was lost. I tried to chant with him. I tried to repeat the words when he asked. He called on Legba and he called on the twins, the first of the Lwa after Papa gave permission for him to continue. He called on Papa Loko—Just Judge—who gives guidance, and Monbo Ayizan—the patroness of initiation—the *first* Monbo, Papa Loko's wife.

There were moments of frustration on Myles's face, only to be replaced by steel-like determination.

On and on it went.

He raised his asson, a great gourd wrapped in beads and snake vertebrae, with a bell attached. He shook it and he cried out, "*Ago! Ezili Danto! Ayibobo!*"

Myles eyes flashed to mine, and he nodded, and I called back, *"Ayibobo!"*

"Ago!" he cried again. *"Ezili Danto! Ayibobo!"*

"Ayibobo!" I echoed.

"Ago!" a third time. *"Ezili Danto! Ayibobo!"*

"Ayibobo!" I answered once more.

And then it happened.

I cannot deny it, even if were able.

Something rose up.

It was like shadow.

It was cold.

It was hot.

Myles stiffened, his body jerked upright, his back arched into a great bow, and God! His eyes rolled up white....

And that was when the brick came through the front window. Our ritual came to an ass-grinding halt.

Myles jolted upright, his arms flung out to his sides. His eyes rolled back to normal—but filled with anguish. "No!" he cried. "No! So close!"

Another brick crashed into the room. A full quarter of the large piece of plate glass now gone.

"Devil spawns!" came a shout from outside the building. "You want to worship Satan? Then we'll send you to him!"

The next object that came hurtling into the room was not a brick. It was a flaming bottle. It hit the table of books and candles with a crash of fire and burning liquid, and instantly the whole of it burst into flames.

"Myles!" I screamed, pinwheeling back, the heat instant and huge. I fell backward, all but in his lap, cornmeal and bowl flying, my feet going out from under me.

"Oh God," sobbed Myles, and he struggled to his feet. "So close," he wept and then grabbed my wrist, pulled me up so that I was standing beside him. We dashed around the raging fire and toward the front door. Except just as he reached for it, just as he began to pull it open, it too burst into flame. The second Molotov cocktail had trapped us in the building.

We were running then, to the back of the big room, a room without another door, and it was in that moment I saw, just like that, my life—our lives—were at an end.

The fire had become an inferno in seconds. So fast!

We were going to die.

Where are you now, oh vodou spirits? I cried inwardly. *Not real. You're no more real than anything my mother believed in!*

No more real than my mother's God. Fake. Made up to help people sleep at night. For people who were afraid of what happens when we die.

And now I was going to find out, wasn't I?

The heat rose higher, and I could not believe how fast it was all happening. It was like the store was made of paper and not cinder blocks and tile and linoleum and steel.

"Taylor!"

I turned to find Myles in front of me. His eyes were wide and desperate, and he looked so dark. In all this bright orange light, why was he so dark?

But it was soot, wasn't it? The room was filling with smoke, and we were coughing, and he pulled at me. "The ground! We've got to get down on the floor! Under the smoke."

I nodded. Under the smoke. But would it really make any difference? Give us ten seconds more of life? I could feel the raging heat. I looked down, saw the hair on my arms singeing, and felt my eyes—*felt* them boiling in my head.

We were going to die. We *were* dying! This was how it felt to die!

"Where are you now!" I screamed, the anger filling my heart. "Where the *fuck* are you now, Manjè Kè? Where are you now, oh, *Bawon Manjè Kè?*"

"Get down!" Myles shouted over the raging sound of the fire and yanked at my arm, pulled at me, pulled and pulled, but....

My foot.

It wouldn't move.

It was stuck. Stuck as if nailed to the floor.

Did my shoe melt to the floor?

But.... But no. I couldn't feel it. I couldn't feel my foot, and as I stood there—the flames catching at my clothes, my hair—my whole leg was frozen.

There was something....

...traveling....

...up my leg!

It was cool and it was hot and it was cool again.

I shook. Felt this... *thing*... this wave... this *force* traveling up my thigh, my torso, spread down my other leg. My arms burst into flames... but... they... weren't... burning! It was cool fire. Heat and ice and then....

I WOKE up.

I was lying back and it was night and there was a man standing over me.

Myles was there too. He was looking down at me with an expression I could not read. His eyes were wide and wet and red. I saw his arm was bandaged and then I remembered.

I'd caught on fire!

But   But I was alive. How? I looked around. I realized I was lying on a gurney. The man I didn't know was an EMT. They were getting ready to put me in the back of an ambulance. A rush of panic went through me. I didn't want to go in there. I looked back and saw the fire trucks, saw the smoking, smoldering wreck that was all that was left of Lucky Charms.

"You are one lucky fucker," I heard and turned my head again and saw Brookhart. She was shaking her head, a complete sense of wonder on her face. "One lucky motherfucker."

"W-what happened?" I asked. I couldn't remember. I was on fire and then I was here. I looked down at myself—knowing I would see a mummy's body, a mass of bandages.

But no. Just a blanket. And my bare chest. Bare chest?

I turned once more to Myles. "What happened?"

"*Manjè Kè*," he whispered.

"What?" But before I could say any more, before he could answer, my eyes…. They were growing *so* heavy—I was falling. "What?"

"Manjè Kè," Myles said again. And then I knew no more.

SHE WAS beautiful.

She had skin like obsidian, and her eyes were large and gold, like polished tiger's eye, her head wrapped in red fabric—like a turban of some kind. She reached down and touched my cheek, smiled, and I felt myself fill with warm and golden light.

The drugs, I thought. It's the drugs….

Rest, my child, she said in a voice like music, like gentle falling rain. But her lips didn't move. It was in my head.

The drugs.

Rest, my Taylor, my son. I will watch over you. You are mine now. I will take care of you. All is well.

I woke up in St. Luke's hospital.

I didn't know that right away, of course. A hospital bed is a hospital bed.

A dream. All a dream. What had happened?

Gay was there. She was dozing in a big chair by my bed, and I saw there were wires and tubes attached to me, but no bandages. I looked and looked, but no burns.

How could that be? How long had I been out? Had I been in a coma? How many weeks? Months? Could it be months?

But no. The hair on my arm was still gone. Singed to the skin, but my skin—it was okay. Not even pink.

Was it all a dream?

"Gay?" I asked, wondering if I could even talk, and yet I did. Full and strong.

She jumped, her large lime-green hat with its wide black band nearly falling off her head. She stood and was at my side instantly. "Taylor. Thank Jesus."

"Gay?"

"I can't believe it. It… it's a miracle."

I looked up into her big brown eyes, saw the wonder there. And the love. Saw her love of me and immense, immense relief.

"Gay? What happened?"

She shook her head, mumbled something under her breath, and reached out and touched my cheek. "A miracle."

"Miracle?" I closed my eyes. *Miracle?*

When I opened them, Gay was gone, but Myles was there. He had pulled a chair up to the bed, and his head was resting on my pillow, and he was snoring softly, and I saw that one of his arms had a bandage from his right hand all the way to his elbow… but wait…. That was it? Nothing else?

How could that be?

"Myles?" I said quietly, remembering the way Gay had jumped, how I had startled her out of her sleep.

He shifted, and I said his name again, and then he was sitting upright, and there it was.

That look.

Just like the one on Gay's face.

Wonder.

"What? What is it?" I asked.

"Oh, Taylor...," he whispered. "You still don't know?"

"Know what?"

OVER THAT day and the next, the story came out.

First from Myles.

Then the articles in the paper. The *Chronicle*, of course. Eye-witness accounts that the paper gave no credence to because it all sounded crazy.

From what I heard, from Myles, from the stories, from the whispers, this is what happened....

One minute, I was me—who else could I be? I remembered. Remembered the roaring of the fire and the smoke filling my lungs, and Myles trying to pull me to the floor so that I could... what? Survive five more minutes and then burn alive? And then the hair on my arms had curled up and burned away, and I felt, *I felt*, my eyes heating up, boiling....

I was dying.

But then I *wasn't*.

I went away—to someplace cool and dark, and yet, so peaceful. I felt arms wrap 'round me and great golden eyes smiling down at me.

I went to sleep. Went into the rocking arms of a woman with skin like obsidian and eyes like polished tiger's eye.

And my body?

WHY, THE Lwa took it.

It is impossible. I can hardly believe it. But what else *could* have happened? Could there be anything less crazy than what those people saw?

A full twenty people told the story.

One minute, I was burning. My clothes, my skin, my hair, all ablaze. I was *on fire*.

And then, I wasn't.

"Like the burning bush," one of the Reverend Doctor's followers said. "He was on fire, but he did not burn!"

I rose up, the accounts read, naked and....

"He was glorious!" said another follower.

"Glorious," Myles agreed.

...on fire, and yet I did not burn.

"He had a heart painted on his face," said someone else.

"A heart?" I asked Myles.

"A heart," he said. "On your face. A big red heart. And there were crows. First one and then another...."

"Hundreds," said one witness.

"Thousands," said another.

"He was on fire!"

"And then the fire, it turned purple."

"Blue," said someone else, but most agree it was purple.

"Purple," Myles said.

"I'll say this only one time," Daphne Brookhart told me, standing by the window of my hospital room and looking out at a clear blue sky. There was only one cloud—like a stretched-out cotton ball. A plane contrail crossed the window's field of view from one side to the other. She was wearing jeans and a T-shirt. I had never seen Brookhart out of uniform. "I'll say this once and never again."

"Say what?"

"You came out of that store, and you was—were—on fire. You. Were. On. Fire. Your hair was on fire and your eyes—fuck me, Taylor—they were gone! But you... you weren't on fire!"

"Like the burning bush," one of the Reverend Doctor's followers said. "He was on fire, but he did not burn!"

"It was like you were wearing it!" She wasn't looking at me. I could only see part of her face, not in profile, but not turned away either. "You was—were—naked as the day you were born, my friend, and the only thing you were wearing was fire. Like it was some big old Bob Mackie costume."

"Bob Mackie?" I said and then laughed. I didn't like the sound of my laugh. It sounded crazy.

She shot a glance over her shoulder. "You think I don't fucking know who Cher is?" she snapped. "I may not be a gay boy, but I *do* like women, remember."

It was the first time she'd said it that way.

Brookhart—Daphne—looked back out the window.

"Then the fire turned blue, and then it turned purple.... And you opened your mouth and your teeth... they was—*were*—they were like *shark's* teeth. They were *huge* and they were razor sharp. You laughed." She shuddered. "Fuck me, Taylor, I don't *ever* want to hear a laugh like that again."

"Daph?"

She didn't seem to notice the name I had used but went on. She had just pulled up, she told me. She and Townsend, and that was when I came out of the remains of Lucky Charms.

"One second the building was on fire, and the next... it was *following* you, Taylor! It was... wrapping around you, and it was so bright I couldn't stand to look at you! I knew you was dead. And that's when I saw you was wearing it. And it turned purple. You laughed!"

She shuddered again.

"That Reverend was there. The fucker was standing there with his mouth hanging open and a Molotov cocktail burning in his hand. I remember his coat catching on fire, and I knew I should do something, but I... I was frozen. I couldn't move!

"You were laughing, and it was like... I don't know. Like crashing cymbals and breaking glass and this... this huge... *roar!* You... you started... *floating* up off the ground!"

I lay there in that bed, listening to all of this. She might as well have been telling me the story of a war, or a school shooting, or who knows what. She was talking crazy. It *was* crazy. It was impossible.

But as she spoke, these images flashed through my mind, and it was as if I could see it.

She started talking again. "And then, Taylor.... You said, 'Reverend *Doctor* Royle Van Young! You liar. You hypocrite. You killer. You murderer. *You* took out their hearts and you *wasted* them. You cast them aside. You didn't *even* eat them!' And then.... Taylor... you flew back! Your body hit the ground. But that... that thing. The thing with the teeth? It was still there. It was like it threw you off like an old coat. It rose higher off the ground... oh, fuck me!"

Brookhart spun around, her eyes wide and crazy, and there were tears running down her face. "It laughed. It *laughed!* And then it had the pastor, the reverend—whatever the fuck he is—*was*—and they—that thing.... God.... It... It dug its face *right into* that man's chest... and then it pulled back and there was blood. I've never seen so much blood! Never."

Brookhart staggered to a chair and fell into it. She dropped her face into her palms, and I lay there forever, trying to believe and believing at that same time, and waiting forever for her to finish.

Brookhart cried. She cried in huge, gulping breaths, and when she finally calmed down... she finished her story without looking up. She said: "There was his heart. It was in the thing's mouth. It was still beating...and then it was gone. Just... gone.

"Vanished."

"And Van Young.... He fell forward like an old doll. And he was dead."

THEY KEPT me at the hospital for three days. They would have kept me longer. They were trying to understand, but hey. Insurance. The insurance people wanted me gone.

The hospital administration wanted me gone.

Because everything that happened was impossible, of course.

GAY KEPT me company. I actually saw her in sweats one day. Sweats! I didn't know she owned sweats. Of course they were bright pink and had rhinestones all over them. But sweats!

She would come to my place in the evenings and make martinis, and sometimes I would just take the Tanqueray bottle and upend it in my mouth.

She let me.

Myles would call, but I didn't answer the phone. I didn't return his calls. I didn't answer the buzzer when someone called me from the lobby, and I didn't answer the door when someone knocked.

Not for two weeks.

But then *she* came calling.

SHE CAME in my dreams, of course.

Black skin like polished obsidian.

Great, glowing eyes.

"He is yours and you are his," she would tell me.

Night after night.

"I don't want this!" I told her. "I don't want it!"

"Too late," she whispered. "You are mine."

Finally, I gave up.

I called him.

"Myles," I said when he answered the phone.

"Taylor. Oh my God!"

"I want to try that coffee. The kind from New Orleans?"

"From Café Du Monde?"

"I don't know what that is."

"It's the best," he said. "With chicory. And lots of sugar and lots of real cream...."

"And not that powered nondairy stuff either."

"No," he replied quietly. "Thick and rich. I can be there in an hour."

"Okay."

I hung up the phone and waited.

Rest, my child, she said in a voice like music, like gentle falling rain. *Rest, my Taylor, my son. I will watch over you. You are* mine *now. I will take care of you. All is well.*

He is yours and you are his.

I sat and I waited.

I waited for my life to begin.

B.G. THOMAS lives in Kansas City with his husband of more than a decade and their fabulous little dog. He is lucky enough to have a lovely daughter as well as many extraordinary friends. He has a great passion for life.

B.G. loves romance, comedies, fantasy, science fiction and even horror—as far as he is concerned, as long as the stories are character driven and entertaining, it doesn't matter the genre. He has gone to literature conventions his entire adult life where he's been lucky enough to meet many of his favorite writers. He has made up stories since he was child; it is where he finds his joy.

In the nineties, he wrote for gay magazines but stopped because the editors wanted all sex without plot. "The sex is never as important as the characters," he says. "Who cares what they are doing if we don't care about them?" Excited about the growing male/male romance market, he began writing again. Gay men are what he knows best, after all—since he grew out of being a "practicing" homosexual long ago. He submitted a story and was thrilled when it was accepted in four days.

"Leap, and the net will appear" is his personal philosophy and his message to all. "It is never too late," he states. "Pursue your dreams. They will come true!"

Visit his website and blog at http://bthomaswriter.wordpress.com/ or contact him directly at bgthomaswriter@aol.com.

By B.G. THOMAS

All Alone in a Sea of Romance
All Snug
Anything Could Happen
Bianca's Plan
Bones (with Eli Easton, Jamie Fessenden, and Kim Fielding)
The Boy Who Came In From the Cold
Christmas Cole
Christmas Wish
Desert Crossing
Grumble Monkey and the Department Store Elf
Hound Dog and Bean
How Could Love Be Wrong?
It Had to Be You
Just Guys
Men of Steel (Dreamspinner Anthology)
Riding Double (Dreamspinner Anthology)
A Secret Valentine
Soul of the Mummy
Two Tickets to Paradise (Dreamspinner Anthology)

SEASONS OF LOVE
Spring Affair
Summer Lover

Published by DREAMSPINNER PRESS
http://www.dreamspinnerpress.com

stitch

gothika #1

sue brown
eli easton
jamie fessenden
kim fielding

http://www.dreamspinnerpress.com

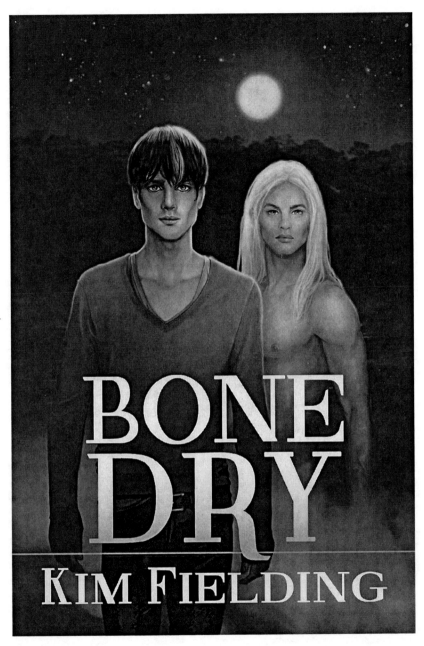

BONE DRY

KIM FIELDING

http://www.dreamspinnerpress.com

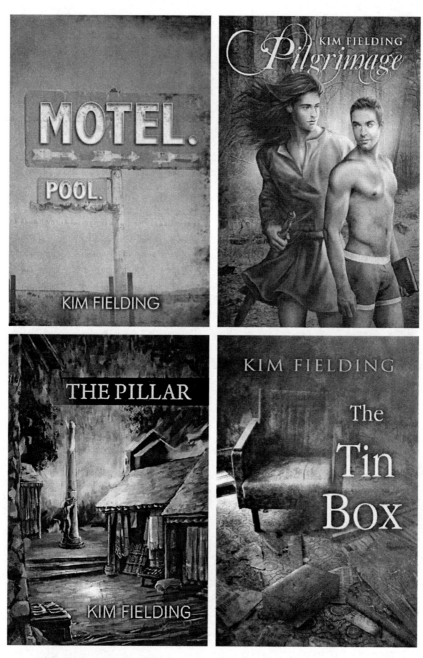

eli easton

the
Mating
OF
MICHAEL

http://www.dreamspinnerpress.com

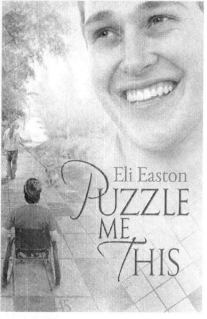

MURDER
ON THE
Mountain

JAMIE FESSENDEN

http://www.dreamspinnerpress.com

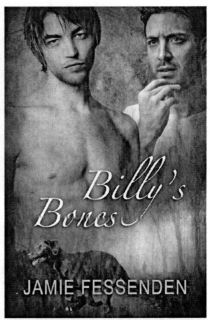
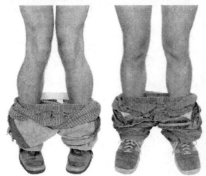
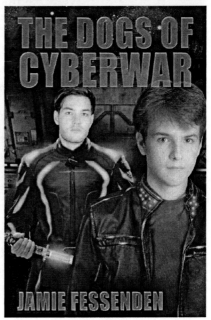

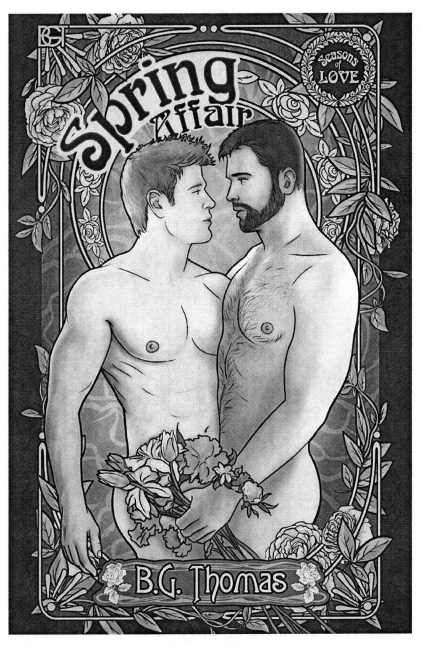

http://www.dreamspinnerpress.com

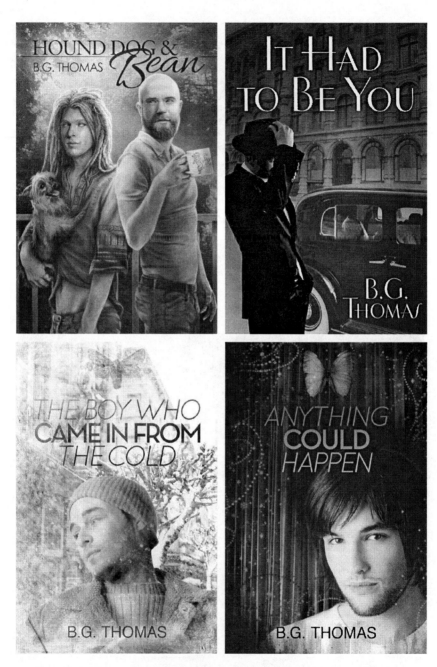

http://www.dreamspinnerpress.com

http://www.dreamspinnerpress.com

CPSIA information can be obtained
at www.ICGtesting.com
Printed in the USA
FFOW01n1950101017
40907FF